Please return/renew this item by the last date shown.

To renew this item, call **0845 0020777** (automated)
or visit **www.librarieswest.org.uk**

Borrower number and PIN required.

Libraries**West**

Illustrations by Steve Leighton

1 3 1519704 3

TALES OF KAPH
on love and death, trees and seas
and other wondrous matters
published by Red Dog Books
ISBN 978-0-9557088-4-8

Illustrations by Steve Leighton ©

British Library Cataloguing-in-Publication Data
A catalogue record for this book is available from the British Library

Red Dog Books is based in Axbridge, Somerset and in Brittany.
Enquiries should be addressed to the editorial office at
Red Dog Books, 29410 Plounéour-Ménez, France.

email: reddogbooks@orange.fr

www.reddogbooks.com

Printed by imprint*digital*.net

PREFACE

The short story as a literary form affirms the "small is beautiful" philosophy. Short stories are tasty little snacks rather than four-course meals; catchy and moving arias rather than epic operas; local footpath strolls rather than long distance hikes. Unlike novels that require days or weeks of reading, these are mini dramas to be read in a single sitting - indeed, two or three could be managed in one go - perhaps with morning coffee, or in the evening armchair, or while reposing beneath a favourite tree. They are brief glimpses into the lives, personalities, ideas and adventures of passing acquaintances.

Some of the stories in this collection concern characters called Kaph - usually a different character in each story. As will be explained more thoroughly in due course, Kaph (pronounced 'Caff') is an acronymic name: K stands for kindness, A for awareness, P for patience and H for humility. These are qualities which, I believe, are worthy of cultivation in our lives. Most of the characters in this book, however, have more normal names and their tales depict varying shades of moral, immoral and amoral behaviour.

All the short stories were written in the first decade of the 21st Century. Most have a recognisable beginning, middle and end but otherwise their subjects, settings, styles and lengths vary considerably. Many have appeared in magazines and anthologies and several have won prizes in short story competitions, including the Canongate Prize and literature festival competitions at Wells, Yeovil and Weston-super-Mare.

Grateful acknowledgements are due primarily to my writing friends: Wes White, Caroline Tapfield, Anna Young, Wendy Mewes, Graham Morton and, especially, Johanna van Fessem. Many thanks, too, to Harold Mewes of Red Dog Books for his excellent work in editing, setting out and producing this book

Steve Leighton
Glastonbury, Somerset
January 2010

By Weary Well
Winner of The Canongate Prize for New Writing, 2001.
First published in "Original Sins", Canongate Books, 2001

The Rod Man
First prize, Weston-super-Mare Arts Festival Short Story Competition, 2008
First published in "Gift", Weston-super-Mare Arts Festival, 2008

Visions of Johanna
Second prize, Weston-super-Mare Arts Festival Short Story Competition, 2009
First published in "Sins", Weston-super-Mare Arts Festival, 2009
Opening lines by Bob Dylan

Words of Wisdom
Second prize, Wells Festival of Literature Short Story Competition, 2007

Doorbell Blues
Second prize, Yeovil Literary Prize, 2005
First published in "My Weekly", May 20 2006

Mr Perkins gets it wrong
Highly commended, Frome Festival Short Story Competition, 2009

Boots
Highly commended, Frome Festival Short Story Competition, 2008

Osmium
Commended, Yeovil Literary Prize, 2008

The Baker of Glastonbury
First published in "Gift", Weston-super-Mare Arts Festival , 2008

Colour of the call
First published in Attack!!!! 5, Wes White, 2006

The Cave
Co-written with Johanna van Fessem

CONTENTS

SHELL

Washed up on the shore, still wet and glistening in the morning sunlight, lay a single white shell, scrubbed and cleansed and hurled to land by the waves, haphazardly deposited upon a virgin surface of flattened sand.

The lighthouse keeper's apprentice halted his stroll along the tideline and stared, suddenly transfixed by that single white shell upon a pristine bed of yellow sand. For many minutes he stood and stared. Into his mind floated the image of his lover's face, a solitary brown mole upon the white silkiness of her cheek, a blemish, some might say, but he took its asymmetric placing as the final master-touch of her loveliness, the imperfection that affirmed the perfect texture of her skin. In the same way, this solitary shell enhanced rather than sullied the smooth perfection of its sandy resting place, the solid reality of its form upon a formless background singing the miracle of existence, the wonder of being. These thoughts, non-verbalised, flashed across the inner screen of his awareness, leaving a trail of quiet joy. Something about this seemingly random sight of Nature's artistic genius touched his soul. He knew, with the certainty of Moses before the burning bush, that he stood upon sacred ground,

He took a step onto the still wet patch of sand, his boot sinking softly in. He reached down and plucked up the shell, clasping it as gently as he would a flower between finger and thumb. He cupped it in his hand, feeling its cold, hard surface, then continued on his way along the beach, leaving only a single boot print and a tiny indentation in the sand.

His name was Kaph, the name traditionally conferred upon all lighthouse keepers as an acronymic reminder of the essential qualities of their chosen profession: K for kindness, for the gift of light freely distributed to all who sailed at night across the sea: A for awareness, the constant vigilance of the watcher in his cylindrical tower: P for patience to endure the long hours of a winter's night: and H for humility, for only a humble man could live so close to the vastness of the ocean and experience the full gamut of her serene and turbulent moods. And Kaph, though but a young and impetuous man, loved his job - a job in which success was measured by the perpetual absence of incident, in which the purpose of a night's work was fulfilled if absolutely nothing happened.

Back in his tiny room on the lower levels of the lighthouse, Kaph sat on his stool and examined the shell he had rescued. He was no expert on the varieties of marine life, preferring to watch the ever-changing surface of the sea rather than consider the abundance of creatures who lived in her depths. But he had spent his life on the shoreline and knew well enough the names of the most common of his aquatic neighbours. He knew the shell to be that of a bivalve mollusc, a cockle-like animal, a tellin, to be precise, but of the strange gelatinous being who once extruded this lifeless outer skeleton he knew nothing. And yet that living blob of organic matter had created, as naturally as a mammal creates hair or an artist creates a picture, an object of matchless beauty: a texture as smooth and firm as polished marble; a shape of exquisite geometry; the colour of ivory or fresh cream, subtly adorned with wisps of ochre; a composition of seven overlapping, inseparable layers; a small masterpiece of sculpture and engineering. Once, this shell had been its creator's home and sanctuary, its vital security, its very definition. Now, that unnamed, unknown artisan had vanished forever into the amoral complexities of the marine food web, its molecules distributed far and wide, its memory totally eradicated, unmourned by its fellows, a brief, unloved blip in the flow of life. Yet, by some unimaginable twist of fate, its legacy remained, to awe the soul of the lighthouse keeper's apprentice.

He thought again of his lover, Maria – she of the white skin, unblemished save by a single, beautiful mole. And thus he named the shell Maria and kissed it and rubbed his fingers lovingly over it and caressed it in his hand. He carried it with him on his duties and it became his link with his beloved through the long nights of lonely watch over the moonless blackness of the sea, through the daily lighthouse keeping chores, through his walks along the beach and across the jagged rocks, through his dreams as the waves thundered against the sturdy walls of his tiny room. It became his friend when his master, Kaph Senior, the lighthouse keeper, grew grumpy or dozed off in his rocking chair. It became his mascot, his comforter when fear or sadness or loneliness assailed him.

Maria was the daughter of the shepherd who grazed his sheep on the coarse grasses of the cliff top. Each evening she'd pick her way down the precarious cliff path to meet Kaph upon the beach. Sometimes, when the tide was out, they'd strip off their clothes and chase each other through the surf, gambolling and giggling as lovers do. Then they'd lie together on the smooth sand just below the high water mark and their lovemaking would synchronise with the rhythm of the waves. They rarely spoke: no words were needed to cement their union or lubricate their playful passion. Then Maria would don her robe and wend her way back up the cliff path to her isolated family croft, while Kaph strolled the beach, dancing with the colours of the setting sun.

But when, in time, his love for Maria had run its course - for he was a fickle young man, alive with the lust of life, and she sought more than transient pleasures in the sand - he placed the white tellin shell that bore her name into his box of treasures and took it out, from time to time, stroking it fondly and reliving his memories of their frolicking.

Next came Sophia, his second love, and for her he found an oyster shell upon the beach, rough on the outside but shining within with mother-of-pearl. Then, for Lizbeth, a golden cockle shell, and a peppered furrow shell for Valerie, a violet mussel for Sarah - girls from the fishing village around the headland, from farms up on the cliffs, from bands of passing pilgrims who trod the path of the Celtic saints,

11

bound for the Holy Well - each one, in her turn, well loved: each one forsaken for the next. By the time he reached the full bloom of his manhood, he had amassed a dozen or more shells in his box of treasures, each a volume of cherished memories, each precious, each perfect - for even the flaws in the surface of a shell, as in the drama of an unfolding relationship, were perfect flaws.

Kaph Senior looked on. He had taught his apprentice the value of constant vigilance, the mark of a true lighthouse keeper. But constancy in love was not a requisite of the profession. A lighthouse was no place for a wife, no place for child rearing. Let those of the land concern themselves with such matters. Those of the rocky shores lived on the cusp of life, enjoying the pleasures of the peopled world but forever looking out into the wild, unfriendly oceans.

So one day, the old lighthouse keeper, well-content that his task was in safe and earnest hands, sat in his rocking chair, gazed out through the thick-glassed window of his room, out across the crashing waves, out into the blackness of the night sky, closed his eyes and opened them no more.

Kaph Junior took over the lighthouse keeper's role and adopted his professional persona. His dalliances with the village girls or the passing pilgrims grew less frequent, and the girls with whom he did entwine gradually became women, but still they looked well upon the rugged features and romantic ways of the shore dweller. And still Kaph found a fitting shell upon the beach to encapsulate the memories of each one of them, adding it to his collection in the box beneath his bed.

And then one day, when middle-age had mellowed his moods, he took his box of shells upon his walk and sat awhile on a shingly bank on the shoreline, picking out first one shell then another, naming each of his erstwhile lovers and savouring the memories in which their names were clothed: Maria first – the white tellin shell – then Sophia, the oyster; Lizbeth, the golden cockle; Valerie, Sarah, Martha, Jill, Jemima... The loves of his life like pearls upon a necklace.

Lost in reminiscences, his attention strayed and the tide crept up on him and the waves mischievously conspired to create a huge breaker that crashed down on him. Soaked to the skin, he leapt to his feet in shock, the box of treasures fell from his grasp and he watched in horror as his several dozen favoured shells tumbled through the salty air to land amongst a million unfavoured, unnamed shells lying in the shingle. He dropped to his knees and began groping in the multicoloured carpet of shells and pebbles, the debris of the sea, searching for his lost loves. Then another massive wave broke, then another, scattering the carpet and, as each wave receded, dragging an avalanche of shells and shingle back into the depths.

Kaph staggered back, yielding, as men must always yield, to the unstoppable power of the sea. Above him, at that moment, the dark clouds parted and the eye of God looked down on him and smiled. Suddenly the lighthouse keeper realised the impermanence of all things, the impermanence, even, of memories. And he saw that he was alone in the world, but he knew that that aloneness was not loneliness. It was the great Oneness that encompassed the sea and the sky and the rocks and the lighthouse and the tiniest particle of sand and the most fragile shell washed up upon the beach. And he saw that that Oneness was nothing more nor less than the entire course of his life, with all its days of harsh and fair weather, all its boredoms and excitements, all its loves, all its cherished shells.

He threw back his head and, being a man of few words, released a mighty roar that echoed back at him from the cliffs.

*

The roar startled a snow goose, preening herself on a nearby rock after feasting on cockles and oysters and tellins. She left her craggy perch and took to the air, squawking her displeasure at the sudden explosion of this human voice into the serenity of the beach, disturbing the reassuring rhythm of the waves. Twice she circled the spire of the lighthouse before heading off on her long northern journey, to the icy breeding grounds that she knew as home, to the longed-for reunion with her long-time mate. But her epic flight belongs to another story of which Kaph knows nothing.

TALES OF KAPH

I have no wish to be regarded as the official spokesman of the Society of Kaph, still less as its public face. Indeed, whether I am even a bone fide member of this strange Society is open to question, as is the very existence of the Society itself. It seems likely that it flourished during the latter years of the Nineteenth Century and enjoyed various periods of resurgence in the Twentieth Century, but such is its nebulous and quasi-secretive nature that I am not at liberty to offer any evidence of its current constitution and membership, other, that is, than myself.

Of its name and its guiding principles, I can be more specific. Essentially, the Society of Kaph is a loosely knit group of men and women who passionately hold a particular view about the nature of humanity, its evolution and the conditions necessary for its future survival. This view is embodied in the letters that form the acronym of the Society's name: K for kindness, A for awareness, P for patience and H for humility. It is towards the perfection of these four qualities that we strive amidst the turbulent waters of our daily lives. These strivings are often illustrated, in the literature and oral communications of the Society, by stories concerning a hero or heroine by the name of

Kaph (or, in some variations, Cath, substituting compassion for kindness and temperance for patience in the acronym.)

The tradition within the Society is that the central character of each Tale of Kaph should be a flawed seeker, an aspirant rather than a paragon of virtue, and that the events of his story should lead him a little further along his path. Yet, lest the potential reader is already raising his defences, the Tales are neither moralising nor proselytising, but are, rather, slices of life to be contemplated, their underlying message usually tacit, appealing more to the intuition than the intellect. These are not parables, rich in encrypted wisdom, but simply stories to be enjoyed for their own sake.

In keeping with the Society's ideal of humility, the tales are usually presented anonymously. They were never intended as enduring works of literature. Indeed, one unwritten rule of the Society – and all its rules are unwritten – is that any written communication should be either passed on or destroyed, never kept. Many tales are either memorised – whether verbatim or in essence – or re-written, each time receiving a different slant or tone or colour from each new teller. Thus the Tales presented here are attributable only to myself, though most, I can testify, are based on stories I have seen or heard, and many, I suspect, have histories stretching back either decades or centuries. I reproduce them here – without, I must stress, the explicit permission or approval of the Society – purely because I cherish the desire that they be more widely read and told, and, unable to provide any provenance for them, I offer them as my own while admitting that I owe much to those who came before me.

By now, I feel sure, my vagueness about the nature of the Society must be annoying my readers. I will endeavour to elucidate as best I can, though I fear my words will prove inadequate.

I believe that the Society was inaugurated sometime in the Eighteenth Century, in what was later called the Age of Enlightenment, by a communion of like-minded persons who sought an advancement of the human spirit within a context that eschewed all religious connections. They met informally and without ceremony, discussing philosophy and psychology and practising, in whatever ways were appropriate, their developing teachings of kindness, awareness, patience and humility. That the Society left no records of membership or written constitution makes it remarkably difficult to trace its history. It is my opinion, however, that it blossomed in Victorian England and sent forth branches across the Atlantic, the Irish Sea and the English Channel. It is tempting to name some names, but that is not the way of the Society. A man's fame or fortune, his standing in society or his worldly achievements mean little for a group in which humility is a keystone. Philanthropic acts are devalued by being made public. Kindness brings its own rewards and needs no advertisement. Patience, by its nature, always goes unseen. And awareness is nameless and shines forth from all eyes. ("One light though the lamps be many", to quote one of the Society's central motifs.) Members have never bragged about their practices, even amongst themselves. They merely did what had to be done.

London in the 1920s became a hotspot of Society activity, as did Cornwall in the 50s, Bristol in the 70s and Somerset in more recent times. Where and how many members currently exist are matters upon which I cannot yet comment.

How, it may be asked, can a society with no recognised constitution, no hierarchy of organisation, no list of members and no central location function as a society? Very informally, it must be admitted. Individual members would meet, talk, exchange ideas and stories, whether in pairs or small groups, in much the same way as any ad hoc group of friends might meet. Cafes have always been the Society's favoured meeting places. Several are known to me, in the major cities and small towns of this country. Indeed, it was in a small town cafe that I first made contact with the Society, as I will now recount.

It was a pleasant place, decorated in a pseudo-Tuscan style, gigantic pot plants in every corner on the flagstone floor, the bare wooden tables scattered with daily newspapers and magazines, the waitresses young, pretty and friendly: the sort of place where you could happily spend an hour or two sipping coffee and watching the world come and go. My first visit was serendipitous. I was in the town on business, an hour to kill before an appointment, the rain started and the cafe, with its soft background classical guitar music, offered a welcome haven.

As I settled with my coffee, my attention was drawn to a middle-aged man at a corner table, dressed casually in blue denim and sandals, a small goatee beard, his grey hair swept back from a vast, creased forehead. He sat back in his chair, hands resting on his paunch, a half-smile constantly adorning his ruddy face, occasionally swigging from the coffee mug which an obliging waitress refilled at regular intervals. On the table before him sat a folded piece of card, announcing his name, I supposed, like a teacher at a school parents' meeting, but rather incongruous in a cafe. A trip to the loo brought me closer to his table and allowed me to read the strange message on the card:

"Philosopher offers free consultations."

Naturally I was intrigued and, over the next half hour, watched intently from my somewhat distant table. Twice, someone entered the cafe, bought him or herself a coffee from the counter and made a beeline for the philosopher's table. He greeted each with a broad smile, beckoning at the spare chair opposite him. Thence, they plunged immediately into intense conversation, the content of which I was unfortunately unable to overhear, although, from the tone and gestures, I formed the impression of a dialectic discussion and imagined Socrates engaged in philosophical questioning in the market-place of Athens. After about ten minutes or so, on each occasion, the visitor stood, shook the philosopher's hand and left. No money was exchanged. The first client – if I may call him that – was a youngish student type, the second appeared to be a housewife upon a shopping expedition. Both left the cafe looking, I must say, quite satisfied with their consultations.

I surreptitiously shifted myself to a table within earshot of the philosopher's. The waitress came across with the coffee flask to replenish his mug.

"Busy today," she said. "No time for your philosophical daydreaming today, eh?"

"Ah, time," replied the philosopher. "What is time?"

17

"A good question," answered the waitress in a jovial tone. She was, I presumed, accustomed to the man's manner.

"I've heard it said," said the philosopher, "that time is Nature's way of keeping everything from happening at once."

He laughed – a quiet but infectious chuckle – and the waitress giggled a little and moved off about her duties. The philosopher slumped back in his chair, hands clasped on his stomach again, and resumed his enigmatic half-smile, his gaze sweeping the cafe. He caught my eye. I smiled. He raised a forefinger and an eyebrow to indicate the empty chair opposite him. Rather self-consciously, I took my coffee cup to his table and sat. His smile broadened. His teeth, I noticed, were in serious need of constructive treatment.

I introduced myself by name.

"Kaph," he replied. I didn't question it.

"An unusual occupation," I commented, motioning towards the card on the table.

"I possess few talents," he said, a deep and relaxed voice. "One thing I can do tolerably well is think. If all I can offer are the fruits of my thinking, then that is what I gladly do."

"So people consult you on philosophical matters?"

"Exactly. Personal problems, largely, but I try to respond from a wider philosophical perspective. I'm not what you might call a counsellor. But most problems, if viewed from a different angle, can be transformed with a little thought. That's what I try to do. Often a sympathetic listening ear is all that's required. To be a listening ear, an independent commentator, is a great privilege. Being a public philosopher, sir, is a truly fulfilling occupation."

"Hardly lucrative," I said, stupidly. "You don't charge for these consultations."

He frowned. "I care little for money. I get by well enough. I give kindness and awareness. Such things do not obey normal economic rules – nor the laws of physical nature, come to that. The more I give, the richer I become."

18

Words of wisdom, indeed. I was beginning to understand this peculiar man. I was beginning to like him.

"May I ask you a philosophical question?" I asked.

"Please do. That's what I'm here for."

Suddenly I was at a loss. The situation had no precedent in my experience. Here I was, conversing with a philosopher of whose credentials I knew nothing, invited to pose a question. Imagine walking in ancient Athens and coming upon Socrates in full flow. What do you say?

"I am a seeker," I said. "But what am I seeking?"

He looked down at his coffee mug for a few seconds, then raised his eyes to mine.

"First, tell me who is seeking."

"I am."

"Tell me who you are."

What was I to say? I had already told him my name. I could have rambled on about my job, my personal history, my personality traits, my likes and dislikes, my hopes and fears, but somehow I knew that that was not what he was asking. I could think of no appropriate reply.

"Tell me who you are," he repeated, and although his habitual half-smile still hovered on his lips, his eyes pierced laser-like into mine.

I held his gaze for what seemed like hours but was no more, I think, than a few handfuls of seconds, then, feeling a great emptiness within, I turned my eyes away from his, as though from the light of the sun.

"I don't know," I whispered, and my words felt, to me, like a desperate, plaintive cry.

"Good!" he responded, slapping a thigh with the palm of his hand. "You have to start with a blank slate. Removing pre-conceived notions is an excellent first step."

I smiled – it came as a great relief – and he smiled too, and in the space between those two smiles, something new was born.

"Words have their uses," he said, "but it is absurd to imagine that one can capture the essence of the vastness of life in a string of words.

19

We prefer actions and attitudes. Kindness above all: the communion amongst men that transcends all languages. Awareness: the light that shines from within. Patience: call it acceptance or surrender, if you like – without it we are in chains. And humility: putting our feckless thoughts and egos in their place, mere ripples upon the surface of Being."

At the time, I failed to make the connection between these words and his name: Kaph.

"So, you just sit here and philosophise each day?" I asked, anxious to inject some sense of normality into our conversation.

"Not every day. Only when the mood takes me."

"You have a more conventional occupation?" I confess that, at the time, I tended to define people in terms of their employment

"Not what you would call conventional," he replied. "Many years ago I left university with little idea about what to do for a living. I visited a careers advice office to enquire about vacancies in the three areas that struck me as suitable to my capabilities. I wanted a job as a philosopher, a poet's friend or a ferryman. 'Not much call for philosophers,' I was advised, 'and, although all poets need friends, most don't pay too well. As it happens, though, you're in luck. We have a vacancy for a ferryman.'

"And so I started my working life rowing people back and forth across a river. Can you imagine a better job? The official cost was a tanner each way – six old pence – but I never asked for money. I left a box in the hold of the boat and collected tips that ranged from a farthing to, on one occasion, a ten pound note. Thus I made a good living by accepting from my passengers whatever they considered their journey across the river was worth."

"And what did you think it was worth?"

"Clearly anything from a farthing to ten pounds. How are we to put a value on things? If your life depended upon it, wouldn't you give your entire life savings to be rowed across a river?"

A good question that I have often since considered.

But I sensed a presence lurking behind me. Another client was awaiting a consultation, and I had other matters to attend to. So I bade farewell to Kaph the philosopher, taking with me just a dim sense that our meeting had changed my life.

*

A few weeks later, finding myself again on business in the same town, I called in at the cafe hoping to renew our acquaintance. The place was bustling, the rich aroma of coffee dominating the steamy atmosphere. I made my way to the corner table where I found the philosopher's seat occupied by a pleasant looking woman, perhaps in her forties or fifties, dressed in clothes suggestive of nineteen seventies hippydom. On the table before her was a folded card proclaiming:

"Storyteller offers story."

I sat in the opposite chair. She smiled - a warm, welcoming smile, I have to say. I smiled in return and proffered my name.

"Cath," she responded.

I had it in mind to ask her if she knew the whereabouts of the philosopher, and also to comment upon the coincidence of their similar sounding names, but, instead and for no accountable reason, I found myself saying, "Please tell me a story."

She looked me over for a few moments, perhaps considering the sort of story that might suit my appearance, then, without further ado, she began. I sat back and absorbed my first Tale of Kaph, reproduced, in my own style and as nearly as I can recall it, elsewhere in this volume – I will refrain from revealing which story.

She told it well, Cath the storyteller. Her voice was soft but expressive, the pace of her narration adapted to the changing events of the tale, her face subtly displaying the various emotions of the central character. I was enthralled. When her story was done and she relaxed back into her chair, I felt like bursting into applause. Instead, I placed my palms together before my chest and bowed my head towards them, a gesture of sincere gratitude that I have long employed. She reciprocated the gesture with a smile.

21

"Do you know Kaph the philosopher who was sat here last time I visited?" I asked.

"We are friends, yes."

"And are there more of you, Kaphs and Caths?

"We are legion," she replied, laughing.

I sensed a man hovering behind me. Cath looked up at him and smiled. Perhaps another "customer" keen to enjoy a story, I thought. Or another Kaph? I stood up, said my farewells to the storyteller, and left.

A few hours later, my business in the town concluded, I returned to the cafe to find Cath still in residence at the corner table, the chair opposite her vacant.

"Is it too presumptuous of me to request another story?" I asked as I sat.

"Not at all. That's what I'm here for."

And so I heard my second Tale of Kaph - totally different from the first in tone, plot, style, even historical setting – and again I was entranced by both the story and the manner of its telling.

"Why?" I asked when she had finished – a word of which I am far too fond.

"A strange question," she replied. "Would you ask the waitress why she brings you a coffee? She waits and I tell stories."

"But she is paid for waiting."

"Why must money be such a crucial factor in the things we do? I like to tell stories and you, judging by your reappearance, like to listen."

"Of course, but that doesn't answer my question."

"Doesn't it?"

*

The next day I made a point of travelling to the town again and headed straight for the cafe. Neither the philosopher nor the storyteller was sat at the corner table. This time the space was occupied by a youngish man scribbling on a large pad of paper. Before him, as before, stood a folded card.

"Artist offers free portrait."

I sat. A few sample portraits were scattered about the table. I could see that they had been executed hastily, but still they possessed a remarkable quality of vitality and, I felt sure, were good likenesses of their subjects.

Before a word had passed between us, the artist was at work, his eyes darting rapidly from my face to his pad, his pencil in constant motion.

"Please smile," he said, after a few minutes.

Now I am not a natural smiler. My face, when relaxed, tends to assume a dour if not downright miserable appearance, often prompting friends and acquaintances to ask me what's the matter when, in fact, I'm feeling perfectly happy. Forcing a smile struck me as inauthentic, even hypocritical, and I said as much to the artist.

He ceased his labours for a moment and looked up at me with such a sweet smile, shining from his lips and eyes, that I could not but respond spontaneously with one of my own, which seemed to please him, broadening his smile and likewise broadening mine.

"A smile is the most simple, most beautiful and most potent act of kindness," he said, "and, I'm sure we are agreed, the best thing in the world to do is an act of kindness. Followed, of course, by another act of kindness. I take this to be, unquestionably, the fundamental spiritual truth."

I nodded. In all honestly, I didn't think I could disagree with this bold assertion.

"So why," he continued, as his pencil danced frenetically across his paper, "do we not spend our entire lives performing acts of kindness?"

I tried to formulate an answer, before realising that his question was rhetorical.

"Three reasons," he said, his speech as quick and fluid as the motion of his hand. "One: we forget. Two: we need to sleep. Three: our egos object. 'Hang on a minute,' they say. 'All this kindness is all very well, but how about doing something for myself for a change?

Maybe I should pay a little attention to number one. Don't I deserve a bit of happiness, a bit of receiving instead of all this constant giving?' As usual, the ego misses the point completely. Its goal is personal happiness but it fails to realise that the road to happiness is paved with acts of kindness."

Thus saying, and allowing me no time to respond, he ripped the page from his pad with a flourish and handed it to me. I recognised myself at once, even though my portrait consisted of no more than a few dozen boldly drawn lines and blocks of shading. Something of my essence seemed to be radiating from the paper. I was indeed pleased with the artist's representation and would be proud for others to view my image. I made to hand the sheet back, but he stopped me with a gesture.

"Please keep it, my friend."

"Thank you," I replied, rolling the paper and placing it gently in my jacket pocket. "A splendid act of kindness."

"My role model is the sun who, every moment of every day, showers the entire Solar System with its kindness, otherwise known as light or energy or the Love of God."

We spoke a while more, of less sublime matters. He asked me where I was from and told me of a cafe in my home town where he and certain friends of his were sometimes to be found. "Perhaps you would care to join us," he added, without being any more specific.

"Certainly, yes," I replied. "May I know your name?"

"I'm Kaph, of course. We will meet again."

With that, he was on his feet, striding off to the counter with his empty coffee cup, and I took it as a sign that I should leave.

*

So it was that I became acquainted with the Society of Kaph. On many subsequent occasions I returned to that cafe, sometimes meeting Kaph the philosopher, sometimes Cath the storyteller, sometimes Kaph the artist, sometimes other men and women, sitting at the corner table, sometimes alone, sometimes in small groups. I frequented, too, the cafe in my own town of which the artist had spoken, a cheery but nondescript establishment along a little used side-street. There I first encountered a youngish fellow offering tarot readings, which did not initially attract me, but I quickly discovered that he read men's souls rather than the cards on his table which served merely as prompts, that he talked of the present rather than the future, and that those four qualities of kindness, awareness, patience and humility were prominent in both his words and his manner.

Kaph the tarot reader introduced me to others who patronised the cafe, and sometimes we would gather together around the corner table, occasionally discussing philosophy but more typically simply telling stories, like friends around a campfire, sleeping out beneath a starry summer sky, or like Chaucer's pilgrims, each with a tale or two to tell. I felt myself welcomed, accepted, at home amongst these people, who, I discovered, embraced all ages and all walks of life, men and women who, it seemed to me, shared my ideals and aspirations and could help me, teach me, ease me along the path that I was travelling, the spiritual way, one might say. And I found that I, too, began to contribute to the group and to realise that giving what little wisdom I had accumulated in my life could be as fulfilling as receiving fresh nuggets of truth from others. I had long felt myself to be something of a loner, an outsider, but now I was beginning to feel a part of something – I knew not what, but it felt good.

A visit to the cafe in my home town became a part of my daily routine, although often I found myself there alone, for it was far from a popular venue within the town, and my new-found friends proved much less predictable in their habits than me. (Rarely, I must add, did we discuss the lives we led in the outside world, beyond the strange intimacy of our cafe encounters.)

Once, alone and about to leave after a coffee and a perusal of the daily paper, I was surprised and delighted to see my original Kaph, the philosopher, enter the cafe. We greeted each other effusively and sat together, exchanging smiles but, at first, few words.

At length I spoke. "You were my first contact with the Society of Kaph and therefore it feels right that you should be the one to, as it were, initiate me properly into the Society – if, that is, you feel I am worthy to join."

In retrospect, my words sound absurd and pompous, and perhaps he thought so too, for he chuckled – he was a great chuckler – and replied: "To be one of us is simple. You embrace the values encapsulated in our name, you practise them in your life as often as possible and spread them in whatever way seems appropriate. Simple as that."

"No initiation ceremony, then?" I responded, inanely. "No revelation of esoteric teachings?"

This time we both chuckled, I in self-mockery.

"Methinks you've been reading too many books," he said. "We're no secret society, if that's what you're after. In fact, we're neither secret nor, in any coherent way, a society. We keep nothing hidden. Why should we, when the truth is abundantly obvious to all who seek it?"

"So what do I actually do as a member of your society?"

"As I said, we're not a society and we have no membership. As to what you do: you practise kindness, awareness, patience and humility. Is that not sufficient?"

I must confess to always having felt rather in awe of those "members of the Society" (what else am I to call them? Kaphs?) whom I had met. In their presence, I felt a certain inadequacy. I was no philosopher, no raconteur, no artist, no soul reader. These were men and women of rare talents. To be frank, I felt out of their league.

"Those I have met all sit at tables in this and other cafes and offer their services," I said. "But what can I offer?"

"You must offer whatever you can. Remember my story – the philosophising ferryman? I offered the strength of my rowing arms and the agility of my mind. So tell me, quickly, without thinking, three things you are good at."

I was glad that he asked only for three. Three I could just about manage. I would have been hard pushed to list any more.

"I'm good at walking," I began, rather tentatively. "I'm a good listener – or so people tell me – and I suppose, without being immodest, I'm quite good at writing."

26

"So there you have it," said the philosopher, opening his hands. "You walk, you listen and you write. Offer yourself."

And that is what I did. The next day, I went to the cafe, sat at my usual table and, very self-consciously, placed a pre-prepared card in front of me.

"Walker, writer and listener offers his services, free of charge."

Before long, customers started drifting in to the cafe, some glancing at my card – not unduly surprised, for the tarot reader and another storyteller often sat here, similarly advertising their talents. Meanwhile I sat back and relished the thought of being a Kaph.

"Ah, just what I need," said a middle-aged man, one of the cafe regulars, plonking himself on the chair opposite mine. "Tricky letter to write and, well, tell you the truth I'm not too good with words. Could you give me a hand?"

We discussed his case – a response needed to an unjustified claim for payment – I hastily drafted a letter and handed it to him. He looked at my scribbling uncertainly and I realised that his literary ineptitude was no relative matter. I found a decent sheet of paper and wrote the letter in my best hand, which is not exactly copperplate but certainly passes muster. He thanked me and shook my hand and I confess that I have rarely felt more satisfied after a spell of writing.

Next, a woman came to sit opposite me, clearly troubled. Hesitant at first, but with ever growing eagerness to unburden herself, she poured her woes into my listening ears. I maintained her gaze as much as possible, nodding my head and offering occasional sympathetic words, but little or nothing that would class as positive counselling. She talked for maybe half an hour, then abruptly stopped, released a deep sigh and a warm smile, rose to her feet and said, "Thank you so much. It's been so useful to talk to you." With that she left, leaving me wondering what, if anything, I had said that had so pleased her.

The waitress brought me a coffee – I hadn't ordered one – and lingered at my table, telling me the sad story of her Alzheimer afflicted mother. I listened. Then another writing chore was presented to me by a cafe customer – I could hardly believe this one: a love poem, naive

27

but heartfelt and clearly in need of some serious polishing. Together we re-worked it, toned up the scansion, substituted a few less corny adjectives, played with a few metaphors, even plagiarised a line or two of a Shakespeare sonnet. I helped him write it out afresh and he dashed off, presumably to meet his beloved.

Thus my day continued, by turns listening and writing, as enjoyable a day as I can remember.

"What's your name?" I was asked by one satisfied customer.

"Kaph," I replied, although not with a straight face. But my name was accepted.

Come day's end, I was still in the cafe. The waitress, a charming woman of about my age, was packing up as I prepared to leave, placing my card in my pocket.

"Plenty of listening and writing," she said, smiling, implying some complicity in my strange day's activities which she had, of course, observed, "But you've done no walking. Will you take a walk with me?"

"Indeed I will," I replied.

But of that adventure I will reveal nothing more.

*

Years passed and the millennium turned. I walked and listened and wrote. I was visited in my cafe by many fellow Kaphs, and, following their clues, I myself visited cafes and meeting places throughout the country where, sitting quietly in corners, I encountered kind, aware, patient and humble people offering their services – always free of charge, of course: the finances of the Society of Kaph have always been zero. I listened to all manner of Tales of Kaph and, at the suggestion of the philosopher, I began to write them down, either as nearly verbatim as I could manage or, later, in my own style. These Tales, I circulated amongst my colleagues (if I may call them that) and collected them together in this present volume. Meanwhile, I followed the patterns of my life and tried, as often as possible – which really means as often as I could remember – to practise the acronymic qualities of the Society, always amazed to discover the simple truth that the more I gave away, the richer I became; the more I let go, the more I received.

Then came a day when, sitting at the corner table in my home town cafe, my card before me, I was approached by a smartly dressed man carrying a small briefcase, a smile on his face, his hand outstretched to shake mine.

"Kaph," he proclaimed, and I was unsure whether he was stating his own name or mine. I smiled and shook his hand.

"I'm an event organiser," he said, sitting down. "That's what I do – organise events."

"Right." I nodded.

"So I'm organising an event. Will you come?"

"Where and when?"

"April 23rd. St George's Day. Noon. Dragon Hill, just below the Uffington White Horse, near Swindon. You'll be there, I hope."

The firmness of his tone did not invite a negative response. "Maybe. Well, hopefully. Yes, of course," I replied.

"Good man. See you there."

He shook my hand again, turned and left the cafe. Kaph the event organiser was clearly a busy man with a mission to fulfil.

*

I arrived early and took a morning walk along the Ridgeway to the ancient long barrow of Wayland Smithy, the surrounding majestic beech trees of which are personal friends of mine. As midday approached, I descended from the ridge top over the ramparts of Uffington Castle. Dragon Hill lies just below the chalk figure of the White Horse: a small, cone-shaped, flat-topped hill at the focus of a wide arc of strange and beautiful slopes, some grassed, some wooded. A bare patch of chalk on its summit marks the spot, according to legend, of St George's dragon slaughter.

But now the hilltop was swarming with people, with many more converging upon it from all directions. Before long, the gathering on Dragon Hill numbered a hundred or more – men and women of all ages, races and states of attire, as motley a band as one could imagine, possessing little in common beyond a name – Kaph – and a love of its magnificent meaning. Many I recognised, including the familiar and well-loved faces of Kaph the philosopher, Cath the storyteller, the artist, the tarot reader of my home town, and others with whom I had become acquainted during my travels. We greeted each other affectionately with smiles and embraces, as we all milled about the hilltop, enjoying the communion, the location and the unseasonably warm sunshine that bathed us, the loving kindness of our role model, the sun.

Kaph the event organiser was there, of course, his suit and tie abandoned in favour of a T-shirt emblazoned with a flag of St George.

"Well organised," I congratulated him as we greeted each other.

"Thank you, sir," he replied. "It's always most satisfying to see an event come together."

"What now?" I asked. After the preliminary meetings and greetings were over, I expected a more formal structure of events to occur – speeches, ceremonies or whatever.

The organiser shrugged and smiled. "Who knows? I simply organise time and place and try to ensure that everyone gets here who wants to be here. After that, well, we'll just see what happens. We have no chairman, no leader, no agenda. It's like those so-called "happenings" back in the sixties – no prescribed structure, no scenario, no script. We gather and we see what happens."

"Ah," I said. "When two or three are gathered together in my name..." The rest of the quote escaped me.

"Quite so," said Kaph the event organiser. "Or like the tale of the hundredth monkey. When just a few share an idea, its field is small. But once the hundredth monkey picks up the idea, suddenly the field explodes to encompass the whole species."

He slapped my shoulder playfully and wove off through a sea of bodies. And we all just stood there on the summit of Dragon Hill, chatting, laughing, exchanging tales, marvelling at the extent of our strange Society, and, very gradually, it all starting happening.

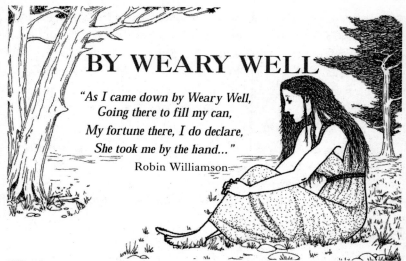

BY WEARY WELL

"As I came down by Weary Well,
Going there to fill my can,
My fortune there, I do declare,
She took me by the hand..."
Robin Williamson

I was weary indeed and in dire need of a thirst quenching draught when first I chanced upon that fateful place known as Weary Well. After days of trudging across wild moors and barren heathlands, the valley seemed like Paradise - meadows jewelled with poppies and buttercups, orchards smothered in blossom, fat-uddered cows grazing in the afternoon sun. Sheltered in a copse of oaks stood the carpenter's cottage, a barn and workshop and, a little way off, the welcome sight of the rough stone wall of Weary Well.

I ran down from the hillside, the lure of water overcoming any caution I would normally have felt upon encountering the haunts of men after so many days of solitary roaming. A pail attached to a rusty chain sat upon the rim of the well. I threw it down into the deep blackness, heard the splash then pulled and pulled until that glistening nectar emerged, cool and clear, the wine of God. I poured it into my eagerly open throat, sighed my pleasure then poured some more. Ecstasy: the taste of water to a thirsty man!

"Water is free to any traveller," came a voice behind me. "Food will cost you a few hours' work."

I turned to look into the face of the carpenter, a short man with bulging arms and massive hands, laughing blue eyes and a smile that was as welcoming as the water from his well.

31

We worked together in the woods till the sun had set, sawing planks of oak and ash and dragging them to the shed by the cottage: strenuous work relieved only by frequent draughts from that marvellous well. We spoke little, both of us men of few words, but I told him, as we supped from the pail, of my roving life, of days spent walking from village to village, following the harvest or any other work that came my way, of nights beneath the holy awning with only the stars for company.

He told me of a different life, a life of sparse adventure, perhaps, but one bathed in contentment and the security of home. Never had he ventured more than a dozen miles from the cottage of his birth. The crafting of wood into beautiful furniture was both his purpose and his joy. Once, he told me, he had loved a wife but death had taken her from him and now his daughter was his one companion.

I met her when we packed away our tools and plodded wearily back to the cottage for supper. No more than fifteen summers old, she was coy yet keen to snatch a frequent glance at me, as gangling as her father was robust, her face almost pretty when it peered out from within the drapes of her matted hair. Her hands were dainty and graceful as she ladled out our soup and cut our bread.

Her name was Placebo - the strangest name I've ever heard. 'I shall please' - and please she did. The carpenter told me that she'd spoken no words since her mother died: no words, that is, save "Yes."

She blushed at this and hid her face from mine amidst her curling locks.

"Is this true?" I asked, wishing to entice her into conversation.

"Yes," she whispered.

"Can't say no," her father told me with a peculiarly unfatherly wink and I, who had lived without the touch of a woman's flesh for far too long, began to feel the stirrings of desire.

He plied me with mead, glad, no doubt, of some more loquacious company than his daughter could offer, and insisted that I should stay the night. I did not gainsay him and he showed me to an attic room, clean but empty of all but a mat upon the boards, a stool and a huge bed, its ends and posts carved with the smooth, swirling patterns that were the mark of his craftsmanship. I flopped onto the mattress, blew out my candle and was asleep at once.

I awoke to a touch upon my unshaven cheek. Moonlight was pouring through a high, narrow window above me, shimmering on Placebo's tangled locks, her moist eyes - no longer coy but wide with longing - her naked breasts which I, bereft of any thoughts of propriety in my hypnagogic state, reached up and cupped in my hands. She lowered her body onto mine.

"Yes," she murmured.

What could I do? What would any man do? Before I knew it, my hands were gripping her buttocks, my lips pressed against hers, my desire burning like a forest fire. She writhed and sighed on top of me as I thrust into her, harder and harder, with the same urgency and delight as I had felt earlier that day, quaffing water from the Weary Well.

I present no excuses for my behaviour, other than suggesting that I was infected by the unstoppable momentum of lust. It shames me, now, that I should have so abused the hospitality of the carpenter. But then, in the bed he had fashioned so lovingly, I gave him not a single thought. I was aware of nothing but the wonder of Placebo's young body, offered with such unexpected and unrequested benevolence as I had never before, nor since, experienced. I confess that I was powerless to resist.

But, in the fury of our passion, the bed began to creak and groan, its legs banging against the floorboards. And then, as we reached the zenith of our lust and relaxed into the afterglow, the door burst open. There stood the carpenter in his nightshirt, a candle in his hand and a look upon his reddened face that any father can well imagine.

He said nothing, just glared, his eyes, it seemed to me, about to explode from their sockets. Placebo leapt from my body and scampered past him out the room. As for me, I just lay there on my back, fully prepared to take whatever punishment the carpenter cared to mete. No doubt I was prepared to die. I would not have argued or resisted.

33

I had no defence. Perhaps I even thought that death was fair recompense for those few minutes of blissful abandon.

For what the carpenter did next, I can offer no explanation, no hint of his possible motive. He turned his back on me, left the room and slammed the door behind him. A few minutes later, as I lay there still, not knowing whether to feel relieved or fearful, I heard a banging outside the wooden door, the banging of hammer on nails that went on and on, a hundred times or more. I knew, without considering the consequences, exactly what was happening. Half a dozen sturdy planks nailed across the door frame with all the permanence of the carpenter's skill. I was sealed up within the room of my undoing. I looked up to the tiny, slit-like window, high on the wall behind me, through which a beam of moonlight still streamed. Its width would barely take an arm, never an entire body. I was trapped. This was to be my tomb, this wondrous bed my coffin.

Presumably I slept - sleep has always been my great escape - for the next thing I knew was daylight bathing the room in a glow of seeming normality and, once more, I felt a burning thirst within my throat. I quickly recalled the events of the night and turned my mind to escape. The window was, indeed, no option and the door as firmly secured as a steel cage. I tried shouting until I was hoarse but no sound responded to my cries, neither from within the cottage nor beyond. I sat upon the bed and contemplated my fate. What was I to do? Nothing, it seemed, but wait. My fate was in the hands of the carpenter and I had no clue as to his intentions. He had appeared, the previous day, to be a friendly and a Christian man, but, knowing nothing of the emotions of fatherhood, how could I predict his reaction to my shameful abuse of his beloved daughter?

And so I waited, alone with my thoughts and self-recriminations, cocooned in my cell with even my luxurious bed now a sour comfort. For two days I waited, driven wild by boredom and fear, by regret and dreams of freedom, by, above all, a thirst that seemed to be sucking the life from me, a torture more painful than anything the carpenter could have devised for me. Or perhaps this was his torture?

34

On the third day, I was stirred from a crazed reverie by a knocking on the floorboards. I hastily removed the mat, located the source of the sound and began struggling to lever up the boards.

"Yes," came a muffled word of encouragement.

First I broke the nails of both my hands, then the blade of my penknife and the buckle of my belt, but the boards would not budge. I cursed the skill of the carpenter.

"Yes, yes, yes." Placebo's voice urged me on.

Finally I managed to rip up a single board and then its neighbour. And there, beneath me, was the dusty face of my erstwhile temptress, staring up at me from between the solid oak beams that supported the upper part of the cottage. It seemed that she had crawled, from her bedroom, along the tiny gap that separated the wooden planks of the downstairs ceiling and the upper floorboards.

She wriggled an arm through the hole in the boards, I took it and pulled and she gradually eased herself into the room. She flung her arms around my neck and tried to hug me but I pushed her away. Pleased though I was to see her, I had no wish to do anything more to incur her father's wrath.

She pointed hopefully to the bed. "Yes?"

"No. Definitely not. Not now. Must get out of here," I managed to say. My mouth was as dry as stone and I had trouble speaking. We were a fine pair - she with only one word to say and I barely able to articulate any. "Water. You have any water?"

She shook her head. Suddenly I had an idea, grabbed her face between my hands and kissed her. As her mouth opened to meet mine, I sucked at her saliva. It was only a drop, but enough to wet my lips. Unfortunately, though, she took it as a preliminary to further intimacy and started guiding me towards the bed. The girl, it seemed, was insatiable!

Finally she grasped the message of my reluctance and pointed at the gap in the floorboards. "Yes?"

I examined the space between the beams dubiously. I am not a small man and the thought of ending up wedged in that dark and dusty

35

tunnel seemed worse than remaining in my prison cell. But thirst is a powerful driving force. I would have tried anything.

"Yes," Placebo decided, eagerly, and she flung herself to the floor and slithered into the gap. It was several minutes before her feet disappeared from view, which did not reassure me.

"Yes, yes." I heard her distant voice urging me to follow.

So began an hour of agony and near desperation. To this day, I don't know how I managed it, but somehow I inched my way through the tiny space, choking on the dry dust, elbows, shoulders, hips and knees rubbed red raw by the rough wood, ribs crushed so tightly that I could barely breathe. I suppose it was no more than six feet but it seemed interminable and, at times, I thought I was completely jammed and would surely break a bone if I forced myself any further. But the light streaming in from Placebo's room, next to my barricaded door, where she had removed a couple of floorboards, goaded me onwards. Finally I emerged, bruised and battered but free at last.

Now she grabbed my hand and pointed at her own bed in the corner of the room. "Yes?"

"No!" I shouted, angrily. I knew that she had just saved my life but I could not forget that it was her carnal craving for my body that had initiated this sad affair in the first place. I tried to calm myself. "First, I need water."

She shook her head.

"The well!" The image, as it sprang into my mind, was like a vision of heaven.

"Yes, yes!"

I ran from the room, hurtled down the stairs and through the cottage door. I was charging down the slope towards Weary Well, too late to take precautions, before I saw the carpenter.

He was sitting on the low stone wall of the well, lifting the pail of freshly drawn, cool, clear water to his lips. It was a hot, sunny day - I hadn't noticed - and he was taking a break from his labours.

I rushed on, careless of the consequences, grabbed the pail from his hands and poured that beautiful liquid into my gaping mouth.

Perhaps my sudden arrival startled him and upset his balance. Perhaps I accidentally pushed him in my eagerness to quench my burning thirst - I just don't know. As I gulped down mouthful upon mouthful, I watched him slowly topple over backwards and fall, head first, into the depths of Weary Well.

The splash, some seconds later, brought me to my senses. I peered into the blackness. Nothing. I thrust my head as far into the gaping pit as I dared and strained my ears. Not a sound. I flung the pail in, its chain securely fixed to the outer wall of the well, scrambled over the wall and clambered down, clinging to the chain and finding ample footholds amongst the rough stones. Twenty feet or more down, my feet splashed into the water. I looked up at a glowing, pure blue disc of sky, high above me. Then, as my eyes grew accustomed to the darkness, I saw two big boots breaking the surface of the water, as still as death. I lowered myself to waist depth and reached out, only to discover that the carpenter's body was firmly wedged into a constriction at the base of the well. Pull as I might, I could not budge him.

By this time, his head had been submerged for a good five minutes and the absence of all movement convinced me of the finality of his state. Whether he had drowned or smashed his head on the well floor, I couldn't tell. And nor did I much care. Panic seized me and I hauled myself, hand over hand, up the chain and tumbled over the wall into the land of the living.

Without thinking, I pulled the pail back up, desperate for more water, but when I raised it to my lips I saw, with horror, that it was clear no more. Clouds of blood swirled around in it, deep red, polluting it with the vital fluid of the carpenter.

Driven by fear and shock, I ran - into the woods and away from that place. For hours I ran until I came upon a stream and washed away the taste of blood and terror, and, I hoped in vain, the memories of my fateful impetuosity. Then, as darkness fell, I slunk into a thicket and spent a restless night with the creatures of the forest floor.

No, I did not return - and that shameful fact has tormented me more than anything. How could I have left Placebo to discover for herself, as she surely would, the horror of her father's death? How could I not claim responsibility for my part in his gruesome end? How could I blot from my mind the whole strange and sorry business? Because I am a selfish coward, of course, although I pretend to myself that it is because I am a survivor, and always have been. No, I am not proud of the fact. I despise myself. I seek not the reader's pity or understanding, for I deserve neither. I tell my tale solely in the hope of relieving my tortured conscience.

*

Some six months later, I happened upon the vicinity of Weary Well once more. I befriended a man in the local tavern and, over our beers, I brought up the subject.

"I once knew the carpenter who lived in the cottage by Weary Well," I remarked, all innocently. "What's become of him, d'you know?"

He told me the tale. Many days after my hasty departure, apparently, the carpenter's body was discovered by the folk from the nearby village, in the blood red water of the well. It needed a rope and horse to winch him out. Within the cottage, the men of the village, searching for Placebo, came across my boarded up door. Eventually, for the carpenter, of course, had done a thorough job, they broke into the room and there found Placebo, lying naked and shaking with fright on that bed on which we had once shared our lust.

"What had happened?" I asked my companion with feigned curiosity.

"Who knows?" he replied. "The girl is a simpleton. 'Yes' is the only word she ever speaks. 'Yes' to everything she is asked. No one could get any sense from her, neither concerning how she came to be sealed in that room nor how her father had died."

I knew both, of course, though I said nothing. She must have crawled back through that tiny passageway, pulling the boards in her room back into place as she went then replacing the boards and mat in my room to conceal all trace of her entry. The reason why was the one thing that eluded me. But Placebo, as I knew full well, was not one to whom normal motives could be ascribed.

"She was taken in by some local worthies," my drinking companion continued, "and, some months later, it emerged that she was pregnant. Now, what d'you make of that, my friend?"

I shook my head, stunned into silence.

"Course, then we understood what had happened. The carpenter, without the comfort of a woman's love for years, had defiled his own daughter. Shamed by what he had done, we can but presume, he sealed her forever in the room in which he had perpetrated the vile deed and took his own life in the depths of the well."

And that, in essence, became the legend of Weary Well. No third party was ever sought, no suggestion that a fugitive from justice - as I imagined myself to be - had fertilised the girl and murdered or, at least, hastened the demise of her father. The only sullied reputation was his and he had atoned for his sin in the only honourable way. The tale was concluded, the legend assigned to local folklore.

But did it ease my conscience? I confess that it did not. And yet I wound my way, that day, with a lighter step and set out upon the rest of my life.

*

Twenty years passed and I found myself, again, at the cottage by Weary Well, my guise concealed by baldness, a greying beard and the scars of many adventures. Placebo lived there still: a grown woman, now - she didn't recognise me but I did her, of course - and with her lived her son, himself a carpenter, strong and stout. Takes after his father, they no doubt said in the village (or after his grandfather, perhaps), but I knew better. He had the look of a rover about him. And did I detect, in his eyes, the glint of a shamefaced coward?

I gave nothing away. How could I? Perhaps I felt a twinge of paternal pride but, with customary insensitivity, I denied it.

I asked Placebo if I might take a drink of water from the well and she smiled - a well-remembered smile. "Yes," she said.

With scant regard for troubled memories, I tossed the pail into the depths of Weary Well and as I pulled it up I became aware of activity around the cottage, of voices in the workshop and children's laughter in the parlour.

"How many children do you have?" I asked.

She raised her dainty hand and spread out the fingers.

"Five?"

"Yes."

So Placebo - I shall please - had done her share of pleasing over the years.

"And your husband?"

She shook her head, her eyes downcast, a flush beginning on her still smooth and youthful cheeks. She was as bashful as she had been when first I saw her, twenty years before.

So why had I returned? Was it sheer curiosity? Or did I seek somehow to atone for my former sins? If God is the only forgiver of sins, then I await the time when I stand before Him. But it was God who made me as I am, and bade me act the way I did. I take exception with the preachers. I do not believe that He who makes the heavenly spheres revolve upon their perfect ways and causes the flower buds to unfurl when the season is ripe should exercise any less control in the lives of men. I have no more free will than the Moon. I am what I am. I do what I must do. No, it is not God of whom we should seek forgiveness, but of those souls whose lives we hurt by our hasty deeds.

"Do you remember me?" I asked Placebo.

She glanced up for just a moment but I could see the dawn of recognition in her eyes. She nodded her head as her flush deepened, and I wondered how she had thought of me over those long years. Had I wronged her? Or had we both just done what our natures and the wiles of circumstance dictated?

"And do you forgive me?" I asked, knowing the only answer she could give.

"Yes," she said.

WORDS OF WISDOM

Sophie had just discovered a new word: pomposity. She liked words like that, words that tripped melodiously off the tongue and gave the impression of, well, pomposity. And now, here was its perfect application - the Headmaster's farewell assembly for the Year 11 leavers.

"Follow your dreams," he proclaimed, clutching his jacket lapels and staring dreamily into the mid-distance. "Set your sights on your goals, set them high and, with circumspect but single-minded determination, go for them. Seize the moment, seize the opportunities that changing circumstances bring, seize on to the unmistakable inner stirrings of your heart."

Come again? thought Sophie.

"Wanker," muttered the girl sitting next to her.

"Whatever aims and aspirations you might have," concluded the Headmaster, "go for them with the utmost zeal and panache."

Nice words, thought Sophie. Zeal. Panache. She mouthed them to herself, relishing their inner sound.

"Prick," muttered the girl sitting next to her.

And then... school was out. It was hardly the euphoria and celebration of that last scene in Grease. Some of the lads ripped off their ties and ceremoniously shredded them with scissors. Some of the girls defiantly lit up fags before they were even out of the school gates. There were a few cheers, plenty of hugs, one or two tears. Sophie wandered home alone, feeling the novelty of her new found freedom more as an unwanted responsibility than a blessing, another chain rather than a release.

The trouble was, she thought as she pondered the Headmaster's pompous words, she didn't have any dreams or goals. Or rather, for she was essentially a pragmatic girl (she liked that word, too), she recognised that all her dreams were unattainable. She wanted to be a Premiership footballer but, being a girl, that was clearly a non-starter. She rather fancied the idea of being a doctor but the most she could hope for was a handful of C grades when the GCSE results came out. An artist, perhaps, but how many people actually made a living out of painting pictures?

"Plenty of jobs going at Tesco," her mother suggested.

Sophie sighed. Sitting at the supermarket checkout was hardly the thrilling, fulfilling life she had envisaged for herself.

"They're always looking for care assistants down at the nursing home," was her father's contribution.

Could be worse, thought Sophie. Could be much better, though. Surely. She'd looked up 'zeal' and 'panache' in her dictionary. Somehow they didn't really apply to care assistants and checkout girls.

She tried the job centre. What was she looking for? One of the little white cards to leap out at her, screaming her name?

That was where she met Bob. They were standing next to each other, both staring vacantly and hopelessly at the bulletin boards.

"Bugger all, as usual," said Bob, more interested in looking at Sophie than the rows of job descriptions. "Fancy adjourning to a local hostelry for a coffee?"

Sophie gave him a quick glance. Scruffy clothes, unkempt hair, hands thrust into the back pockets of his jeans. Not exactly her type, she thought, although she had not the slightest idea what her type might be. Then, unaccountably, the Headmaster's speech flashed through her mind. "Seize the opportunities that changing circumstances bring." "Yeah, why not?" she replied, smiling for the first time that day.

"A touch of serendipity, us meeting like this," he said. How could she not fall for a chap who used a word like 'serendipity'? So fragile and innocent was her heart, a flower barely opened, that a single word was enough to conquer it.

So began the wild and reckless phase of Sophie's life. Bob lived in his own flat - well, a bedsit, actually - drove his own car and pursued a lifestyle that Sophie had never before encountered. Bohemian, he liked to call it - another word that appealed to her although she didn't really know what it meant. It seemed to involve not working, spending rather a lot of time in bed, smoking rather a lot of hash and talking rather a lot of crap with other Bohemians - or good-for-nothing, layabout, druggy, spongers, as her father preferred to call them. Sophie was sucked in. Getting a job seemed low on Bob's list of priorities - if, indeed, the concept of prioritising had ever occurred to him. A perfunctory weekly visit to the job centre was the extent of his efforts to find employment. Money seemed to appear from somewhere, probably from his well-off father who, Bob claimed, was happy to support his son's attempt to make a name for himself as an artist. Not that Sophie ever saw him applying paint to any of the blank canvases that littered his bedsit, but he and his mates rambled on about expressionism and post-modernity and other phrases that sounded good to Sophie and became included in her developing vocabulary.

"Bollocks!" Her father dismissed her attempts to justify her new boyfriend's artistic inclinations. "The bloke's clearly a no-hoper."

"Can't you find yourself a decent boy and a steady job?" her mother pleaded.

But Sophie had rapidly outgrown the hopes her parents had lovingly woven for her. She moved into Bob's bedsit. Autonomy and independence were her latest words. Spontaneity and self-sufficiency - words she rolled around her mouth and released into the world like sparkling soap bubbles, watching them drift away and burst into nothingness.

"You won't get a penny from me!" her father roared at her as she left home with a couple of suitcases. "We'll see how long your precious independence lasts. Autonomy my arse!"

Her mother slipped her a few tenners as she left. "Make it last," she whispered. "And try to get a job, dear."

Money continued to trickle into Bob's life from sources he never explained. He gave her enough to buy food and he kept her glass full whenever they went out drinking. She came to see this as payment for her services as cook, housekeeper, laundry maid and bed companion. Her father would have added whore but Sophie felt that she was doing nothing that she didn't freely and, for the most part, joyfully decide to do. It wasn't that she was in love with Bob - or so she told herself, love being the one word she felt unworthy to use - merely captivated by a life of which she had never dreamt, and relieved to be free of the expectation, from home and from school, to make her way in the world. Freewheeling, Bob called it, which evoked the image of gliding downhill on her bicycle, the wind blowing through her hair, careless of what lay at the bottom, of the effort required to pedal back up.

Bob had a way with words that she found irresistible, a playful verbosity that rivalled her ex-headmaster's. "My little wallaby," he called her, which probably wasn't very flattering but the way he pronounced 'wallaby' always made her giggle. "Make us a beverage," he'd demand, rather than simply ask for a cup of tea. "A brief perambulation?" he'd suggest when he fancied a stroll. And the words he whispered to her during their lovemaking - though she'd never repeat them - were more poetic than anything she'd ever heard at school, little onomatopoeic jewels she treasured in a secret compartment of her memory.

She began to experiment with Bob's paints and the experience of watching the rich colours spread and grow and flow, like a living being, over a huge, bare canvas was truly - another word she loved - cathartic. And the names on his watercolour palette filled her with as much rapture as the colours themselves: ultramarine, vermilion, alizarin, cerulean blue, burnt sienna.

Bob looked on, neither praising nor criticising.

"It conjures up the taste of anchovies, the sound of tumbling cataracts," he commented upon looking at one of her creations. "Real synaesthesia."

Sophie reached for her dictionary. Words like that oozed through her mind like melting honey, thrilling her like the touch of Bob's fingertips, sliding down her back.

But, for all his fancy words, he never told her that he loved her. Such clichés belonged to a world he despised. For him, it was enough to enjoy the moment.

After a few months, though, the enjoyment began to pall. When he wasn't stoned, Bob became moody and his idleness deepened, bordering on sloth. Sophie grew restless. At first, she had been awed and bewitched by the fact that he was five years older than her, but now it seemed that the age difference had been reversed, that he was the naive and immature one. Once, his solipsistic soliloquies had sounded like music from a higher world. Now, as she familiarised herself with her dictionary, they collapsed into self-indulgent prattling.

When, finally, he and his mates decided, on an impulse, to spend the last weeks of the summer in Ibiza, she gave up on him.

"What's the problem?" he asked. For him, nothing was ever a problem. "Living's really cheap, out there. Come on, it'll be great. Truly transcendental. Romanticism personified."

"What about the plane fare?"

"Get it from your old man. That's what I'm doing. That's what filial affiliation's all about."

So Sophie left Bob with his sophistic arguments, his fancy words, his selfish fantasies and his stoned mates. She returned home, depressed. Her father wore his "I told you so" expression and her mother, more sympathetically and rather tentatively, suggested, "How about trying Tesco?"

On her way to the supermarket, resigned to the inevitable, she bumped into her old Headmaster, Mr. Pomposity.

"How goes it, Sophie?" he greeted her cheerily, having abandoned, for the duration of the holidays, his headmasterly tones.

45

"Still looking for a job," she replied, wearily.

The Headmaster, always one for fatuous platitudes, offered her the benefit of his oft-delivered but rarely solicited advice. "Follow your heart, girl."

Where was her heart? she wondered. In Tesco? Certainly not. With Bob? Equally certainly not. But the thought of Bob rekindled the image of those enticing empty canvases and delicious tubes of paint, the memory of how beautiful it felt to bring them together, to watch the colours flow.

"D'you reckon I could get into college on an art course?" she asked suddenly.

"I reckon you can do anything you want to do," declared the Headmaster, seizing the opportunity to deliver more of his favourite words of wisdom. "Decisiveness, that's the word. Decisiveness and perspicacity. Perspicacity and consequentiality. Not forgetting zeal and panache, eh, girl? Zeal and panache: those are the words."

She turned away from Tesco and started walking briskly in the direction of the college. Decisiveness was the word that had taken root in her mind. She liked the emphatic sound of it, the four staccato syllables, like firmly planted footsteps marching into the future.

Words, she thought, are like the colours on a painter's palette: beautiful in themselves, perhaps, but, when put together, so much less than the finished picture.

ZEN AND THE COLOUR OF ORANGES

A story of a tree

Roshi Kashumo, one-time abbot - or roshi - of the Zen monastery at Kanazawa, delighted in the cultivation of a single orange tree that grew in the monastery courtyard. Although not, in general, a gardening man, he lavished love and attention upon this one tree, following the principles he had learned in his youth from a bonsai master: carefully picking out the growing shoots, rigorously pruning the upper boughs and curling wire around the stout lower branches to direct their growth. Over the years, the tree took on the gnarled and sculptured appearance of a true bonsai, yet it grew to a height of twelve feet and was regarded by many to be the most beautiful orange tree they had ever seen. Kashumo's meticulous pruning resulted in a profusion of blossom and a crop of oranges that would have proudly adorned a tree of twice the size. Each orange, slightly smaller than average, was perfect in both colour and shape, fitting neatly into the cupped palm of the Roshi's smaller than average hand.

It was said that the tree regularly bore exactly 365 fruit each year, allowing Kashumo to enjoy one for his breakfast every morning. Although a pious and self-disciplined man, the Roshi - small of stature and gentle of speech - relished the pleasures of the senses as well as any man, and no sensory experience pleased him more than the taste of cool, fresh orange juice to start his day.

47

The monks of the community, of course, would never touch Kashumo's oranges but contented themselves with the less pampered fruit that grew in the monastery gardens. Kashumo personally picked his own exemplary crop and placed the luscious, shining orbs in a wicker basket beside his mat in the zendo where, even in grey twilight, they glowed with the orange light of the sun that had nourished them. Very occasionally, he would offer one to a guest, thereby denying himself his full annual quota of breakfasts. To be a recipient of such a gift was a singular honour.

Once, according to legend, the Emperor of Japan visited the monastery and, knowing the tale of the oranges, anticipated receiving the choicest specimen from the Roshi's wicker basket. But Kashumo, who regarded all men as equal and was in awe of nobody, declined to make the gesture. Later, he noticed the Emperor's servant boy gazing longingly at the fruits as they shone in the candlelight and, with a kindly smile, he handed the boy one, to the astonishment of all present. The Emperor said nothing. The entire company of monks, courtiers and guards watched in silence as the boy carefully peeled his orange, slurped noisily at the juice and chomped at the flesh. Not wishing to discard any part of the Roshi's gift, he scraped off the pith with his teeth and placed the outer skin into the soles of his sandals as extra cushioning.

The Emperor could contain himself no longer. It was not the custom, in those days, for anyone, even an Emperor, to question the words or deeds of a Zen Roshi, but nor was it the custom for the Emperor to be anything less than the focus of attention and the prime receiver of favours. Not one for hiding his feelings behind tact, the Emperor said, as respectfully as he could, "Why do you dishonour me by so honouring my servant boy?"

The courtiers nodded their heads. A good question indeed.

"An act of kindness dishonours no one," replied the Roshi, with a smile. "You expected a gift and feel aggrieved that you did not receive one. This boy, I could see, longed for one of my oranges but expected nothing, of course. Longing without expectation! You must concede that even an Emperor is no match for such power. How could I resist?"

The Emperor, for all his imperial arrogance, was educated enough to know that the quality of wisdom is second only to the quality of kindness, and here were both displayed in a single action. He bit his lower lip and, with an evident absence of sincerity, returned the Roshi's smile.

That night the servant boy was taken away from the Emperor's entourage by the monks and shown to a privileged bedchamber overlooking the courtyard. During the night the Emperor's bodyguard burst in to the boy's room, their swords raised, intent upon slaughter - whether acting on the Emperor's orders or inspired by their own jealousy is not known - but the monks, ever alert, had whisked the boy away and secreted him in a cave in the garden.

When the Emperor left, the next day - after a breakfast with the Roshi that was devoid of oranges and low on conviviality - the boy was offered for adoption to a local Samurai family. There he was trained in the art of swordsmanship and, years later, led a successful rebellion against the Emperor.

"Such is the power of happenstance: a single orange may change the course of a nation's history," said Kashumo, an old man by that time, but still capable of uttering a pithy epigram for every occasion.

Naturally enough, the monks of Kanazawa came to regard Kashumo's orange tree as a sacred object and they would bow reverently whenever they passed it while crossing the courtyard about their daily business. When Kashumo heard of this practice he rebuked the entire community.

"Why do you revere this particular tree?" he demanded. "Has God neglected to touch all other trees with his presence? If my orange tree is sacred, then so too are all orange trees. And if all orange trees are sacred, so too are lemons and limes, cherries and almonds, elms and firs."

"Then why do you devote such care and attention to that one tree?" asked one of the monks.

"Because it is the tree I see each day through the window of my bedchamber, my first vision of the outside world. If you see a fir tree through your window, or a cherry tree, or a lump of rock, or a pile of dirt, then direct your love towards that. When awareness alights on any object, then that object proclaims the wonder of the Godhead."

Kashumo, as head of a Rinzai Zen monastery, would set koans upon which his monks would meditate in their quests for enlightenment. A koan is an unanswerable question that pushes the thinking mind to and, hopefully, beyond its limit. "Who am I?" is the most fundamental of all koans, the ultimate enigma of human thought, while "What is the sound of one hand clapping?" is the best known in the West (although it is doubtful whether this koan was ever used by the Japanese Zen masters).

Kashumo achieved a certain fame for his choice of either absurdly simple or fiendishly convoluted koans with which to bamboozle his most intellectually arrogant pupils. Often he would pick an orange from his wicker basket, hold it up before a novice monk and propose a koan such as, "Is the fruit named after the colour orange or the colour after the fruit?" or "Why is an orange orange?" or "The orangeness of an orange is its colour. What is the manness of a man?" or, strangest of all and an aphorism that came to stand for the highest ideals of the Zen aspirant, "When an orange rots on the kitchen windowsill, a crane flies off to the south. How can this be? What is the secret that connects all beings?"

And it is said that many a monk, sweating for days or months or years over such a koan, would suddenly experience the opening of his mind's eye and rush to the Roshi with his answer.

And if the Roshi was satisfied with the answer he would smile, pick an orange from his wicker basket, toss it to the monk and say, quite calmly, "Good. You have it. Now enjoy it."

The orange tree, planted as a pip by Kashumo when still a young man, grew old with the master. Its limbs became twisted, its skin wrinkled and furrowed, its exuberance subdued, its fecundity tempered. And yet it was destined to survive its benevolent patron by many centuries.

Some fifty years after Kashumo's death, towards the end of the Seventeenth Century, the renowned poet Basho visited Kanazawa during one of his contemplative walks across Japan. Kashumo's orange tree still stood in the courtyard, cared for with devotion - although somewhat less empathy - by subsequent Roshis of the monastery. It was springtime and the branches were covered in blossom, so Basho was unable to indulge his dream of plucking a fruit, peeling its wonderfully orange skin and sucking at its flesh. Nevertheless, he commemorated the occasion by sitting in meditation beneath the tree and composing a suitable haiku:

> *Kashumo's tree blooms.*
> *We sit beneath its branches*
> *To await the fruit.*

Years after the days of Kashumo and Basho, in the late Nineteenth Century, the ancient orange tree was toppled by a small earthquake. Its roots remained embedded in the soil, however, and, even from its supine position, it sent forth its flowers each spring and annually produced a modest crop of oranges.

The Englishman Christmas Humphreys, who did so much to popularise Zen Buddhism in the West, once visited the monastery and came upon the tree. It lay on the ground of the courtyard, its boughs bizarrely twisted and tortured by age, but still a few healthy young shoots sprung from it, still it retained its legendary beauty and still a few of its fruits reached delicious ripeness. Mr Humphreys, a well-respected scholar of Japanese cultural traditions, pleaded for and was granted a taste of one of the latter generation of oranges from Kashumo's tree.

"The essence of the sun was contained therein," he later declared, "and so too was the essence of Zen." With his characteristic penchant for hyperbole, Humphreys went on, "I saw that orange as a symbol of the very nature of Zen: a hard, smooth, impermeable, beautiful and perfectly shaped outer skin which, once pierced, yielded a juice that was both sweet and acid in equal measure."

Kashumo, with characteristic scorn for overblown pomposity, would have laughed. He was a simple man who simply loved to eat an orange for his breakfast.

And the orange tree itself, the true hero of my story, would have given the words of the English scholar not a single thought, for, being a tree, it had neither capacity for nor need of thinking. While Kashumo and Basho and Christmas Humphreys came and went, it grew, as trees do: it absorbed sunlight, water and carbon dioxide: it blossomed, produced its orange fruits and silently basked in its own Being. Such is the way of trees.

POOTER

My father was a lighthouse keeper: a strange, littoral profession, between the jagged ship-crunching rocks and the roaring vastness of the ocean. I often used to imagine him silently patrolling the balcony of his lonely pinnacle in the sea, peering into the blackness for signs of vessels in distress. His was a noble and romantic calling, I liked to think, lighting the mighty lamp and keeping watch through the long, dark nights of winter: a life in which success was judged by the complete absence of incident.

Perhaps I was mistaken. Another possibility was that my lighthouse keeping father was a myth created and perpetuated by my mother to explain her husband's removal from our family home. But it was a myth which my siblings and I were happy to accept and to augment with our own imaginings. Was all his furniture rounded, I wondered, to fit against the walls of his tall, cylindrical, red-and-white striped home? Did he sleep in a curved bed? And did he have a toilet in his lighthouse? Perhaps he had a hole in the wall – quite high up above the crashing waves, of course – and he went directly into the sea.

One day, when I was ten and my father showed no signs of ever migrating from his lighthouse, my mother presented us with a small cardboard shoebox.

"The legacy of your father," she said, simply.

We opened the box excitedly, expecting exotic treasures washed up on the rocks from shipwrecked galleons. But it was full of shells. My brother, Peter, was disappointed and mooched off in a huff, but not I. I was enthralled by these seashore wonders. They weren't especially remarkable shells – just your average selection of winkles, cockles and clams – yet each one was perfect. And even those that were flawed had perfect flaws. I imagined my father strolling the beach, each low tide, eyes downcast, searching. He'd stop, bend to pick up a shell, turn it slowly in his hand and nod his approval. I like to think I inherited his sense of rapture at the ordinary miracles of nature.

*

My father's surname was Pooter, and I am Matthew Pooter. A strange name. Literally everyone, when I have to give my name, expresses surprise and asks me how I spell it: as though Pooter could be spelled in more ways than one. Well-read people usually smile and bring up the name of Charles Pooter, the straight-laced hero of Grossmith's "Diary of a Nobody". I read the book long ago. I'm quite fond of the poor old twit, but he's not exactly a role model. He works as a lowly clerk, goes to extraordinary lengths to be terribly polite and proper, and his idea of a good time is to wander across the common with his chums Cummings and Gowing.

But I know of no one else who shares our family name.

"So are you related to Charles Pooter?" I'm sometimes asked.

"No. He's a fictional character," I reply with barely concealed irritation.

"Ah, really?"

"But my father was a famous lighthouse keeper."

"Really?"

Well, he was famous in our family, at least.

*

My mother was once a dancer on the London stage, later a gym mistress at a girls' prep school. Then a freak trampolining accident deprived her of her agility, her confidence and her livelihood. For reasons that I never understood, she became a watch repairer, in the days when it was still cheaper to repair a broken watch rather than discard it and buy a new one. She worked from home, a solitary and meticulous occupation, a magnifying glass permanently wedged into her eye socket, her fingers moving with the grace and precision that had once infused her entire body. But the intense concentration produced a throbbing headache that came to be a persistent feature of her inner landscape. She turned to opium for relief – I've no idea how she came by it – and sank into a miasma of private visions and comfortable numbness, listening to Mahler or Bruckner and dreaming, perhaps, of her former glory days or her ever-absent and rarely-mentioned husband.

My older sister was an astonishingly pretty girl, and as naive and selfish as only astonishingly pretty girls can be. I can't remember her ever speaking to me except to criticise, mock or insult. When she was seventeen and I was twelve, she eloped with the hippy son of the local vicar and they both disappeared to live in a yurt in the wilds of Ayrshire, never to be seen again.

"Gone the way of your father," my mother would mutter, leaving me to wonder what way that was. My childhood seemed to be full of the comings and goings of other people. The Pooter legacy, my brother called it.

My brother Peter was so unlike me that I often wondered about our common progeny. He was - and still is - one of the few people I have ever known to be truly happy in his work. He drove an earth mover: a huge, yellow monster shifting rock in the local quarry. Each wheel was twice as tall as a man, the driver in his lofty cab appearing the size of a child. And it moved like a lava flow, slow and all-consuming, transforming the earth.

Peter was eighteen months older than me. He still is, and still he never lets me forget it. An eighteen month age gap might have been quite significant when we were both kids, but its importance has tended to diminish as the years have drifted by – except, that is, in my brother's eyes. Consequently, like millions of second sons, I have suffered all my life from a younger brother complex. I have always felt a bit vulnerable and inadequate, dwarfed by other men in their huge earth movers, trying to shape the world.

*

The shape of my world changed, quite by chance, one morning when I met Soapy.

It was in a crowded Clifton cafe, a place called Bodkins, a favourite watering hole of mine. I was preoccupied with something or other and, on a whim, ordered a peppermint tea. The atmosphere in the place was steamy and smoky, which I found perversely comforting after the cold air of the street. I eased my way through the sprawl of tables and chairs, mostly occupied, to my usual table by the window where I plonked down my mug of tea, and myself, and reached in my pocket for my notebook, feeling that a line of poetry was about to emerge.

Almost at once, another identical mug of tea was plonked down on the table beside mine and a woman flopped herself into the chair opposite me. I looked up. At first I couldn't see her face, concealed behind a mass of dark curls cascading over her shoulders, but as she swept her hair back behind her ears with both hands, she looked me full in the face. Her eyes were huge, deep blue, sparkling, fringed with long black lashes. Her lips were slightly open, uncertain of whether to stretch into a smile. God, she was beautiful!

She spoke: "Tell me the first thing that comes into your head."

"I'm sorry? Why?"

Those were the first words that passed between us, and so succinctly did they encapsulate our respective personalities that we might just as well have never bothered to converse again. She was all spontaneity, openness, playfulness and eagerness to explore. And I, already, even in that first exchange, was apologising for myself, questioning.

She laughed and I laughed with her and our laughter broke the magic spell of that perfect moment.

It was then that I noticed the extraordinary coincidence of our meeting. We were dressed identically. We both wore blue denim jeans, blue and white trainers of the same make, and black T-shirts bearing a Guinness logo. We were both drinking herbal tea from identical mugs, and she, like me, had a notebook and pen in her hand. To an observer, we could have been twins, deliberately emulating each other.

(Except that she wore her clothes so much more elegantly than me. Her jeans were tight fitting around her hips; mine too baggy. The Guinness logo on her T-shirt, stretched over the mound of her breasts, was smooth and clear; mine was crumpled. And her hair was exquisite; mine a mess.)

"Nice get up," she said, casting her eyes over my clothes.

"Yours, too," I said and we laughed some more.

Then we talked a little. She talked. I listened. At least, her mouth opened and closed and sounds poured out. Presumably they represented words that joined to make sentences that conveyed some kind of meaning. I just stared in wonder.

She paused to sip her tea, her eyes still fixing mine over the rim of her mug.

"What's your name?" I asked.

"Soapy. Soapy Cringle."

"I'm sorry?"

"Soapy."

"How d'you spell it?"

She laughed. I never laughed when people asked me to spell my own name.

"Actually, I was christened Sophie," she explained, "but when I was young I had a problem with the 'f' sound, so I always pronounced my name as 'Soapy'. Pucking silly, I know, but it stuck, the way childhood labels tend to stick. Now everyone knows me as Soapy."

"Nice to meet you, Soapy," I said, trying out this new name.

"And you?"

"Matthew Pooter."

"Superb! I used to love pooters. I'm a big fan of entomology."

She was one of the few people I had ever met who professed a familiarity with a pooter. It's a glass flask with two tubes attached. One has a funnel-shaped end that fits over a tiny insect. The other tube goes in your mouth, you suck – or poot, as it's called – and your

57

specimen is whisked up into the flask. It's the most efficient method of collecting small insects.

And Soapy Cringle, who shared my dress sense and, it turned out, had never read "Diary of a Nobody", was an expert pooter. How could I fail to fall for her?

*

We became very good friends: Soapy and I. Eventually lovers. Even this, like our first meeting, happened by accident. I was a shy and rather feckless young man, bewitched by the opposite sex but failing to understand how any of their number, and particularly this utterly beautiful representative called Soapy, could feel anything other than a mild repulsion towards any of my own sex, and particularly this tortured and self-doubting specimen called Pooter. Yes, we were friends, but the notion of advancing our relationship to a more intimate level struck me as a wild presumption. The consequence was inertia. (Like my missing sister: in Ayrshire).

Then, one evening, we were in her flat, drinking a bottle of wine and enjoying a freely flowing conversation. I stood up and stumbled over something – her floor was always littered with stuff. I fell and found myself pressed against her, as she sat on the edge of her bed. We were touching. Neither of us moved. The moment had come. All at once it all happened – a great unleashing of pent-up passion. We both surrendered to it.

I won't go into the details. You'll have to imagine what happened next. As I said, I'm a bit of a shy type.

*

Where does shyness come from?

When I was a boy, my mother had a pair of black knickers. I only saw them on wash days, of course, hanging out on the line in the back garden. Embroidered over the crutch area, in pink letters, was the phrase, "Come inside". I thought it a rather strange message and, in my innocence, I asked her why.

"Your father bought them for me," was her only response.

I should have asked her, then, whether this purchase was before or during his lighthouse keeping life. But I didn't. We never talked about my father.

"There are many things, Matthew, that are not fitting subjects for conversations," she often said.

In my mother's case, virtually every topic fitted this category. She was as taciturn as Soapy was loquacious. But they were both, I have to say, very good looking women.

*

Our love affair was short but very sweet: a matter of weeks only, weeks that were to define my personhood and forever be recalled as the glorious springtime of my life. But they were weeks of bliss and torment in equal measure. I suffered from the debilitating delusion that I was simply not good enough for one such as Soapy. How could she love me? Although she said she did. The album of the day was Jackson Browne's "Late for the Sky", which we, along with most young lovers of our generation, pretended was our personal anthem. I can still recall the haunting words:

> *"You never knew what I loved in you; I don't know what*
> *you loved in me:*
> *Maybe the picture of somebody you were hoping I might be."*

I imagined that she was just toying with me for a while, amusing herself till someone better came along: such were my perverse, self-pitying thoughts. She possessed charisma, an ebullient personality and a beautiful body. She could have had her pick of Clifton's most handsome, dynamic men-about-town. So why should she be interested in a scruffy, poverty-stricken, poetry scribbling, neurotic no-hoper like me? It struck me as a valid question. But I successfully kept it at bay during the magnificent first flush of our flowering affair.

Our incompatible energy levels posed the greatest problem. She was a great flitter. I'm more, as befits my name, a pootler. I pootle leisurely along. She flitted energetically, unpredictably, whimsically. Like an

59

insect flitting from leaf to leaf, she was too quick to be caught in my clumsy pooter.

But our few weeks together, like my father's seashells, were perfect. And even their flaws were perfect flaws.

*

Soapy and my brother met, somewhat against my better judgement, during that intense period between our first encounter and our first sexual consummation. He was passing through town and he called in on me unexpectedly. I had arranged to meet Soapy in Bodkins, the cafe where we first met, a place that had become our regular haunt. I didn't want to miss her so, rather reluctantly, I took him along. I suspected that it would all end in tears, and indeed it did.

"This is my brother, Peter," I introduced him.

"You must be joking," said Soapy.

"No. Why?"

"Peter Pooter? You must be joking." And her face fell into a wide grin as she sat next to me at our table.

"It's my name," said Peter. I could see that, like me, he was instantly bewitched.

"Peter Pooter pooped a pot of pootled poppers," said Soapy, bursting into a giggle.

"Sorry about her," I said.

"It's okay, Matthew. We Pooters get used to such things." He was grinning. He didn't take his eyes off Soapy. Her hair was tumbling all over her face as she shook with laughter.

"Pleased to meet you, Peter," she said, slowly calming herself.

"A chap can't help his name," said Peter, in a tone of mock apology.

"Peter just dropped in," I said, trying to regain some semblance of normality.

"I didn't even know you had a brother," said Soapy. "Would you believe it," she addressed Peter, "he never even mentioned your existence."

"Charming," said Peter.

"So where d'you live?"

"Right now, up in Gloucestershire. I'm working on a new by-pass."

"Doing what?"

"Earth moving. That's my job."

"Wonderful!" said Soapy. "Sounds like a path with a heart. So tell me: how did you come by your amazing name?"

"It was my father's. As first son I suppose I sort of inherited it."

"Your father? You never told me about him, either, Pooter," she said, flicking only the briefest of glances in my direction. She always called me Pooter: I took it as a term of affection.

"Our father was a lighthouse keeper," said Peter.

"You never told me that, Pooter." She turned to me, her eyes wide open in delight. "A lighthouse keeper! How absurdly romantic! And what about your mother?"

"She used to be a watch repairer," said Peter, "before she went mad. She was once a ballet dancer."

"And are there any more of you Pooters?"

"There's our sister. Somewhere in Ayrshire, 'pparently. We don't keep in touch."

"What's her name?"

"Polly."

"Polly Pooter? Polly Pooter kettle on." She threw back her head and roared with laughter. "Pooter, why didn't you tell me all this? It's priceless."

I shrugged. "Well..." I began, but Peter jumped in.

"Our Matthew's not exactly into families. He couldn't wait to leave home. Tell you the truth, he's a bit of an intellectual snob, what with his poetry and his degree and all, and me working as an earth mover, and Polly married to a half-wit in Ayrshire, and Mother virtually out of it, and our father... well, the least said about him the better."

"Why?"

"Why? Well, it's just that nothing's ever said about him. Except that he's a lighthouse keeper."

61

"So he's still alive? And still a lighthouse keeper?"

Peter looked at me. I raised my eyebrows. He'd brought up the subject and, after all, he was my older brother. He could reply.

"That's a good question," he said. "A very good question."

Soapy looked from Peter to me and back again. "And the answer?"

"Like all good questions," answered Peter, "it has no answer." Then he made a rapid subject change. "So tell me, how did you two meet?"

"We just sat down together," said Soapy. "At this very table, in fact. Both dressed the same and both drinking peppermint tea. Simple as that. We just fell into each other's lives"

"And I bet he's been trying to get into your knickers ever since, eh?"

Jesus! Can you imagine it? This was still several days before that bottle of wine in Soapy's flat, and my delightful brother, who's used to exchanging crudities with his road-building mates, comes out with a comment like that. I could have killed him. Instead, I laughed, hoping that we'd all laugh together and make light of it.

"Yeah, he's been trying," said Soapy.

"But not succeeding, I'll bet."

"Not yet," she said, and I swear she flashed me a provocative glance, although, by that time, I was intently studying the dregs at the bottom of my coffee cup.

"Don't worry," said Peter. "He'll probably get there in the end. Talking of knickers, Matthew, d'you remember that black pair that Mum had. 'Come inside' written across the crutch. You wanna get a pair of those, Sophie."

"Soapy," said Soapy.

"For Christ's sake, Peter!" I snarled across the table.

"Sorry. I embarrass him, you see. I think the whole family embarrasses him. Actually, I think the whole Universe embarrasses him. Don't worry, Matthew. I'm only joking. Your little Sophie here's a great chick. Far be it from me to tell her what a prize prick you are."

Yes, I remember, now, why I rarely review the memory of this unfortunate encounter. Most of the pages of my book of Soapy reminiscences are lovingly well fingered. This one is seldom opened. I hate to form stereotypical judgements but, like all of us, I inevitably do. If you imagine the appearance, personality and conversational manner of a typical plant-driving road builder, then you have Peter perfectly. And if you want a clearer image of me, while we're talking stereotypes, well, let's just say that, at the time, I had a newly acquired degree in philosophy, very long hair, no job and no money. And Soapy? No, I think she defied stereotypes. Femme fatale, perhaps?

I had virtually dropped out of the conversation, cringing in my chair while Soapy Cringle quizzed Peter Pooter about his earth moving activities. Contrary to my initial expectations, they seemed to be getting on remarkably well, but Soapy always got on well with everyone, and I will grudgingly concede that Peter, for all his coarseness, possessed a certain primitive charm and good looks of the rugged, unpolished variety. After a while, I retreated to the loo and sat there seething and sulking for a good ten minutes. When I returned, Peter was on the point of leaving.

"Gotta hit the road, Matthew. See you again soon." He slapped the back of my shoulder rather too forcefully, picked up Soapy's hand, kissed it rather too passionately, winked at her rather too conspiratorially, held her gaze rather too lingeringly then left rather too dramatically. Bastard, I thought.

"He certainly says what he thinks," said Soapy.

"He just doesn't think about what he says," I replied.

"I like him," she said. "And I want to meet your father, the lighthouse keeper."

"Me too," I muttered.

*

She left me about three weeks after that wine-fuelled evening of delight in her flat. She went off to India. I never saw her again.

To be fair, she'd been planning the trip for months and, at one point, she'd suggested that I accompany her. But I couldn't possibly afford it, and neither did I feel inclined. I'm not an adventurer. I once went to Holland and once spent a weekend in Paris: that's enough overseas travel for me, thank you. But Soapy had a longing to see the world. In particular, her dream was to visit the ashram of Ramana Maharshi on the slopes of the holy Mount Arunachala in southern India. A large, smiling photo of the old chap adorned the wall of her flat. He looked a pleasant enough sort, but I wasn't really into gurus or Eastern religions. Soapy was. Ramana had actually been dead for some thirty years, but his memory and his teachings were alive and thriving. Soapy wanted some first-hand contact.

I expected her to return within a month or so. I kept her seat warm for her, both in my heart and my life. But she stayed away for a year, then two. She'd apparently found what she had been looking for. I should have been pleased for her, but jealousy and rejection were my dominant feelings. I got on with my life. I didn't find anyone else. I continued to nurture the hope that one day she might return to me, just as I had spent my early life hoping that one day my father might come home from his lighthouse. He didn't. And neither did Soapy.

After a few years, I happened to bump into an old friend of hers, a woman named Heather whom I had met once or twice.

"Heard anything from Soapy recently?" I asked her.

The smile dropped from her face. "God, haven't you heard?"

"Heard what?" I knew this wasn't going to be good news.

She led me off to my favourite Clifton cafe and bought us both a peppermint tea – the house speciality – before speaking.

"We kept in touch," she began. "The occasional letter. Soapy loved it there. She'd begun an apprenticeship with an old Indian herbalist on the ashram. I went out to visit her – my boyfriend and I were travelling around Asia for a bit. God, it was dry and unbearably hot down there. We got a train to the nearest station where we'd arranged for Soapy to pick us up. She'd borrowed an old jeep from someone. Anyway... D'you really want to hear this?"

Why did she ask that? Of course I did. I nodded.

"You know she was always a crazy driver. And the roads were no better than dirt tracks. A wheel got caught in a rut, the whole thing turned over, Soapy was thrown out and the bloody jeep landed on top of her."

She didn't embellish the story, I'll grant her that. I stared at her.

"She's dead, Matthew. Crushed to death in an instant."

How did I receive this news? Stoically, I believe. At one time, I might have felt that a world that no longer contained Soapy held no further place for me. At one time, I would have been inconsolable. But the flow of time had carried me on upon my idiosyncratic course and my memories had found comfortable shelves on which to rest themselves in the store cupboard of my mind. Like the lifeless shells in my father's shoebox, I took them out, brushed them off, polished them up and basked in their beauty, from time to time, then put them back and pootled on upon my merry way.

So my central feeling, I believe, was one of unselfish grief. For such a radiant and vivacious life to be snuffed out so suddenly – so needlessly – seemed such a waste. She deserved a better death, a hero's death. But who amongst us can choose the manner of our death, just as we cannot choose the circumstances into which we are born.

"We stayed for her funeral, of course," my bearer of bad news continued. "It was held at the ashram where she'd lived her final years. They burnt her body on a pyre. Presiding was the old herbalist she'd worked with. It was all conducted in Tamil. They scattered her ashes on Mount Arunachala: an immense, pyramid-shaped hill.

"I brought home her few meagre possessions – virtually nothing. A clay bowl, a few clothes – it was so damn hot over there that no one seemed to bother much with clothes – a few old letters from me and a postcard from you, I think. Picture of a lighthouse."

*

She'd asked me, once, why I'd never made an effort to locate my father. Surely the records of lighthouse keepers were accessible at Trinity House, the headquarters of the lighthouse service. And surely there could only have been one called Pooter.

"True," I mused. "No doubt it would have been possible."

"So why didn't you ever try?" she asked. "Why don't you try now?"

There was no answer I could give that she would understand. There was no answer that I understood myself. Some things, I might have said, are best left as myths and mysteries.

I had it in mind to visit all the lighthouses of Britain – for no other purpose than that I felt a great affinity for lighthouses. I started, naturally enough, at Land's End, staring out across the boiling sea to the Longships and Wolf Rock. From there, I walked to Tater Du and Pendeen, then on to the Lizard on England's most southerly point. After that, my resolve dwindled – lack of perseverance has always been my greatest fault – and I returned home.

I finally wrote to Trinity House, not to seek information about my father but enquiring about the possibility of employment for myself. I had decided to become a lighthouse keeper. But the unstoppable march of technology was against me. The final few flesh and blood lighthouse keepers were rapidly being phased out, replaced by soulless robots. My father's profession had become redundant. I was unable to succeed him in his noble vocation, denied my rightful place in the family business.

Instead, I found a job as a laboratory assistant in a university biology department. My boss was a beautiful entomologist who reminded me of Soapy. I often stood behind her as she bent down to peer through her microscope, admiring the firm roundness of her buttocks. Maybe one day I'd ask her if she'd like to join me in a mug of herbal tea.

She specialised in fruit flies, tiny insects that breed so speedily that studying their genetic changes across numerous generations is a relatively easy matter. My task was to catch the little things in their vivarium and prepare them for her examination. My main tool was a glass pooter. Pooting was my occupation. I had become a pooter.

A DEATH IN THE FAMILY

Dark and secret shadows lurk in the histories of most families, if one digs down a generation or two. The strangely soiled undergarments of my own family have their origin in a single incident, the consequences of which have rippled through my entire life - indeed, my very existence is a result of them. I speak of it now in the certainty that no evidence of a crime will ever be unearthed and that my words will be construed by all who knew my father and my grandparents as nothing more than a rather warped fiction.

My grandfather, who may be regarded as either the hero or the villain of this story, was the Reverend Joseph Gogently, vicar of our sprawling rural parish. Unusually for a country vicar, the Reverend Gogently supplemented his meagre stipend with occasional work as the local slaughterer and butcher. Called out by neighbours in the many smallholdings surrounding the village, he would slit the throats of pigs and sheep, shoot cattle in the head with his oddly named humane killer or wring the necks of hens and turkeys for squeamish housewives. He'd then proceed to hack their bodies into manageable chunks with his daunting array of saws, cleavers and knives. Usually he was paid in kind with legs of pork, salted and stored in the vicarage cellar, sides of lamb or plucked poultry carcasses, hung from hooks in the cool pantry. My grandmother was an accomplished cook and dinner invitations to the vicarage were highly prized in those meat-rationed years following the war. The Bishop himself was a regular and ravenous visitor.

No one - not even the Bishop who had a soft spot for the genial vicar and the delights of his wife's dinner table - seemed at all concerned that a man of God should practise such a gruesome sideline. But then the Reverend Gogently was a man of unorthodox views, accepted by his unquestioning parishioners and ignored by the well-fed Bishop. The Church, it seems, was prepared to tacitly tolerate the peculiar ways of the vicar of a backwater parish.

Although he diligently upheld the ethical teaching of Christianity, my grandfather had no belief in the dogma. The story of Jesus was, for him, just that - a story that he recited in church, each Sunday, with as much conviction as a father reading a fairy tale to his incredulous children. It was simply a good story, to be taken, like his pork, with a pinch of salt. Becoming a vicar had been more a lifestyle decision rather than a matter of faith. Always a modest and self-indulgent character, he had taken a fancy to living in a well appointed vicarage, to the image of sipping afternoon tea with his parishioners and to the prospect of only working one day a week. Entering the cloth had been a career option as valid, in his youth, as joining the armed forces or becoming an accountant. He wore his dog collar as a barrister wore his wig - an outdated symbol of his chosen profession.

As for his slaughtering activities, it was generally thought that he was the ideal man for the job. Who better to kill with compassion, secure in the belief that his bestial victims faced the prospect of a glorious return to their Maker? After all, in the minds of most, were not death and the Christian teaching intimately entwined?

The Reverend Gogently enjoyed his work. The fear of death, he would claim, only exists in the human mind. Animals, being incapable of thought as we know it, have no concept of death. They are aware only of life. They never consider a time before they were born and they never contemplate the possibility of the world continuing after they die. They live in an eternal present. And when the Rev. Gogently drew his shiny steel blade skilfully across their necks, they would feel, perhaps, only a moment of burning pain followed by a rapid slide into unconsciousness. And that was that: the end of their timeless life. Clean and simple. One moment living in the vastness of eternity. The next, gone forever.

As far as I know, my grandfather himself never considered that his butchering activities ran contrary to the message he proclaimed from his pulpit each Sunday. The Apostles had killed and gutted fish, had they not? He was simply committing the final act in the long process of animal husbandry that was the lifeblood of the farming community he served. After all, weren't domestic animals reared entirely for the purpose of dying? Wasn't that their raison d'être? And wasn't the moment when his knife severed their carotid arteries or the bullet from his humane killer obliterated their brains or the jerk of his two hands snapped their windpipes, wasn't that the moment of the consummation of their being?

Has anyone ever claimed that Jesus was a vegetarian?

*

Killing men, of course, was a different matter. But my grandfather never killed another man. That was something he left to the next generation of Gogentlys.

My father, Robert, only child of the vicar and his wife, grew up as a nervy, introverted and rather spoiled boy. To be frank, he was something of a disappointment to my grandfather who had hopes of siring a deep-thinking academic or, at least, a craftsman who might have continued in the family butchery business - a business that the Rev. Gogently always regarded as an art form rather than a trade. But Robert, my father, was a peculiarly feckless youth, repelled by the sight of blood, nauseated by the stench of dead flesh in the utility room at the back of the vicarage where the vicar kept his knives and chopping boards and mincing machine, and too frightened to venture down to the cellar where once he had encountered a pig's head dangling from a hook, staring at him, he fancied, with a look of vengeful malice.

But Robert was well loved by his parents, his mother feeding him more bacon for breakfast each morning than most of his school mates saw in a month, his father introducing him, at an early age, to the wonders of wine and whisky that he himself deemed essential to bring each evening to a satisfactory close. The life of a vicar's son, it must be said - despite the obligatory early rise, smart suit and front pew seat every Sunday - was one to be envied.

My grandparents were apt to dine, from time to time, at the Bishop's Palace. The Bishop could not suffer little children so Robert was always left at home with a baby sitter, whose services were dispensed with once my father reached the age of fourteen. And that was his age when the incident happened that was to transform the lives of three generations of Gogentlys: my father's, my grandfather's and, of course, mine.

Alone in the vicarage one Saturday night, the adolescent Robert ensconced himself in his bedroom, tuned his transistor to Radio Luxembourg (a hint of the era of which I speak), picked up his cricket bat and set about practising his strokes in front of his wardrobe mirror - untypical behaviour, I admit, for a teenage boy given the run of the house on a Saturday night, but cricket was the one activity at which my father excelled - even at fourteen he opened the batting for the village team - and there, before his bedroom mirror, he indulged in his favourite fantasy: an heroic innings at the crease at Lords, the Aussie bowlers mocked before a jubilant crowd.

The tinkle of breaking glass dispelled the dream. Robert's bedroom was at the rear of the vicarage. The rest of the house would have been in darkness. Either someone had broken in or one of the household cats was up to some mischief. Robert crept down the stairs, his cricket bat still in his hand. He switched on the hall light at the foot of the stairs and there before him, emerging from the dining room, stood the intruder.

What happened next took no longer than a second to enact. The intruder froze - a smallish man clothed in black, a look of utter surprise on his face as he stared at Robert, a stocky boy for his age, dressed in cricket whites with his bat poised for attack. The intruder turned, intent on a hasty retreat into the dining room and, presumably, out through the window by which he had entered. Robert, buoyed with confidence after his triumphant innings at Lords, filled with outrage that a burglar should be violating the sanctity of his home, too shocked to formulate any coherent thought, instinctively did what he did best. Focusing on the man's head as though upon a spinning full toss destined for the boundary, he executed a masterful offensive stroke that would have had the crowds in the stands at Lords on their feet in rapture. The flat of the bat made contact with the intruder's head as he turned to flee. The sound was less resonant than that of willow on leather, the follow through less certain. But the poor man flew, not into the sky for a six, but headlong against the hall wall where he collapsed in a heap on the carpet.

For a while there was no movement: Robert with his bat over his left shoulder, the heap on the floor as still as a bundle of old clothes: no cheers from the crowd, just a numbing silence, external and internal, as my father slowly realised what he had done.

My grandparents, when they returned a few hours later, found him sitting on the bottom stair, bat between his legs. He pointed to the heap on the floor. My grandfather investigated while my grandmother took her son in her arms.

"Everything's going to be all right," she whispered.

And everything would be all right. They adjourned to the drawing room and were on their second glass of recuperative brandy before any of them spoke. Then Robert, with remarkable composure, related the few facts of the matter.

"Well, the man is dead, that's for sure," said my grandfather, although this confirmation was unnecessary. "No bleeding, thank God.

The skin wasn't pierced. But the blow must have caused massive brain damage. He would have died instantly, of that I think we can be certain."

"I'll call the police," said my grandmother.

"I think not," said the vicar in a tone that invited no discussion. He was not a domineering man, my grandfather - no household tyrant. His manner, whether in the home or the pulpit, befitted his name: always gentle and even-tempered. He lost as many arguments as he won. But in this matter it was clear, right from the start, that he would have his way.

My father and his mother must have looked aghast. Was it not obligatory to report immediately any death?

"There's little doubt that he was a burglar," my grandfather told them. "Clearly he smashed a small pane of glass, undid the window and climbed into the dining room, presumably assuming that, with the car gone and the house in darkness, he was quite safe. But he stole nothing, it seems. I took a quick look in his pockets.

"Then there's the manner of his death to consider. The impact of the cricket bat was on the back of his head. Hardly conducive to a plea of self defence."

The implications of these brief comments were clear to my grandmother and my father. No doubt the legal technicalities concerning the defence of one's property were as uncertain then as they are today, but what was certain was that there was trouble ahead: a police investigation, the usual publicity that any violent death entails, a possible manslaughter charge, a major trauma in the life of a boy on the threshold of manhood, the repercussions of which would undoubtedly be long-lasting if not permanent. Some, it was true, might call him a hero. But there would be others who would call him a murderer.

"But..." my grandmother spluttered. "Of course we must call the police."

"Must we?" replied my grandfather.

Can you imagine this situation? Your only son, the object of your love and devotion, has just killed a man in a brutal, albeit spontaneous and understandable, outburst of violence. What do you do? Hand the matter over to the authorities and wait for the slow-moving, ugly wheels of justice to churn through your lives, possibly shattering them forever? Probably yes: so alien to most of us is the reality of death, so intimidating is the lifeless hulk lying in the hallway.

But the Reverend Gogently was a man well accustomed to death. It formed an integral part of his day-to-day work. Barely a month went by in which he did not have a grieving family to comfort, a body to bury, a sombre funeral soliloquy to deliver. And as a slaughterer, of course, he was skilled at dealing with dead bodies, as comfortable with a corpse as with a living being. Furthermore - and this was perhaps the crucial factor - he was a free-thinker, a philosophical anarchist who based his decisions on the voice in his heart rather than the mores of society. His moral code was, I believe, deeply considered and robust, but it was certainly far from normal.

Did they question his plan? I suspect not. My grandmother and my father, in their state of shock, were only too happy to abnegate responsibility. Besides, everyone trusts the judgement of a vicar - even his family.

The first thing they did was carry the body down to the cool of the cellar and stash it in a cask used for the salting of pig carcasses. Then they swept up the glass in the dining room and replaced the broken pane with a piece of hardboard. The story, should anyone ask, was that Robert had had an accident while playing with his cricket ball on the drive. The hallway appeared free of any incriminating evidence. The lack of blood was indeed a fortuitous blessing. Finally, Robert cleaned and rubbed linseed oil onto his bat, the way he did each weekend before a match.

The next day, the vicar made a few discreet phone calls. In the jacket pocket of the deceased he had found some small change, a girl's photo, a half bottle of whisky and a letter bearing the name Jack Palmer with an Exeter address. His enquiries elicited a sketch of the life of Robert's victim. Jack Palmer was a Cornish man, aged twenty-two. He had left his home some years before to seek work in Exeter, staying in a boarding house - the address on the letter - from which he had suddenly disappeared, presumed bound for Bristol and a job opportunity. His parents, it appeared, had virtually forgotten about him. The letter in his pocket was a brief, chatty missive from his younger sister - the girl of the photo - who loved him well enough but evidently was not expecting to see him in the near future.

They waited a week. No local gossip surfaced suggesting anything unusual had happened, any strangers seen in the village. The newspapers, which they scoured thoroughly, gave no hint of a missing person. Of course they didn't. The Reverend Gogently was loath to admit it of any man, but Jack Palmer was not a man of any account: a loner, a petty crook, a drunkard, no doubt. He would not be missed. Like so many young men, off to seek their fortunes, he had simply vanished into the chaos of the wider world.

"And yet," thought my father, "he was once a lad like me, with dreams and desires, fears and passions which I, in a moment of madness, snuffed out forever."

The experience had a profound effect upon his impressionable young mind. A strange rite of passage from boyhood to manhood it may have been, but that was how he came to view it.

As for the body in the cask in the cellar - here the tale takes a macabre turn. My grandfather, quite capable of dealing dispassionately with a lump of dead flesh, be it porcine, bovine or human, hacked it into pieces with his cleaver, removed the internal organs and burned them in the furnace that supplied the vicarage's hot water, pushed the chunks of pink meat through the mincer he used to make pork sausages, crushed the bones to bone meal in the machine designed for the much stouter bones of pigs and cattle, and fed the pulverised remains to the two sows he kept in a sty at the end of the vicarage garden.

No, I can't imagine it. These sound like the actions of a psychotic murderer, the scenario of a horror film. How could my grandfather have done such things? Yet he did them for the love of his son.

Within a week, not a trace of Jack Palmer remained.

(The sows, it must be said, were the only living things to benefit from Jack's demise. Not only did they enjoy the bonus feed, but, their flesh no longer fancied by the occupants of the vicarage, they were allowed to live to a ripe old age and were eventually buried, uneaten, beneath the compost heap.)

Life in the vicarage - this, too, I find hard to believe - soon returned to normal. My grandfather continued to tell stories of Jesus in his church each Sunday. He baptised, married and buried his parishioners according to their requirements and dispatched their livestock in the same perfunctory manner as ever. My father grew up into a fine young man, diligent at school then off to university to study law. He never again played cricket - which I can understand - but turned to tennis instead, regarding his racket, perhaps, as having less potential as a lethal weapon.

After five years, the death of Jack Palmer was forgotten, or, at least, never mentioned. Perhaps he existed on some missing persons register somewhere. Or perhaps not. At all events, there was absolutely nothing to connect him to the happy family home of my forebears.

And here my story might have been concluded were it not for a niggle, a festering wound that would never heal in the depths of my father's psyche - in his conscience, one might say, if such an organ exists within the immaterial world of consciousness.

My father had acquired, not surprisingly, my grandfather's oft-expressed views on the subject of death. Death was simply the end of life, as all things must end. The span of everything in God's creation is measured in time, from the puniest ant to the highest mountain which, one day, will lie as dust at the bottom of the ocean. Even the glorious sun, the scientists tell us, is not eternal. One day it will burn itself out. So what absurd human arrogance is it to suppose that our souls might live forever? What gross presumption to imagine that we might contravene Nature's basic law: for everything its season? Man's great problem is not death itself but the fear of death, generated by his peculiar capacity for conceptual thought. It is the fear of death that haunts us, sometimes polluting our entire lives. How lucky are those who fall asleep at night, oblivious to that fear, and simply never awaken. Or those to whom death comes in the blink of an eye. Like Jack Palmer. In a moment his felonious plan is thwarted, his only thought that of escape. He turns, the bat strikes and that is his final thought. The end. No time for fear or panic. The life of Jack Palmer is over.

But what of those he left behind? This was the thought that haunted my father, from adolescence into manhood. Secretly, he had kept the address of Jack's family home in Cornwall, from his sister's letter. At the age of twenty, he decided to pay the family a visit.

Of course they had not forgotten their long-lost son and brother. And of course my father could not confess his secret, for it was a guilt, now, that he shared with his parents and he could not betray them.

The Palmers ran a guesthouse. My father stayed - one night, then two, then an entire week. He fell in love with Jack's sister: twenty-two, unattached, as pretty as the white-sanded bay on which they lived. She fell for him, too, a dashing young law student, a promising future, the son of a country vicar.

They married and bought a cottage in the village, half a mile from the vicarage. And that was how, a few years later, I entered the story. It's strange to think that, if my uncle had not been a burglar, if my father had not killed him with a cricket bat, then my parents would never have met. But thoughts like that are best not pursued.

*

My father never told my mother about the death of her brother, of that I am sure. I have some sympathy for his motives. What good would it have done? Destroy a happy marriage, more than likely. In the event, a congenital heart defect did the job more efficiently and probably less painfully. She died suddenly when I was fifteen. I miss her still.

He never told me, either - our relationship was congenial but not intimate. He left it to my grandfather to reveal the family skeleton. I was twenty, he well over seventy, a placid old man - a widower, by then - who spent his days pottering in his garden or walking in the woods.

76

He abandoned Christianity entirely when he retired, becoming a sort of New Age Buddhist. But he kept his butcher's knives sharpened and occasionally plied his alternative trade when some old timer in the village requested his services.

He told me everything, one mellow summer's evening as we sat in his garden. I can recall the occasion perfectly: the sounds of birdsong, of insects flying about their business, of sheep bleating in the fields as the golden disc of the sun sank behind the woodland trees – a wonderful pastoral setting in which to hear such a gruesome tale.

Naturally I was shocked. I'd always assumed my family to be a staid and conventional bunch, living secluded lives bereft of adventures. To suddenly have my father, by then a respected solicitor, portrayed as the murderer of my uncle: my grandfather, a dignified country vicar, as a butcher of human flesh – these images were hard to take. The fact that they had both committed grievous crimes - crimes for which they could still be imprisoned - was not something I could accept without considerable mental revolt.

"You think we did wrong?" asked my grandfather, his voice as gentle and untroubled as ever.

"Well, yes," I had to admit. "Don't you?"

And then he smiled and expounded to me his conclusions drawn from thirty years of cogitation on the events of that fateful night.

"To be sure, we broke the laws of the land," he began, "and I am fully prepared to plead guilty and face the legal consequences should our transgressions ever be discovered - as, I believe, is your father. But did we do wrong? Your father acted spontaneously, perhaps instinctively, filled with a young boy's rage and fear and the basic human urge to defend his property. He lashed out. There was no thought of wrong doing in his head, probably no thought at all. His was no deliberate, premeditated act. He merely swung his bat - unfortunately a little harder than was necessary.

"And what of me? Was I wrong to conceal the death of your mother's brother? Was I wrong to dispose of his body in a manner that most people would regard as unspeakably hideous? The man was dead -

nothing could change that. My motives were towards the living: towards preserving the life of my family. Selfish motives, you might say, but were they wrong? Certainly they were right for us at the time. And I deemed, after not inconsiderable thought, that they were even right for Jack's family. They assumed that he had ventured off to some city to seek his fortune. They hoped that, one day, he would return but, knowing his character, that hope was undoubtedly tentative. Would it have been better to destroy that hope and replace it with the horror and grief of the reality of Jack's fate? Your mother sometimes spoke fondly of her brother and wondered, in a wistful sort of way, what had become of him. Her thoughts of him were entirely positive. Would knowledge of the truth have served her better?"

"But..." I struggled to find a response. "Are there no absolute standards of right and wrong? Aren't murder and deceit simply wrong, no matter what personal justification you might find for them?"

"Are they? Where exactly do these absolute standards reside?"

"In the mind of God?" I suggested.

"Do you suppose that God, the omnipotent power of the Universe, has created a world in which wrongness and imperfection can exist?"

A good question. What did I, a twenty-year-old man searching for meaning in my life, know of God?

"On my travels I tread upon an ant and crush the life from it," continued my grandfather. "Meanwhile, in the depths of space, a comet, following its prescribed pathway, crashes into a planet, smashing it to smithereens. Is either event wrong? Is either beyond the Will of God?"

"But..." I was floundering. My grandfather was a consummate philosopher; I a novice, toying with ill-defined ideas. "But what of morality? What of the concepts of right and wrong?"

"They're just that - concepts. They exist as thoughts within the human mind. Like the concept of death."

"You believe, then, that nothing is wrong?"

"If it happens, then it is right. Perfection is actuality. Every event is either inevitable or impossible. If it happens, then it is a part of the unfolding reality of the Universe. Who are we to say that it is wrong?"

"This is not exactly the teaching of Christianity," I ventured, hoping to appeal to his clerical sensibility.

"Did I say it was? But look at it this way. Christianity teaches that God is perfect. How else can one define God? And if perfection exists in the Universe, then it must exist everywhere. If one moment is perfect, then so are all moments, for each moment develops out of the past and its consequences stretch into the infinite future. Christianity teaches that the death of Christ on the cross was a perfect moment, a pivotal point in the history of the world. Would you describe that death as wrong? But if you regard Christ's death as perfect, as 'meant to be', then so was Judas's betrayal, so was Pilate's sentence, so was Cain's slaying of Abel, so was Adam's biting of the forbidden fruit. And so was your father's killing of Jack Palmer. Were any of these acts wrong? Adam, Jesus and Jack Palmer lived and died so that we might experience the reality of this moment."

"But surely you can extend this argument into absurdity," I objected. "Were the deaths of millions in the stinking trenches of the First World War wrong? Was the gassing of the Jews in the Nazi horror camps wrong? Is any murder or rape or theft really wrong?"

He shrugged and smiled at me. "Can you look into the mind of God? We may pass judgements on the events of our own lives. Society may pass judgements on events in the wider world of humanity. But what kind of judgements, if any, does God pass on the happenings in his perfect Universe? God looked and saw that it was good - that's what the Bible says. He didn't see anything wrong in his Creation. Others may believe that something called evil also exists alongside goodness. Myself, I regard such an idea as absurd, an almost blasphemous contradiction. I no more believe that a man can go against the Will of God than that the sun can choose not to rise tomorrow. Maybe I'm wrong - I accept that possibility - but if God disagrees with me, well, he's left it a bit late to tell me so.

"And how can you, my grandson, tell me that I should have acted differently when, if I had, most assuredly you would never have been born?"

A good point, I had to admit.

*

My grandfather, the Reverend Joseph Gogently, former vicar of our parish, died peacefully in his bed, one drizzly November night. The whole village turned out for his funeral. "He was a good man," many told me, and I could not disagree.

His successor, the new vicar - a dour fundamentalist type - droned on about salvation, eternal life, the glorious day of judgement, "not dead, just sleeping" - all that stuff. My grandfather, of course, would have loved to argue the matter. According to his philosophy, his life, like this story, had simply reached its end.

THE ROD MAN

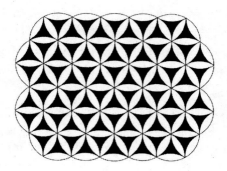

The gift comes from the Universal Spirit, given as freely and naturally as a branch snapped from a tree in a storm. In fact, the gift *is* a branch snapped from a tree in a storm: an almost straight rod, the length of a man's arm, smooth but for a node where a new twig is forming at one end, and a spike of torn wood at the other where the branch was wrenched from its mother tree: a staff of ash, stout and grey.

The recipient is a man from such an ancient time that we feel compelled, in our imaginations, to clothe him in bear skin, to give him a shaggy beard and matted hair, a mud caked face. Picture his primitive life, wandering the forests and plains, hunting for boar and deer, gathering berries and roots, communicating with his tribes people with monosyllabic grunts, with gesticulations and facial expressions, for his inner world, as yet, is free of the tyranny of words. But he is a true man, like us: his consciousness vast and spotless, his mind sharp and vital.

He picks up the ash rod from where it has fallen in the woods and turns it in his hands, wondering. He is about to make a discovery that will change his world, that will set his species upon the road to civilisation, that will shape the minds of his descendants for millennia to come.

What does he do with his gift? Does he shape its rough end into a hunting spear? Does he use it as a weapon to beat his fellows? Is he inspired to collect more such rods and construct a dwelling? Or will he rub it vigorously against another and form a fire? All these things his peers have done before him, mastering their wild world. But our man is different. He is about to discover symbolism, to create beauty.

He takes the rod back to his camp and lays it on the sandy ground. The rough splinter at one end of the rod sticks into the soil. The man looks at it.

And then, whether by accident or some mysterious divine guidance or the sudden explosion of an idea in his mind, the man turns his rod about the fixed end, and the sharp node on the other end traces a curve in the sand. He continues to turn the stick. The curve continues. Now he grasps what is happening before his startled eyes. He takes care, firmly holding his rod, gently turning it. Finally, he snatches it away.

There, in the sand, is a perfect circle.

His kinsmen gather around, amazed by what they see etched in the earth – a shape unseen in nature save in the face of the sun, the full moon and the iris of the eye, or, so transiently, in the pattern of ripples in a pool when raindrops fall, or the multi-coloured arc of the rainbow. A circle. Their man has created the form of God using nothing more holy than a rod from the woods.

They shrink back in awe and wonder. The man grasps his rod to his chest and feels a surge of joy and pride. Now is he set apart from his fellows. He has the power to capture the face of the sun in the sandy soil. Others before him have made images representing buffalos and deer, men and their hunting ways. But our man has created the form of perfection. The circle is an infinity of points, each uniquely orientated yet each equidistant from the centre. There are no special points in a circle, no corners. It is the perfect egalitarian shape, the ultimate symbol of wholeness, of God.

Awash with inspiration, he replaces his rod on the ground, its spike upon the circumference of the circle. He turns it again, slowly and deliberately, making another circle, and another shape is born where

82

the two circles intersect: the vesica piscis which will one day be honoured in the design of pyramids and cathedrals.

He stares at his new shape, and the first inkling of its meaning and mystery stirs in his mind.

Then the power of the gift flows through him like a flood. He places the point of his rod on the upper point of the vesica and turns it again. Another perfect circle appears in the sand, interlocking with the others. He continues, for now he grasps the technique, moving his rod around the original circle and placing its point on every crossing of circles. Now six circles surround the first and a perfect six petalled flower is formed at their centre.

Ah, the beauty of this pattern on the earth! The rod man drops his miraculous stick and steps back to marvel at his wonderwork. His fellows are already on their knees. Even their strongest warrior, their nimblest runner in the hunt, their most fecund mother, their oldest, most wrinkled matriarch, even these most honoured ones of the tribe cannot match the magic of the rod man. He is feted, exalted. The finest site around the campfire is reserved for him. The most succulent cut from the roasting joint is handed to him. The cup of fermented apple juice is passed first to him. The prettiest young women vie for his favours.

The rod man clasps his gift tightly to his breast. He does not understand, but he feels - a strange fluttering in his stomach, a tingling in his fingers, a vivid clarity in his sight - that his world is now a different place.

The man with the rod becomes the magician, the wise man. He discovers more, for now his fellows expect it of him. He discovers that he can repeat the six-petalled pattern over and over again, that he could cover the whole sandy plain with these perfect pictures. He discovers that, laying the rod upon the ground between the points of his pattern and scratching along its length with another twig or a stone, he can create straight edged shapes of staggering symmetry. First a triangle, then a square, a hexagon, a six-pointed star, an octagon. These are sights never seen before, save in the depths of the parts of plants. These are shapes that hint at the order of all things.

The rod man, in his time, hands down his gift to his son, and he to his. Over the millennia, his descendants are called magi, priests, the makers of civilisation, the guardians of truth, the geomancers, the scientists. From the first simple circles and their interlocking shapes, from the first radius – the length of the rod – all shapes and numbers and geometric forms emerge like the natural opening of a flower. The whole of mathematics, man's mighty symbolic representation of his Universe, is derived from a single rod laid upon a sandy soil.

The first rod, the gift of the Universal Spirit, and the first man to revolve it on the ground, have long since rotted into dust, their atoms circulated throughout the world. Their legacy is likewise everywhere.

*

My two-year-old granddaughter picks up a crayon and scribbles joyfully on paper. Sometimes she can roughly copy very simple shapes, but she is a long way from even approximating a regular square or triangle and many years from making accurate drawings of these figures. Yet, with a suitable stick in her sandpit, she creates a precise circle, the most fundamental and perfect of all figures. She is descended from the Rod Man.

TOPAZ

My colleague, the eminent philologist Dr. Bob Sole, delighted in the playful hypothesis that, through some unspecified mechanism of cause and effect, people's personalities are often reflected in their names. Or was it vice versa?

At first, I dismissed the idea as nothing more than the latest example of the good doctor's whimsical eccentricity. Now I'm not so sure. Perhaps in support - or perhaps in refutation - of his outrageous suggestion, I present the strange case of Topaz Bolero, one of my creative writing students.

When I first scanned the list of names for my new class, my attention was immediately attracted by Ms Bolero's. A singularly strange name, you must admit. The image of some exotic beauty sprung involuntarily into my mind. Topaz Bolero. A name to rival Pussy Galore or, if not a Bond girl, then at least the daughter of a colourful Sixties pop-star. Being relatively unattached and only on the lower fringe of middle-age, I began to fantasise a steamy affair with the alluring Ms Bolero behind the closed door of the tutorial room.

A girl with a name like that, ran my spurious reasoning, would surely be instantly recognisable amongst the unfamiliar faces of my first-year class. I leant back in my chair, feet up on the desk, in eager anticipation.

First through the door ambled a couple of lads with shaven heads and virtually identical baggy trousers and canvas shirts. They both nodded at me, unsmiling, and sat together at the table at the back, next to the radiator. C plus students, I assessed them. B minus at most. Next came a skinny young man wearing an overlarge jacket and a skew tie, a brand new leather briefcase clutched protectively under his arm. Intellectual type. He'd probably freak out at the first lateral thinking exercise.

Then, in walked a glowing vision of loveliness - curtains of black hair curling down over a splendid pair of perfectly hemispherical breasts struggling to escape the confines of a tight T-shirt bearing the image of pouting red lips. She smiled at me and her white teeth gleamed, her dark eyes shining like sumptuous black cherries.

"Ms Bolero?" I ventured, hastily removing my feet from the desk.

"Na. Sheila Green. This the right place for the writing fing?" A practised huskiness in her voice almost drowned her Cockney drawl.

I gestured for her to be seated as a crowd of ten or more students pushed through the door and finally settled themselves at desks with as much grace as a herd of hippopotami hitting the local water hole.

The register I'd been given listed the students in the order in which they'd signed up for the course, rather than alphabetically.

"Thomas Walker?" I called out.

"Here, Sir," came a reply from the front desk – the nerd with the new briefcase.

Continuing down the list, the rest of the class responded largely with inarticulate grunts and occasional raised fingers of acknowledgement.

Finally: "Topaz Bolero?" The name seemed to roll off my tongue like liquid honey.

The students pricked up their ears and glanced curiously around as a modest whimper emerged from the back row. My imagined glamorous temptress, it appeared, was a tiny, mousy haired, spotty-faced, bespectacled girl with hunched shoulders, clutching her grey coat to her chest as though fearing the full blast of an Arctic hurricane. I tried to make eye contact with her but she seemed to be fascinated by her own firmly joined knees. Even much later, as I cracked a few jokes and got into a bit of ice-breaking banter with some of the more confident students, I noticed that Ms Topaz Bolero's pose remained unaltered. Her gaze stayed fixed on her knees, as though they had assumed the irresistible allure of the bestseller we all hoped one day to write. She didn't say a word as we discussed the structure of the course and ran through a few basic ideas of creative writing. When the class was over and several of the students hung around chatting, she vanished into her own self-contained anonymity. That night, when I tried to picture her in my mind, I could form no more coherent image than that of the checkout girl at Tesco.

And yet the homework assignment she coyly left on my desk at the end of the second class was sheer brilliance. I'd chosen as a topic, as is my wont, a randomly selected word from the Concise Oxford Dictionary. Thomas Walker, in the front row, had done the picking with a bony finger.

"Custard," he announced, and a questioning murmur spread around the class.

"So there you go, custard it is," I decreed. "Any length. Any style. Let your imaginations run riot."

Most of the submissions were, frankly, pretty dire. Well, I suppose there's not a lot to say about custard beyond its taste, colour and viscosity. But Topaz Bolero handed in an immaculately word-processed, two thousand word polemic on the subject: spectacular imagery, intricate double-entendres, incisive dialectic in support of her preposterous thesis that custard originated in 4th century China where it was regarded as sacred: dry irony masterfully combined with literary allusions and contemporary style parodies. Without a doubt, A plus material. I was impressed.

We took an unscheduled break in the middle of the third class and I accosted Topaz by the coffee machine in the corridor.

"Might I ask how you came by such a delightful name?" I asked her in as friendly a tone as I could muster.

"Bolero's Spanish. My great grandfather was a Spaniard," she replied, a soft voice but she delivered her words with more aplomb than she ever revealed in her physical posture.

"And Topaz?"

She blushed and studied her plastic coffee cup intently. "Apparently, when I was born, I had a peculiar translucent yellowness to my complexion. My mother was reminded of the topaz ring she wore. Turned out I was jaundiced."

I laughed spontaneously and, in retrospect, rather insensitively. Her blush deepened.

"It's a beautiful name." I tried to redeem myself.

She shrugged. "It's a burden I carry through life."

I mentioned Topaz to Bob Sole: we occasionally discussed our students in the staff common room over pre-prandial drinks.

"I've never come across a Topaz before," he said. "Except, of course, for William Topaz McGonagall, the notorious Scottish poet. And I've no idea how he came by his middle name."

This prompted me to devise a rather wicked homework assignment for the next class. I took in a book of McGonagall's poems and read out the well-known "Tay Bridge Disaster". McGonagall took himself very seriously but his poetry was unremittingly dreadful. We creative writing tutors often use him as an example of how not to write poetry.

"So, this week's task: a short poem in the style of McGonagall."

Most of the students couldn't handle it. They couldn't quite grasp what made McGonagall's verses so bad that they were almost good. Thomas Walker made a passable effort, choosing, as his theme, the London underground bombings – a clever choice but a lack-lustre poem. Sheila Green missed the point entirely and read us a poem about a sexual encounter in a teashop in the Cairngorms on a rainy Sunday. Topaz, surprisingly, had used the actual name of Scotland's worst poet as her subject, and her offering, as always, was a superb parody:

The Scottish Victorian poet of whom
It is said phrased rhymes from his womb to his tomb,
McGonagall his surname and William his first
And a middle name twixt them with which he was cursed.
For all his life long he was straining his mind
A suitable assonance hoping to find.
He had no quibble with the name of McGonagall -

He simply pretended he came from near Donegal.
Less easy was finding a rhyming for William
Till intestinal pain afflicted his ileum.
But how could he cope with the middle name Topaz,
A word with no rhyme - and that really pissed off the old bugger.

She read it out, hesitantly at first, but with growing confidence and even a hint of theatricality. I burst into laughter and applauded enthusiastically. The rest of the class gave her funny looks or fiddled with their pens. No, they weren't the brightest bunch of would-be scribblers I'd ever taught.

During the sixth class, the discussion turned to the subject of how the students should market themselves as potential writers. Someone brought up the matter of adopting a pseudonym. I suggested, following Dr. Sole's line of thought, that perhaps they should consider pseudonyms that reflected their personalities, or, at least, the style and content of their writing.

"Something a little naughtily frivolous for me," offered the glamorous but unexcitedly named Sheila Green - merely another C student, as it turned out. "I'd like to keep the Green but I think I'll change my first name to Theresa. Theresa Green. Geddit?"

The class tittered and Ms Green expanded her expansive chest in appropriate appreciation.

"Absalom Kipper," proclaimed one of the shaven-headed, baggy-trousered twins, and no one questioned the provenance of such an absurd appellation.

"I think I'll stick with Thomas Walker," said Thomas Walker.

"And you, Topaz?" I asked. "An advantage, surely, to enter the publishing world with such a distinctive nomenclature." It was the first time I had ever directed a question at her in the public arena.

"I'll write under the name of Jane Smith."

Such was Topaz's standing in the developing social structure of the class that this strange remark was completely ignored as others tested their ridiculous noms-de-plume on their assembled peers. I confess to having felt unaccountably sad for the girl. She possessed such a wonderful name and created such beautiful prose - her next assignment, the story of a doomed love affair between an Irish mole-charmer and a schizophrenic Dutch hill walker, nearly had me in tears - that her chronic shyness could only be viewed as a severe psychological disability. I wondered how much her very name had contributed towards the growth of that disability. As she had said, it was a burden she had always carried. It can't be easy when every innocent utterance of your name is met with either astonishment or incredulity.

I brought up the matter with Bob Sole, later that day, as we partook of tea and crumpets in his private study.

"As I always maintain," said the doctor, "the name reflects the personality and the personality reflects the name."

"Surely not in this case, Bob."

"I disagree. Consider the facts. Bolero - a dance that begins as an understated, reserved exercise in manners but gradually reveals a deep hidden passion. Topaz - at first glance an unremarkable yellowish stone, but polish it and hold it up to the light and its translucence is beguiling, its mystery sublime. Do we have, here, an acceptable description of the character of your Ms Topaz Bolero?"

I nodded my assent.

"And take, too, your Sheila Green," he continued. "In appearance, a stunning figure of a woman, but we're talking personality not physical appearance. Like her name, she is commonplace and homely, reliable but uninspiringly predictable. As for Mr Thomas Walker: Thomas is a doubter, lacking confidence. And Walker – a pedestrian. The chap's a doubtful plodder. I rest my case."

As I left, I noticed the name plaque on his study door. "Dr. Robert Sole. Philology." R. Sole, I thought and repeated it with a satisfied grin. Dr. R. Sole. Perhaps there was something in his outlandish hypothesis of names, after all.

90

ASHANTI

She was still young when the Palmer family moved in - little more than a teenager. For several months they ignored her completely. They were never great gardeners, their efforts largely destructive: mowing the lawn, dead-heading the daffodils, cutting back the shrubs and uprooting the plants they saw as weeds. Their goal was a minimal maintenance garden: an undemanding place to sit in the sun on a Sunday afternoon.

Finally they turned their attention to her.

"What kind of tree is that?" asked the boy.

"An ash, I believe," replied the father in a slightly pompous manner, clearly happy to impress his son with one of the half dozen trees he could confidently name. Not really difficult. In summer, her delicate compound leaves were almost unique amongst trees. In colder seasons, her hard black buds were an instant give-away.

"A beautiful tree," said the mother, laying her fingertips on the smooth, grey trunk.

"Badly placed, though," said the father. "It's going to cast a lot of shade over the lawn. I think we should have it down."

The ash tree felt threatened. Of course she couldn't understand human words, but she could feel the energy behind them.

"Let's not be too hasty," said the mother.

"Maybe I can climb it when it gets bigger," said the boy. "Maybe I can have a tree house."

She liked the boy. He might snap off a few of her twigs with his clambering antics, or even carve his initials on her sensitive skin, but she felt him to be a friend.

Spring came and at last her leaves unfurled and she basked in the warm love of the sun and she knew herself to be so alive, so blissful.

"We must give it a name," said the boy.

"It's an ash, I told you," said the father.

"No, a proper name. Like mine. Like Christo."

That was his name: Christo Palmer. His father objected to the ungainly shortening of Christopher, but his mother loved it and the epithet stuck.

"Don't be silly," said the father. "Trees don't have personal names."

"Why not?"

"I think it'd be fun," said the mother.

"So do I," said Christo. "What is it, a boy or a girl?"

"Don't be silly," said his father. "Trees are hermaphrodite. They contain both sexes."

"How do they do that?" asked Christo.

"They just do. That's the way with trees."

But the mother was unsure. She reached up and examined one of the newly emerging flowers - the ash was only in its second year of blooming - snapped it off and rushed indoors to consult one of her books. Five minutes later, she was out again.

"She's a female," she proclaimed. "Ash trees come in separate sexes."

"Ridiculous," her husband mumbled.

"So what shall we call her?" Christo persisted.

The mother closed her eyes and leant a while, one hand resting on the smooth bark of this fellow female being. She breathed in deeply several times, while her husband sighed irritably and turned away. She liked to commune with Nature, this human mother. She intuited. She channelled. She touched the spirit of things. She favoured all alternative ideas, and the more strongly her husband rejected an idea, the more strongly she favoured it.

She removed her hand and opened her eyes. "Ashanti," she whispered.

*

Ashanti felt the Palmer family establish their roots in their new home, spread their branches, blossom into creativity, etch their mark into this patch of soil they shared with her. She radiated love towards her neighbours and they, it seemed, reflected a little back. They established a harmonious relationship with each other, or so she felt, for Ashanti, like all of her kind, was an elegant and graceful tree and the Palmers, for the most part, were mild-mannered and respectful.

Christo Palmer grew from childhood into adolescence. His father, James, grew from a bigoted and tense youngish man into a bigoted, tense and unhappy middle-aged man. Mary Palmer, the tree whisperer, grew ever further from him. Hers was a life with which Ashanti could readily connect. Mary Palmer stroked the earth and embraced the sky. She sucked in the sunlight, transformed its energy and let it pour forth in a torrent of creative projects. Her ideas were unpolished, it was generally admitted, but her zest and commitment were infectious and her circle of friends - "strange, arty types" as her husband labelled them - expanded like the ripples from a stone plopped into a still pool. She distributed her attention and influence

93

as Ashanti spread her seed keys: freely cast into the wind to find welcoming soils in far-off places.

Christo loved his mother and loathed his father in equal measure. His father was the only person who called him Christopher - a sound that screeched through his consciousness like fingernails across a blackboard. He never argued with his father - he quickly learned the fruitlessness of such behaviour - but glared his disapproval or sunk into sullenness in his company. When Mr Palmer was away - he was a sales manager, obliged to spend brief periods at "head office" in London - Christo and his mother danced and sang and spread gleeful disorder across house and garden.

Ashanti instantly felt the joy of those dancing days - like a black cloud suddenly moving from the face of the sun - and, it sometimes seemed, she fluttered her feathery leaflets as her human hosts cavorted around her.

What did she think of the Palmer family?

Of course she didn't think anything. Thinking is strictly a human activity, requiring words. Trees have many things that humans lack, but they don't have words. They feel, though, as all living things feel. And trees, with their ancient pedigree, their graceful grandeur and their undisputed place at the pinnacle of life, can feel the most subtle and the most majestic of moods, the swirling energies and ever-changing tunes of emotion, the slow turning of the seasons. For what is time to a tree? Trees inhabit eternity where all things are known and felt.

*

Christo loved Ashanti. He climbed daily to her ever-heightening summit, scampered amongst her lower branches, sat on the grass and leant his back against her grey trunk, dreaming, reading, picnicking, camping beneath her in the summer months, glimpsing stars between her silhouetted, filigree leaves. And, of course, it was to Ashanti that he took his first love.

They were both sixteen. She was a black haired beauty called Sappho. She had hurled Christo's life into a seething cauldron of

94

desire. They were way beyond the preliminary kissing stage when, one sunny afternoon when his parents were out, Christo led her to the soft grassy bed beneath Ashanti's boughs.

"Have you done this before?" Sappho whispered.

"Yeah. Course. Well, no, actually. Have you?"

"Yeah. Well, no, not really. Have you got...? You know."

He produced a single foil-wrapped condom from his shirt pocket. It was the last of a packet of three he'd bought months before, after he'd first kissed Sappho. The other two had been used for practice purposes. This one was it. They lay back on the grass.

Ashanti can feel it all: the love, the excitement, the urgent desire to make seed while the sap is rising fast. She feels the quickening dance of lust as the two young bodies writhe beneath her. She tastes the ecstasy, like the touch of pollen on her ripe and yearning stigmas. She shares the sigh of consummation. She relaxes with her human friends into the afterglow of peace and love.

"Yes," whispers Sappho.

"Yes," echoes Christo.

"Yes," the feeling flows up and down Ashanti's xylems and phloems.

*

Father Palmer did not like Sappho.

"She'll come to no good," he declared. "You mark my words. A chap like you can do a lot better than a girl like that."

"But I love her," retorted Christo.

"Don't talk such nonsense, Christopher. What can a boy of your age know of love?"

Ashanti, sensing the encounter from her placid listening post in the garden, felt a violent storm swelling up in her young friend, thundering through his tender green branches. He snapped under the unfamiliar force of his own emotions.

"Why can you never see anyone's point of view but your own?" he yelled. "You expect me to be just like you: a boring, intolerant, stuck-up, old fart. Well, thank God I'm not. I've had it with you. You're nothing but a chain around my neck."

Christo fled from home that very night, taking his bicycle and a rucksack of camping equipment. He and Sappho went to live with a group of travellers in an unofficial yurt camp in the nearby woods. He gave up school, swapping his academic studies - at which he possessed little talent - for an intensive course in circus skills - at which he showed great aptitude.

His father disowned his only son. "Nobody talks to me like that," he bellowed at his wife, "least of all a member of my own family."

Mary Palmer never bellowed, and she never argued with her husband. Her strategy, finely honed over many years, was to completely ignore him. She slipped Christo a wodge of tenners before he left and made sure he was regularly supplied with additional money whenever he needed it. She missed her son, but her life, like Ashanti, had sturdy branches spreading in all directions, all of which were alive and fruitful.

James Palmer, it soon transpired, missed both his son and his wife, who was always either absent or taciturn. He missed his former life. His job, through no fault of his own, collapsed beneath him. Unemployed, alone, his youthful dreams long forgotten, he sank into depression. One day he sat beneath Ashanti and wept his heart out.

Ashanti felt his pain - a tacit understanding, an unexpressed empathy - and a single, sudden shudder shook the leaves of her many limbs.

*

Mary Palmer was at a week-long crystal healing workshop in Glastonbury when James Palmer decided he'd had enough of life. Always a meticulous planner, he saw that his affairs were in order, left his will and insurance policy on prominent display on the kitchen table, selected a length of stout rope and a stepladder from his garage, checked that everything was switched off in the house, then walked slowly down the garden.

He was not a likeable person, he knew that. He was disliked by his family, by the friends and work colleagues he no longer possessed, and, he had to admit, by himself. His life appeared vacant, a worthless succession of empty days. The single thing he really enjoyed, it dawned on him, was sleeping. Eternal sleep: what more could he desire?

He slung his rope over one of Ashanti's boughs, secured it, fashioned the end into a noose-like knot, climbed the ladder, inserted his head, pulled once on the rope to check it was fast, then stepped off into the cool vastness, shimmering with crystals of sunlight that slipped through Ashanti's gently fluttering canopy...

*

Ten years later, Mary Palmer - who loved to hug trees but had omitted to hug her husband when he needed it most - decided to sell the house. She had a new man, a new life, new energies pulling her in new directions. Christo was travelling the world with Sappho, in no need of a home. James Palmer was but a seldom visited, rarely cherished memory.

Ashanti was a fully grown queen of an ash tree, the pride of the neighbourhood, the fecund mother of countless smaller ashes, a stately matriarch amongst trees.

Mary visited her on her final day in the house, enfolded her trunk in a lingering farewell embrace, pressed her cheek against the roughening bark, breathed in her ashy scent.

And Ashanti gathered up her vital sap and slowly oozed a single teardrop through the lenticels of her wood.

THE SEA AND THE SKY

They'd told him of The Sea, of how it went on forever, but he hadn't believed them. Only God and Time went on forever. Of the former he was unconvinced and the latter was so incomprehensible to him that he dared not think on it. God and Time - so said The Sage - were mysteries not of this world but of the next. The Sea, however, was very much of this world. Beyond the mountains and the forests, beyond the fields and pastures, beyond the wide plains where men built cities and spent their lives pursuing strange and insubstantial goals, there sat The Sea, basking in its unending vastness.

They'd told him to imagine a lake that stretched further than the eye's gaze, that touched the sky in a line as straight as a rope pulled taut between two poles, a lake that grew and shrank twice each day, echoing the phases of The Moon: but he could not imagine such a wonder. They'd said its water was clear and cold yet tasted vile and not only refused to slake the thirst but made one thirstier still. And boats the size of houses, they'd said, sailed out across this water till they were but distant specks - and many that travelled over that infinite liquidity did not return.

So it was that Kaph resolved to see The Sea and look for himself upon the edge of the world. He was young and adventure called him. His kinsfolk called him mad. His place was here, in the woodlands and mountain valleys, herding the deer and boar, tending the corn. One day he would take a wife and raise a family, earn his place amongst the elders of the village. But The Sage blessed him as he set upon his way, knowing that, above all things, a young man should seek a taste of the unknown. Follow the river, he told him, and Kaph obeyed, for The Sage knew many things and, though he had never seen it for himself, he knew that all rivers flow eventually into The Sea.

For days he walked, leaving far behind the haunts of his youth, the rugged, wooded uplands in which he had been born and raised, while the river widened and the valley slopes grew gentler, the meadow grass more lush, the crop fields flatter and more prolific. Then he came upon towns with buildings as tall as trees, and roads as smooth as slate, and cities so full of men and women that he wondered how they ever knew the names of one another. All these sights were new and strange to him and he marvelled at them, thinking how rich and varied and complex were the lives of men. Yet nothing could detain him long for he held fast to his vision of the endless Sea, the most marvellous sight of all.

Those to whom he spoke upon his way broadened his vision. The Sea was fierce and cruel, some said, prone to sudden anger, eating into the soft cliffs of the shore, swallowing up those who would sail upon it in search of fish or trade with other lands. Others spoke of its beauty, its ever-changing colours, its constant movement and its music that could soothe the troubled mind, of the vast larder of creatures that lived within its depths or scuttled about its margin, of its sandy beaches, its banks of smooth pebbles, its chalky headlands, its craggy rocks, the muddy mouths of rivers, the crystal clear waters of its reefs. For some it meant the frontier of the place they called their homeland, for some the start of journeys to new lands, for some the source of their daily livelihood, for some the dread of their worst nightmares. And for some, like Kaph, it meant the lure of mystery.

The days of his walking stretched into weeks and months and years, for the people of the towns and cities were not as friendly as those of his native hills and they looked aghast at him when he asked if he might share their food or the comfort of their homes. He learned that labour was required in return for these favours and this he gave willingly, using his strength and stamina to work in their craft shops and hostelries and building sites. And to some he gave the knowledge that The Sage had taught him, for wisdom and contentment, he discovered, were gifts that these people seemed not to know nor, for the most part, to value and respect.

They asked him of the derivation of his name and he told them that The Sage had conferred it upon him when he was a child, an acronym to remind him always of the four qualities that characterised a good life: Kindness, Awareness, Patience and Humility. This they found strange, unsurprisingly so, for Kaph could see that it was fame and riches, intoxication and the pursuit of pleasures that motivated them and, to himself, he called these people Frips and saw that the cities were overrun with them. But some admired his simple ways and listened as he recounted the discourses of The Sage on the wonder of Awareness, God's gift to mankind; and the magic of Kindness which, in the giving, always benefited the giver as much as the receiver and grew in quantity and quality as rapidly as it was given away; and Patience which was the peaceful, accepting trust that all was as it should be; and Humility, the divine realisation of the essential emptiness of the human mind.

Some there were who listened to his words and came to call him their friend: a few, too, who knew him as their lover, for he was young and strong and good to look upon, firm in his resolve yet gentle and vulnerable, and he came to know that womenfolk everywhere loved these things. So he lingered awhile in the places that pleased him, enjoyed the company and colloquy of men and sampled the pleasures of the women who fell for him. But none, not even the fairest or the most loving, could put a permanent brake on his restless feet. The call of The Sea would return to his mind and ever he would pack his meagre bag and head onwards, following the flow of the river as The Sage had bade him.

Then came a day when the river broadened to a mile or more and its banks were lined with sticky mud, and the screams of unfamiliar birds filled the air, and the wind grew chill and carried a scent that Kaph had never smelled in his upland home. At last he saw The Sea, distant still but unmistakable in its uniqueness, flickering with slivers of light as the sun danced upon its ever-moving surface, stretching as far as he could gaze, merging, in the sultry haze, into the blue greyness of the sky. He sat down upon the dusty road and stared long and hard until his eyes had grown accustomed to The Sea's unfamiliar formlessness and his heart had assimilated the joy of this long awaited revelation. Then he walked slowly on, savouring the sight of The Sea expanding to fill his entire field of vision, marvelling at its famous vastness.

He left the road and clambered over the rocks that the coastal folk had erected to defend themselves from the encroaches of their massive aquatic neighbour, then plodded across the yielding sands and stumbled over banks of shining pebbles until he reached the water's edge. The mighty, undulating roar of the breaking waves entranced him, filling the arena of his hearing, a thousand individual voices, he fancied, mingled into one, like the bustle of people in the market places of the cities through which he had passed; louder yet more harmonious, more serene. It was like no other sound he had ever heard, so different from the rush of wind through the trees or the constant babble of the river, for The Sea possessed a haunting melody and a pulse that calmed and finally matched the rhythm of his breathing, in and out, in and out, until he felt that he was listening to the vital breath of the world.

He removed his boots and let the waves engulf his legs until his feet were numb with cold. He scooped up a cupped handful of the wondrous fluid and tasted it, spitting it out at once; amazed that such an abundance of clear water should be less palatable than a brackish pond. Then he walked slowly forward, his feet sinking into the shifting

101

sands, massaged by the rush and retreat of tiny stones. The coldness crept up his body, but he heeded it not. This was what he had walked so far to feel, to know The Sea with a thoroughness with which he knew the land and the air. The water reached his chest. His arms floated up in front of him. He pushed himself free of the sand and launched himself into this new element, letting it hold him with the barest movement of his limbs. Buffeted by the foaming waves, he made his way into deeper, calmer water until his feet could no longer find solid ground. Then he turned onto his back and stretched out his arms and legs, giving himself to The Sea, relaxing in its cold but comforting and secure embrace. His ears, below the surface, no longer heard the crashing music of the shore. All sounds were muted, otherworldly, as he drifted gently out with the ebbing tide. His mind, now that his yearning was satisfied, was still and happy, thinking neither of the past nor the future. He felt the empty, limitless potential of an unborn babe, floating in his mother's womb.

He opened his eyes and saw nothing but The Sky above him, an ocean of untainted and exquisite blueness through which rolled occasional billowing masses of grey-white cloud like silent, magical landscapes. And a new thought came to him - so new, so huge, yet so simple that he wondered that he had never thought it before. The Sea does not go on forever, he thought. Here I am at its edge and there are other edges on other, far off lands. But The Sky! Ah, The Sky! It has no edges. Up and up it goes, never ending, never changing. The Sea has its shores and its bed and its wavy surface, but there is no skyshore, no skybed, no surface to The Sky. Even the night-time stars are no more than tiny islands of light in the infinite blackness. The Sky truly goes on forever.

I must explore The Sky, he thought, as his arms and feet kicked off towards the shore. I must tell The Sage.

But The Sage already knew. The Sage was a Sky watcher. He was waiting patiently for Kaph's return.

DEATH OF A GOOD MAN

1. THE NEIGHBOUR

Yes, he was a good man, old Joe: a good neighbour. No noise, no trouble, always a cheery greeting, a smile, a brief exchange of pleasantries:

"Morning, Joe. How you doing?"

"Ah, hello there, Simon. Well, thank you. And yourself?"

To be honest, I suppose that was as far as it usually went, which suited us fine, Martha and me. I mean, friends you can pick, family you can escape from if the going gets tough, but neighbours, well, they're there for life, just the other side of a six inch wall or over the back fence. You don't want to get too chummy, just so long as you rub along comfortably. Joe would come in to water the plants for us when we were on holiday, feed the cats, that sort of thing. I'd give his upstairs windows a clean, when I was on the ladder doing my own. Once or twice I'd pick him up in the car if I passed him walking home from the shops, carrying a couple of carriers. Martha would occasionally pass a cuppa to him if they were both in the backyard together, on a summer's day. That was pretty much the extent of our relationship. Like I said, we considered ourselves lucky to have Joe as a neighbour: never any trouble. The most we heard of him, sometimes, was his radio through the kitchen wall - usually Radio 4, the low drone of voices – or his record player, an ancient tin box of a thing. Joe's musical taste was firmly stuck in the sixties.

As for old Joe's history, we knew very little. Strange name: Joe Stikans. Latvian, I believe, although Joe himself was born in Birmingham – second generation immigrant. Spent most of his working life at Bourneville, first on one of the chocolate conveyor belts, ending up in some office job. He was never a high flyer, although he was quite bright. I gather he went off to university sometime in the sixties, but dropped out after a year or so. Then he travelled the world for a bit, took a look at Latvia but didn't much like the look of the place so he came back to Brum, back to the chocolate factory. He was married once, but not since we knew him. Divorced? Widowed? No idea. Not a matter we ever touched upon. But he had a daughter – Isabel, her name. She came to call on him occasionally, but never stayed long. I got the impression they were just duty calls – you know, checking everything's OK with the old man. We'd hear her knock on the front door.

"Knock, knock."

"Who's there?"

"Isabel."

"Isabel who?"

"Isabel necessary on a bicycle."

Then we'd hear him laugh. He'd got a lovely laugh: not particularly loud but really genuine sounding – and infectious – a sort of deep chuckle type of laugh. I never knew Isabel to laugh. Presumably she'd been subjected to this "knock, knock" routine since childhood and she was well past laughing. She'd stay maybe an hour or so, then we'd hear the front door slam and she'd hop in her car and be gone. Nice looking girl. But we never spoke.

Joe retired long before we moved here – well, not exactly retired. I gather the firm had been seeking a few redundancies and Joe had volunteered. I think he was in his fifties. Ever since, he's not worked, so far as I know. He just lives here, eking out his redundancy pay, presumably, and a meagre pension. Never a big spender: no car, no TV even, no holidays, a simple life by any standards. But this much I will say: he seemed happy with his lot. I never heard him moan, never bitter, never resentful, never jealous. He was content – and, let's face it, you don't often meet a content man these days.

He wasn't that old when he died – mid sixties, something like that, which is nothing. Always seemed a healthy chap. He didn't take much exercise, it's true, and maybe he could have been a little overweight – but not excessively, mind. He didn't smoke, hardly drank, so far as I know. A man of few vices, one might say.

Anyway, you don't expect a man of that age to just die, just like that. Certainly not in the house next door. A real shock, it was. A real shock. No one deserved to go like that, Martha kept repeating. Certainly not old Joe. He deserved something better than a lonely, lingering death in a cold home.

We'd not heard a sound from him for a week or two – no radio, no tinny blues music through the wall, no sign of him in the backyard.

"Maybe he's gone away somewhere," I suggested, but Martha was having none of it.

"When did Joe ever go away?" she said. "And surely he'd have told us. No, I don't like it, Simon. Something's not right."

So she sent me round the back, into his backyard. I peered into his window – Joe always lived mainly in his back room. And there he was, sat in his armchair, his head flopped down onto his chest. My first thought was that he was asleep, taking an afternoon nap, and I was about to creep away before he woke up and saw me staring through his window. But there was something about him: his face – grey, shrunken, lifeless. I knew he was dead. For some reason, I tapped on the window, hoping to wake him, I suppose. Then I freaked a bit. Jesus, I've never seen a dead person before – not in the flesh, so to speak. Seen thousands on the tele, but never in real life. I was spooked, I don't mind telling you. My heart was beating wildly, my stomach felt tight and my fingers were trembling. I suppose I should have tried the back door – he usually left it unlocked during the day – but, well, I'm ashamed to say that I didn't care to look any more closely. I hurried back to our place and Martha, soon as she saw my face, she gasped and stared wide-eyed at me.

"Think we'd better call the police," I said.

2. THE DAUGHTER

I received the call at work, at the worst possible moment. I was with a customer, and a big deal was rapidly approaching completion. I run a music shop. It's a good little business: I like it. "The Music Stand" – not my choice of name. It came with the place when I bought it a few years back. The majority of my business is with schools, but it's mostly low profit stuff like sheet music and recorders. But I keep a few pianos in the shop and here was someone showing definite interest. Sell a piano, and that's the rent taken care of for a couple of months. He was a rich chap, you could tell, wanting a piano for his wife for their silver anniversary. I could almost see a wallet full of fifty pound notes bulging through his trouser pocket.

And then the phone rang.

"'Scuse me," I said. "Maybe you could try giving it a tinkle yourself. See how it feels." I could tell he didn't know the first thing about pianos, and normally I would have left the phone, but I was on my own in the shop.

"Hello. Music Stand."

"Isabel?"

"Yes."

"Simon Weston here."

"Yes. How can I help?" I was sure I'd never heard the name before.

"It's about your father. I'm afraid he's died."

"Ah, right." Suddenly the penny dropped. Dad's neighbour. Simon, the bloke next door who cleaned his windows. I was pleased to have put a face to this disembodied voice. I'm not good with phone calls. "Sorry. What did you say?"

"I said, I'm afraid your father's dead."

"Ah, right." I mean, what did he expect me to do? Break down and weep piteously into the receiver? The man with the bulging wallet was hesitantly tapping a few keys with a single finger. He needed help, quickly, or I'd lose him.

"What happened?" I asked into the phone.

"Perhaps you'd better come over."

"Right. I can't make it just now, but I'll be there as soon as I can. Goodbye." I didn't want to start asking questions, nor to express any shock. What's my piano buyer going to think if he catches on that my father's just died? He's going to be gone pretty sharpish. When you've got a bite like that, you don't let it slip away. I was in business woman mode. No time to dwell on my father lying dead in his horrible little house.

God, I'm a heartless bitch, aren't I? Simon Whatever-he's-called must have been horrified. I could just imagine what he was saying about me to that fat wife of his.

Dad's dead. Okay. I could deal with sadness and all that a bit later. Sometimes I really hate myself.

But I clinched the deal on the piano. Five grand! Yes!

The undertakers had removed his body by the time I got round to the house. First the police, then his doctor from the local health centre, then the undertakers. They didn't hang about. The smell, presumably. That back room was reeking – like, I don't know, rotting meat, I suppose. They'd opened the window wide, but it was still there. And knowing that it's the stench of the decay of your dead father's body makes it so much worse. It almost seemed disrespectful to cover your nose.

I knocked first on the neighbours' door. The chap, Simon, seemed a bit frosty, but the wife was full of the usual sympathy and insisted on pouring me a cup of tea that had already been made – several hours previously, by the taste of it.

"We're so, so sorry," the wife gushed. "Your Dad was such a good man."

Then Simon related how they'd found him, called the police and then called me.

"Your Dad gave us your contact numbers some time ago," said the wife. "You know, just in case."

"Yes, and thanks for calling me. And I'm sorry I was rather abrupt on the phone."

"Death affects us all in different ways," said the wife. "There's no accounting for how we might each react. Simon was shaking for an hour or more. Real shook up, he was."

"Well, there's no need to bother Isabel with all that, Martha. She's got her own grief to worry about."

Actually, I wasn't worried about anything, and, at the time, I wasn't exactly feeling grief-stricken. I'd just put a deliciously large cheque in the bank and I was feeling quietly jubilant. But I had to put on a bit of a show with these neighbours. Dad always said I was a good actor.

"So what did the doctor say?" I asked.

"Natural causes," said Simon. "Seems he's had a dicky heart for some time. Looks like it just packed up on him."

"Right." Dicky heart? That was the first I'd heard of it. I knew his liver was none too special, but his heart? But what did I know? Dad was always "fine". Those could well have been his last words: "I'm fine, thanks." He spoke more about the weather than the state of his own health. He could ramble on for hours about the changing sky – clouds, sunshine, precipitation, air pressure, he knew it all in immense detail – but ask him about himself and he was simply "fine". I'd stopped asking, long ago.

"The doctor called the undertaker," Simon continued. "He was here in minutes. We asked if they could leave him till you'd arrived, but they said they ought to take him off."

"A bit... You know." Martha pinched her nose and grimaced discreetly.

"Probably been sitting there for a week or more, poor bloke," said Simon.

The two neighbours glanced at each other – a touch of shame and guilt, I fancied. For a week they'd been sitting here in their cosy little room while, literally a few feet away, through the wall, Dad had been slowly rotting. But I held nothing against them. I didn't even know the names of any of my own neighbours.

So I drank my tepid, stewed cup of tea and said I'd better take a look at Dad's house – I don't exactly know why. It just seemed like the right thing to do.

"Back door's open," said Simon. "Take your time, love."

I don't quite know what he meant by that. I don't expect he did, either.

Dad's kitchen was clean and tidy, not even an unwashed cup or teaspoon. He was always hot on household chores – not that he regarded them as chores. He just did what had to be done. He just "got on with it". That was the constant refrain: "Just get on with it, girl." He never said it angrily or impatiently. He just said it – his few, brief, oft repeated words of wisdom. "Get on with it, girl." And I did. I've done okay with my life, I like to think. I knew he was proud of me and, though he rarely said it, it's quite something to know that your Dad's proud of you.

The back room. I'd never known him to ever enter the front room. I peered into it, later. Absolutely empty. An old carpet on the floor but nothing else at all. He sat and ate and listened to the radio and played his records and entertained his very few visitors all in the back room. Yet even this room felt remarkably empty. Maybe you could call his style minimalist. No pictures on the wall, no ornaments, no stuff lying around in corners, no piles of paper on the table, nothing really to suggest that he'd been living here. Well, he hadn't for over a week. I'd never noticed, before, how stark his living room was. Not cold. He had his little gas fire on most of the time, but even without that, the atmosphere always seemed cheery. It was a room that felt lived in even if it didn't look it.

Mind you, I'd never been in that room without him sitting there in his armchair. Now his absence transformed the place. Apart from its extraordinary small number of furniture items – one armchair, a small table, two small wooden chairs, a sideboard on which sat an ancient record player, a stack of records and a small radio, and a low table supporting a chess set – this was a truly empty room. Were it not for the stench of death, you would not believe that a normal human being had ever lived here. He really was a strange man, my Dad.

Then my eyes fell on the biscuit tin on the sideboard – an ancient relic of decades past, a battered Constable on the lid. He called it his correspondence box – not that he did a lot of corresponding. I opened it, and there, on top of a few papers, was an envelope with my name on it. God, no, I thought. Surely not a suicide note.

I considered stuffing it in my handbag and looking at it later, over a glass of wine, well away from this empty room, but before I knew it, I'd opened it – it wasn't sealed – and was staring at a single sheet, written in his usual, impeccable but over-large handwriting:

"My dear Isabel,

Well, that's me finished. Please don't be sad. I've had a decent innings. Mustn't grumble. Sometimes good, sometimes bad, sometimes happy, sometimes sad. Now this particular lamp has burnt itself out. But remember what I always used to say: 'One light though the lamps be many.' So now it's your turn to keep the light shining.

Here's some cash for my funeral. Keep it a quiet affair. Cardboard coffin – they do them, these days. Quick cremation. You hang on to the rest – there's nothing else. Ask Simon, next door, if he'll take all the furniture down the charity shop. Keep the chess set and give it to Bill, will you?

You're a good girl, Isabel. I love you. Take care of yourself.

Dad."

Of course, that set me weeping. I'm not usually a crier, but now it simply poured out. I don't know exactly why I was crying. We'd never really been that close, or so I thought. But, I don't know, those few lines set me off. He was such a good man, my Dad. I don't think he'd ever told me that he loved me – at least, not that I could remember – and I'm damned sure that I'd never told him that I loved him – which I suppose I did, now that I came to think about it. Oh, God! Why is it all so difficult, this business of families and love and other people? Why are we all so feeble and fragile and vulnerable?

A wodge of notes came out of the envelope. My lucky day, I remember thinking, which at least brought a sort of smile to my face as I sniffed back my outburst of grief. Good old Dad. Always thought of the practicalities.

But was this a suicide note? It was undated and looked as though it might have been sitting there in the biscuit tin for weeks, months even. Natural causes, the doctor had said. And presumably the police would have spotted anything that might have aroused suspicion. Perhaps he'd had some premonition. Or perhaps he was just being prepared – ever the Boy Scout, keeping things in good order.

He left home when I was five. I didn't see him after that for ten years. Of course, I only ever heard Mum's side of the story. Dad had an affair with another woman, someone from his office. He said it was nothing more than a temporary infatuation; that it would blow over before long, like a dose of flu. But Mum kicked him out. Eventually it did blow over, but by that time Mum had found another bloke. So that's when Dad got this pokey little terraced house. They got divorced, Mum re-married and Dad has lived alone ever since. Once I'd grown up, I got in contact with him again and we'd developed a father/daughter relationship of sorts. I went through a divorce myself, few years back, so I feel I have some insight into what happened with Mum and Dad. No, I don't. I was too young, at the time. And every relationship is different. And we never talked about it, Dad and I, neither his divorce nor mine. A pity. It's too late now, of course. I think that's perhaps why I cried.

I must contact Bill, Dad's one and only chum. He'd come over every week or two and they'd play a game of chess and drink a bottle of port between them. The game took hours, and they never spoke during it, just kept supping their port and topping up each other's glasses and staring at the board. Dad told me once that they were pretty evenly matched, so they'd agreed to take it in turns to win. And so they did. I've never played chess myself, but it struck me as rather odd to spend hours playing a game when you'd already agreed beforehand who was going to win. "What's the point?" I'd asked Dad. "For the fun of it," he'd answered.

111

He was strange, my Dad. On the surface, he appeared perfectly normal and conventional – one might well say boring – and I can't help feeling that he didn't really achieve very much in his life, a life bereft of incident and adventure. And yet, scratch below the surface and you exposed a truly remarkable masterpiece of humanity. I think Dad would have liked that image – not about himself, but about all men and women.

I put the chess set in its box – which, as I anticipated, was neatly stowed in the sideboard – and headed back to Simon and Martha's. They were good neighbours, really. Dad could have done a lot worse. They each gave me a hug as I left. I took a tenner out of the funeral money Dad had left and bought a bottle of port on my way home.

Here's to you, Dad. And, yes, a bell is necessary on a bicycle.

3. THE FRIEND

I was away when Izzy called. On the festival circuit. A friend of mine runs a mobile ostrich burger bar and we do all the summer festivals. They sell like hot cakes, our burgers and steaks: good, healthy stuff, more like pork than poultry. Anyway, we rake in the dosh and, taking it in turns to cook in the van, we get to see some of the music and soak up the atmosphere. I'm still an old hippy at heart. So was Joe, come to that. Of course, he dressed reasonably normally and his locks had long since fallen out, but he was still one of us. We're a breed apart, we ancient ageing hippies. Joe would have said that was bullshit. He reckoned that, back then in the sixties, we were simply pulled along by the flow of fashion and some of us found a rock to cling on to and never moved on. Maybe he was right, but I like my pony tail – even if it's grey now – and my beads and shoulder bag and crazy clothes. I bring a much needed splash of eccentric colour into our drab modern world: that's how I see it.

No, I wasn't really shocked when Izzy finally got hold of me and broke the news. Joe spoke to me much more than he did to his daughter – not a lot, mind: he was a pleasantly taciturn sort of chap – but, well, I was his oldest mate and it's a bit tricky telling your immediate family that you're dying. Especially for Joe who'd enjoyed almost perfect health for most of his life, the bastard. Pretty much the first time he ever went to the doc's was when his liver started playing up – sozzled with port, I suspect. It was only then that they discovered he'd got a faulty heart valve – always had, apparently – and his heart, to compensate for the problem, had blown up to nearly bursting proportions. That was just over a year ago. Joe was wondering why he was having trouble exerting himself, but he took it to be the first sinister sign of approaching old age. And he always was a lazy sod – never too keen on exerting himself.

An operation was a possibility – replacing the buggered valve or something – but it seemed his poor old ticker was definitely on its last legs. Joe wasn't too bothered. Well, of course he was, really, but he's always been a bit philosophical about death and mortality and all that stuff.

"A time for everything, and everything has its time," he'd often say. "When you watch a beautiful sunset, for instance, it reaches its magnificent peak then gently fades to blackness. Or a piece of music: it may be stupendous, but it's bound to end sometime. Or you're eating a delicious meal: great, but it can't go on forever. Pretty soon you've had enough. Meal over."

You can't argue with that sort of thing. But most people do. I want to live forever, they scream. Why? Even a mountain will one day crumble into dust. Even the sun will burn itself out in a few billion years. A mayfly lives for a single day. We manage to get seventy odd years, if we're lucky. Time enough for a good life, I'd have thought.

So Joe's heart finally packed it in. No, I wasn't shocked when Izzy told me. Neither was she, I think. Too wrapped up in her own affairs, if you ask me. But no, I've always had a soft spot for little Izzy. I knew her as a tiny tot. It really cut Joe up when he didn't see her for ten years, after the divorce. They'd lost a huge gap in their relationship, a wound that would never be healed, although I believe they both tried. Trouble was, like most of her generation, she was into money and Joe most assuredly wasn't. Possessions didn't interest him at all. "Why should I want to own things when the whole world is mine?" he used to say. You can't answer a question like that.

Throughout his life – not many people know this – he gave away half of all the money he earned. Paid his rent first, of course, then split the rest fifty-fifty. Even after he'd given up work and was living on a pension. Any charity he fancied benefitted from his remarkable generosity: maybe Oxfam one week, then the local church roof appeal the next. Sometimes I'd seen him hand a tenner to a beggar in the street. I pulled him up on that one. These guys are professionals, I told him. He's probably got a posh car parked around the corner, thanks to mugs like you. Either that or he's got some crippling habit to feed.

But Joe wouldn't have it. "He wants money, I don't. So why not let him have it?"

The truth was, Joe didn't want anything. Not quite true. He wanted to win at chess. I could tell. His mind was totally locked into the game. He was good – but I was better. So I let him win every other game. Well, what did it matter to me? Joe enjoyed winning, so why not let him win? Although not so often that he came to think of me as a walkover – that way the enjoyment would have palled. But his enjoyments were few, so I was happy to indulge him: chess, port, an occasional stroll in the park, listening to his bloody hippy music – the bloke never realised that popular music has moved on over the decades – and watching clouds: that was pretty well his lot.

Watching clouds? you're probably thinking. Oh yes.

"Better than the tele," he'd tell me. "Constantly changing beauty. I sit in the backyard and gaze up at the sky and watch the clouds roll by and, I tell you Bill, I'm truly happy."

And he was: I believe it. So there you go.

Izzy gave me his chess set. I know for a fact that it was worth a darned sight more than all the rest of his possessions put together. But Joe wouldn't have known that. And even if he had, it wouldn't have mattered to him.

114

4. THE GOOD MAN

Well that's pretty well it, I think. That's enough for me. Almost time to turn off the lamp and go to sleep. It's no big deal. Far easier to die than to cope with someone else's death.

I'm happy to die. Why shouldn't I be? We've all got to go sometime. So let's see what Mother Nature has in store for me next. Bring it on, as the kids say. Bring it on. I'm ready.

This armchair. Just sitting here. Breathing. In, out. In, out. Slowly. Gently. No need to hurry. No need to hold back. Just let go. In, out. In, out.

How I love this armchair by the window, looking up into the clouds, watching time flow steadily on. How I love this house: simple, pure, the perfect final resting place of this human being called Joe Stikans. And how I love this world: this magnificent outwardness, this warm, intimate inwardness. Thank you. Thank you. Thank you for being.

Old beating heart, you've done all right. Nearly time to stop. Two billion beats – I worked it out once. Two billion beats without stopping. You've done well.

You'll do well, too, my Izzy. No doubt Simon will find me here before long and let you know. Don't worry: everything's in order. And go easy with your life, my darling daughter. Find the time to stop, once in a while, and look to the beauty of the clouds.

And Bill, my old friend. I expect you know I let you win every other game we played – but you never let on, and nor did I. A tacit understanding, that's what we had. A precious thing. Take care, Bill. It's a cold world out there for a delicate soul like you.

And, hey, good luck Earth. Good luck humanity. Together I hope you pull through all this global warming business. Simple living and kindness: those are the keys. I won't be here to see it, but I know you can do it.

Still breathing. In, out. In, out. This one small lamp almost burnt out, though the One Light will shine forever: that much I know. Dreams: so lucid, so wonderful. And brief periods of wakefulness, eyes open but not focussing, familiar patches of colour. Finally just the awareness of awareness itself. And the breathing. In, out. In, out. And the odd words, drifting like clouds across the inner screen. Ah, the sweetness of it all. Ah, the rich vastness of the present. Ah, the privilege of being. The gratitude. So grateful. So grateful. So grateful...

BOOTS

Day's end. The long black shadows of the bare beeches in the copse oozed across the farmyard like a pool of spilt oil. Matt turned off the tractor's engine and slumped over the wheel, weary but content with the afternoon's work. Muck spreading up in Big Dell, preparing the land for the winter. Time for supper then maybe a few pints in the pub.

"Boots!" came the customary shout from Mother as he closed the back door of the farmhouse and lowered himself onto the stool that had sat there, in the scullery, all his life and probably all his father's life. He pulled off his mud-caked boots, placed them side by side on the edge of the pile of assorted footwear that littered the flagstones, and reached for his slippers, placed equally neatly, awaiting his aching feet.

In the kitchen, Mother was bent over the sink. She didn't turn. She knew Matt's sound. "Right," she greeted him.

"Right," Matt responded, sitting at the table. That was the conversation over with. Matt rolled a fag. As he lit it, Mother plonked a mug of tea in front of him. He raised his index finger a few inches from the table. She nodded slightly and returned to the sink.

Ten minutes later, the back door slammed.

"Boots!" shouted Mother.

117

The sound of two Wellingtons thrown to the floor preceded Danny's entry. He snatched up Matt's mug and drained what was left of his tea.

"Bit of a rush today, Mother," he announced. "Off into town. Don't bother with no supper for me. Them bloody cows was moody tonight. Typical when I'm in an 'urry. And that number twenty-eight got teat trouble again, Matt."

"Patsy," said Matt.

"Bloody Patsy. They's just numbers to me and she's a right bugger of a number."

"She's fine. You gotta be patient with 'er. She's a good little milker."

Danny stuffed a slice of cake into his mouth from a plate Mother had placed on the table, and he made for the door. "I ain't got the time for your bloody gentle touch," he spluttered through a spray of crumbs. "Ain't got time for bloody cows at all. Caravans, that's what we wants in them fields. Make some decent money from the bloody tourists."

Neither Matt nor Mother appeared to acknowledge his oft-repeated opinion. They listened to his footsteps, dashing up the stairs, two at a time, clattering across the floorboards of his room.

In ways, Matt envied his younger brother – envied his self-assurance, bordering on arrogance, his energy, his ambition, not to mention - as he never did - his success with women. In ways, he despised him. Their father had given everything to the farm including, finally, his life. He'd been on his own, fencing up in Big Dell, a mile or more from the farmhouse. A length of barbed wire had sprung back and caught him in the eye. He'd tried to make it home on the tractor but, unable to see, he'd misjudged the slope of the hill. The tractor turned over, crushing the life from him. Matt had been fifteen, Danny ten, shielded from the horror of it all and quick to forget. To Matt, though, it seemed that they owed it to his memory to carry on. It was something that he'd never questioned. Besides, he loved the farm. He loved the familiar rolling hills, the woods, the hedgerows, the jobs that arose naturally from the gradual march of seasons. And he loved the cows, every one of them. It was an old cliché but they said, down in the village, that Matt, like his father before him, loved cows more than people. He talked to them more, at any rate. And why not, he thought. You could say anything you liked to the cows and they never mocked you or tried to put you down. Or you could say nothing at all and they never thought you were dense or stuck up or too shy to stick a sentence together. He could share the silence of the cows and they could share his - and that, he thought, was a precious thing. He fed them, he milked them - alternating days with Danny - he tended to their afflictions and he kept their home in good order. Yes, he loved them and, he never doubted, they loved him back in their quiet bovine way. There were no complications with cows. No games. No need for the fast and clever talk at which Danny seemed to excel and Matt was completely inept.

*

He sat at his usual barstool, that evening, and supped from the same tankard that his father had once used. He knew everyone in the pub but his conversations rarely extended beyond a brief exchange of pleasantries.

"Right then, Matt?"

"Right then, Bill?"

"'Ow goes it then?"

"Fine, mate. And you?"

"Ripped off at the market again today, Matt. Bloody sheep prices 'ave gone crazy. How'd they expect us to survive?"

Matt listened sympathetically to the troubles of all his neighbours and nodded his head in agreement but he never ventured any troubles of his own. They've got problems enough, he thought. They don't want to hear about mine. And so his acquaintances wandered off to find more loquacious companions and Matt sipped from his tankard and rolled his fags and thought about tomorrow's jobs. Did he really want to be like them, forever moaning and gossiping? He wanted to joke with them, to be sure, but somehow all his attempts at humour

119

seemed to fall flat and when they laughed it was only because he'd get the punch line wrong.

He'd stay at home of an evening, sit with Mother in front of the telly or fiddle about with the farm books, were it not for Gill. They'd been at school together, grown up as neighbours, if not quite as friends. She'd been the regular barmaid for years, always smiling, joking, flirting. All the local chaps had had her - at least once - all, that is, except Matt who'd never tasted the delights of any girl and probably, he was inclined to think, never would. Danny had someone new in tow every week. If he wasn't milking the next day, his bed was rarely slept in. Matt looked on with a mixture of wonderment and disgust. The only girl he wanted was Gill.

"You look down tonight, Matt." She leaned across the bar and gave him one of her delightful smiles.

He glanced up at her then rapidly returned his attention to his tankard. "Me? I'm fine."

"'Ow're the cows?"

"They're fine, thanks."

"Danny out on the town again tonight?"

Why did she always spoil it by mentioning Danny? "S'pose so," he muttered.

Gill returned to her barmaid duties. Conversing with Matt was hard work. But she liked him, she always had. True, he wasn't much of a looker and certainly nothing of a talker. He wasn't like the other lads. Born into the wrong era. He belonged to the time of her father, or even her grandfather, men who loved the land they worked and treated their stock as equal partners in the daily struggle for survival. Gill, too, felt herself to be part of some past generation when life was simpler and more immediate, when conversation was largely dictated by the passage of the sun across the sky, by the changing weather and the flow of seasons. She'd tried the modern life - messing about with the boys, dressing up and heading into the clubs in town with Danny and his mates, joining in with their hollow banter, deriding the ancient traditions of the village in which they all lived. She'd watched her contemporaries move off to jobs in the city or marry young and start child rearing in the tiny brick boxes on the new estate. She'd listened to their constant moaning about prices and politicians and the state of the world. She pulled pints and flirted with the punters in the pub but her heart was out in the fields, in the woods, beneath the open skies. Perhaps Matt would understand her. But she was trapped behind a persona of frivolity and superficiality that she had unwittingly created for herself and he was locked in a strange cage of taciturn self-consciousness from which he seemed incapable of escaping.

*

Gill was strolling the footpath along the ridge that skirted Big Dell, the boundary between her father's land and Matt's. These were the few hours she devoted to herself, after lunchtime closing and before her evening stint. Her mother had suggested a tour of the shops in town but Gill had opted for solitude and space and greenery. A cold autumn wind was blowing a flotilla of wispy white clouds down from the north, racing across the light blue sky, the sun sinking into a huge grey bank, like a range of unexplored mountains on the western horizon.

There, on a stile, sat Matt, a roll-up dangling from his lips, gazing at the sky and the naked trees of the wood in the dell while his Friesians ambled carefree about the lush green grass of the field.

They both hid their surprise at the encounter and greeted each other nonchalantly.

"Matt."

"Gill."

She stopped a few yards away from him and followed his gaze to the west. Half of the sun had disappeared into the cloudbank leaving a semicircle of burning gold, just tolerable to the eyes, tingeing the peaks of the nebulous mountains with a thousand shades of orange and pink and purple.

They were silent for many minutes. Just looking.

"Colours that man forgot to name," said Matt.

"Colours that put language to shame," said Gill.

Matt nodded. They were seeing the same thing, Gill and he, and the pleasure of their common vision was more than doubled by the sharing. Vastly more.

The sun sank lower, a tiny arc of burnished bronze scattering its brilliancy over the rapidly greying landscape while, high above, the blueness deepened and the scurrying wisps were touched with candy-floss pink. The wind died down, respecting the mood of another day's end. The bare boughs of the giant oaks in the wood were still. The rustling of the ochre beech leaves in the hedgerows gently faded. Even the cows in the field ceased their munching and maintained their dignified silence. Seconds turned into minutes then dissolved into timelessness. They shared the perfect beauty of their native land.

Gill shivered involuntarily as the cold air penetrated her flimsy coat.

Matt turned to her and smiled. "Tea? Back at the farm?" It was the first time he had ever invited her anywhere.

"Yeah," she said.

*

"Boots!" shouted Mother from the kitchen as they opened the back door.

Together they sat, back to back, on the little stool in the scullery, removed their boots and placed them neatly, side by side, on the flagstones.

THE CAVE

Kaph, the village Elder, had led an exemplary life until, at the age of fifty, he fell under the grip of an uncontrollable passion. Surely the madness of love is an affliction of youth: so ran the murmurings in the sleepy village. A young man may be excused, perhaps even pardoned, for abandoning all to chase after his sweetheart. A young woman, forsaking her family for the love of another, may be understood, if not forgiven. But such maladies of the heart belong to the young and the foolish. Surely a man of fifty - an Elder, no less, who had achieved his status by dint of hard work and moral steadfastness, who had sired and raised a goodly family and earned the respect and admiration of his entire community - surely such a man was immune from emotional tempests and the lures of the flesh.

But Kaph was truly smitten. One look into the eyes of the beautiful stranger who had chanced upon the village, and his sanity deserted him, his accumulated wisdom vanished like a bubble burst - or so it seemed to his fellows - his life of ease, social standing and apparent contentment overthrown in an instant.

"I saw the whole world reflected in those hazel eyes," he tried to explain to his concerned peers. "I heard the voice of my destiny as clearly as the peal of the Sunday church bell."

"Nonsense," retorted his closest friend. "You've been bewitched. Show a little strength of spirit, man."

"But how can I resist the inevitable?" Kaph replied, seemingly calm though his heart was churning and spitting like an overheated pot of broth. "I feel that I know this lady as intimately as the song in my soul. Even now, her memory is like the warmth of sunshine on my face. You say I am bewitched. From within, I feel liberated."

His friends despaired of him. His wife wept with the pain and humiliation of his rejection. His children despised him for his selfishness. The villagers threatened to remove him from his exalted position of Elder, presiding over their affairs, if he could not return to his senses. But Kaph, suffering a week of agonised ecstasy after the beautiful stranger had continued on her way, packed a small bag and, with downcast head, slunk away from his home, knowing that he would find no peace except in her company. And never did he return to his native village.

They spoke of him often, those he left behind, and the legend of the love-torn Elder was passed down from generation to generation. And many a young man wondered how a man of such advanced years could be wracked by such a youthful passion. And many a young woman secretly pined for a love so powerful. He was a weak-willed misfit, said many, dismissing their once respected Elder. She was a witch, said others, recalling the hazel-eyed stranger who had tarried in the village for no more than a day. But memories are fickle and, as the tale was retold, the stranger's image was transformed, for some becoming a wizened hag, for others a radiant temptress. And Kaph himself was pictured by some as a feeble and perverse old man while others, recalling his days as a woodchopper, imagined a noble, handsome figure for whom middle-age brought that life-transforming experience that is often spoken of in the legends of heroes.

In time, the village died, its people drifting off in pursuit of their various fortunes. Even its name faded from maps of the locality. But the name of Kaph continued to burn brightly in the country's folklore and the myth that grew around his name, down through the ages, served as an inspiration to those, of whatever age, who sought the perfection of love.

For two years, so the myth recounts, Kaph roamed willy-nilly across the land, living off charity and the fruits of the wayside. Who can say what thoughts passed through his mind, what motives stirred his heart? Was he searching for his beautiful stranger or was he simply yielding to the restlessness that he knew would plague him until - as he knew with irrational certainty - their paths would cross again? Was he happy in his wandering or was he tormented by the guilt of leaving his family and his village, or by the unfulfilled ardour of his love? Myths make no mention of their heroes' feelings, leaving us to imagine ourselves walking in their shoes, animating their bodies with the colours of our own personalities. Was it weariness that caused him to cease his roaming when he discovered the cave, or was it some premonition, some glimpse of his destiny? I like to believe that those two years on the road changed him in ways that only the solitary rover can understand; that all concepts of time gradually dropped from his mind; that the years of his life meant no more to him than the wrinkles on his face - which, lacking a mirror, he never saw; that he finally found himself in the bliss and contentment of the present moment.

And finding himself in the present moment, he looked around and saw a wondrous gorge, cutting through the high cliffs to a shingly beach where the waves of the ocean broke gently on the shore. There, amongst the ivy-clad rocks, he came upon the cave, just tall enough to take his height, just deep enough to provide protection from the wind and rain. And there he made his home, lining the cave with smooth stones that lay strewn across the grassy hills, carpeting the floor with ferns, fashioning what meagre furniture he needed from driftwood and rocks he found on the beach, feeding on herbs and berries and the bountiful larder of the sea, knowing the peace and beauty of Nature, desiring nothing but to be as he was.

In time, men and women came to him, for legends spread quickly, even in the remote hills, and seekers are forever keen to share the company of remarkable men. They came singly, for such was the custom, and each one found Kaph sitting at the mouth of his cave.

125

They offered him what victuals they had and he brewed up beverages of camomile or rose-hip or raspberry, depending on the season, or milk from the few sheep that roamed the coastal cliffs. And they sat together, gazing at the wondrous valley or down along its length to the sea. Each visitor told his tale and Kaph listened silently, nodding and smiling at times, but saying nothing himself. And none could resist the temptation to ask the hermit's advice on whatever question or dilemma or problem perplexed them - what should they do, where should they go, how should they pursue their dreams. Kaph gave no answer, but led each stranger down the winding path to the beach and there, after searching a while in the sand or shingle, he would pick up a shell, or a twisted piece of wood, or a pebble, or a curl of dried seaweed, and hand it to the questioner.

Some saw at once the answer to their question, an image in the subtle colours of the shell perhaps, some pointer in the shape of a stone, some personal reminder in the twists and gnarls of a twig. Some, of course, saw nothing but a shell, a stone, a lump of wood.

"I don't understand," they would complain.

"Look," said Kaph.

"But what am I meant to see?"

"Look," said Kaph, the only word he spoke.

Some, inevitably, were disappointed. They would leave Kaph in his cave and wander off across the cliffs, still holding his gift in their hands; and perhaps in an hour, a day or a week, the answer would dawn on them and they would marvel at the hermit's wisdom. Or perhaps not.

Thus it was that the name of Kaph the Elder, the hermit, the silent counsellor, became renowned along the southern shores and his tiny cave became a place of pilgrimage for the desperate, the curious and the few true seekers of life's open secret. He turned none away, greeting all with the same welcoming smile, the same beaming eyes, granting all the same steady attention, the same careful selection of some small gift from the seashore to encapsulate the answer they

126

sought. The very letters of his name, so it was said, enshrined the qualities of his soul: Kindness, Awareness, Patience and Humility.

Here the legend blurs, as legends do, leaving one to imagine what one wills. One day, as Kaph is gathering berries in the shrubland, a woman approaches his cave, a beautiful, hazel-eyed stranger. Kaph returns to find her peering into the dim interior. She turns, surprised. Their eyes meet...

*

She had been wandering all her life. When she was little, her father had sat with her on the box of their wagon, showing her how to rein a horse along the highways and byroads of the countryside. The wagon was brightly coloured, decorated inside and out with painted flowers. She loved to gaze at them, lying in her cot at night, trying to fix them in her mind.

Her mother wove baskets and her father mended kettles and pans and earned a living thereby: and sometimes he'd sing the melancholic songs of their people in exchange for drinks in the taverns. She was the oldest of five. For as long as she could remember, she'd helped her mother making the fire, gathering firewood, keeping the children out of mischief, washing the clothes and cooking. But as she blossomed into a young woman, she grew tired of the never-ending chores of her daily life. She yearned for more space for dreaming, for thinking, for practising her art. Her fingers were restless, only happy when they held a brush, dancing with the joy of flowing colours.

When she was sixteen, they married her to a boy of thirteen, the son of the leader of their company of wagoners. But the strange demands of marriage repulsed her. That very night she ran away to lead her own life, taking with her only her paint box and pencils, her mixing pots and colour powders, her favourite painted planks of wood as evidence of her prowess in decoration, for she had it in mind to live the life of an artist.

She roamed far from the tracks that her family took: always north in summer, south in winter. Instead, she headed west, coming to lands that had never known the footfall of the travelling people. She offered her art to the people of the villages through which she passed, and they, whether through sympathy for the girl or genuine appreciation of her flowers and garlands, bade her paint their cupboards and chests, their cradles and wooden spoons. At night she slept in her blanket in the forests or copses, beside a running brook, or in the fields where roe deer and foxes approached her in her sleep to gaze at her closed eyes and wonder at her deep and constant breath.

As the years past, her floral paintings underwent many changes. Where once they had been primitive and gaily coloured, now they grew in depth, subtlety and sophistication. A new mood had entered them. She started to paint the moon and the stars and the sun, trees and castles and beasts. These things she painted for her own pleasure – rarely at the behest of a customer – expressing the feelings and insights of the dreams that welled up within her soul, like a constantly seething cauldron of creativity. This inexhaustible well was her home and her solace: this and the path that connected one village with the next, sometimes losing itself in woodlands and marshes, or leading, perchance, to a secluded mountain lake, into which she would dive to catch the setting sun. At times, of course, she was lonely. But the wild world befriended her and, for the most part, she was content.

One day she emerged from the woods to find a field where three brown horses came to greet her, swaying their heads, coyly treading towards her. She had always loved horses. She stroked their noses, ran her fingers through their manes and shared her bread with them. Then off they trotted, turning as if beckoning her to follow, across the meadows and down into a valley where nestled a dreamy village. Children were playing around the well in the centre of the village, and the clang of iron on iron rang from the smithy. She struck up conversation with the women, standing or ambling on the green, and asked if she might see the village Elder – for usually, if the Elders approved of her artwork, then the people of the village would look more favourably upon what she had to offer.

He was a man of about fifty years, ruddy and fine looking with the strong arms of a woodchopper and a face both intelligent and sensitive. He looked at the sample wooden panels she carried. Then he looked into her eyes and asked her to paint the cradle he had crafted for his first grandchild-to-come. His eyes were a strong sky blue, and his look was strangely penetrating and magnetic. She had to fight with herself to turn away from him, yet still his look attracted her back and she felt a thrill of joy from his gaze and an unfamiliar anxiety that she was glad to channel into her work.

It took her a day to finish the cradle. He seemed well pleased, and when he paid her he looked at her again. Now the blue eyes, soft and vulnerable, gazed questioningly into hers. And her solitary heart fluttered under the force of his look. She blushed and turned her face from his, bade him a curt farewell and hurried upon her way. Maybe others in the village would request her skills, but, for reasons that she did not understand, she felt that she could not stay.

She made her camp, that night, on the hill where the three brown horses roamed, feeling that she needed their company, feeling reluctant to leave the village behind her. At sunset, she knew that she was waiting there for him: the respected Elder, the woodchopper, an ageing man with wife and children and a grandchild-to-come. She waited all night, thinking of his face, the look of his eyes. She waited there for two days more. He didn't come.

*

In the two years that followed, a remarkable change occurred in her painting. Between the garlands and the leaves, between the sun and the moon and the stars, she started to paint his eyes: two kind, soft, searing eyes that seemed to see into her soul. She told the people whom she met that they were the loving eyes of God, and she achieved a certain fame for those divine eyes amidst the flowers and foliage. Many asked her to paint them above their doors or around their beds, on their prayer books and even upon the coffins of their departed.

But she was no longer content. Each time she painted those eyes, he was looking at her again, and his look was the eternal restlessness of her life.

One summer's afternoon, she followed a footpath through cultivated fields to the high sea cliffs of the southern shore. There she spied a secluded little bay where the surf lapped gently in, depositing shells and seaweed on a narrow strip of yellow sand. She wanted to be on that beach for a while, to listen to the sea and let her weary heart be rocked to sleep by the sound of the waves.

Climbing down to the sea through a rounded, grassy gorge, she came upon a small cave. A twisted elder tree grew over the entrance. She approached, curious to peer within, attracted, it seemed to her, by a sweet mystery that lurked in the atmosphere of the place.

The cave was almost circular with a domed roof. Someone had strengthened the curving walls with flat stones from the seashore and fields. A small niche had been created on the right side. In its shade stood a candle, a jug of milk and a large clam shell. Fresh ferns lay on the floor and, in the deepest recess, a heap of ferns formed a scented bed for the night. Clearly someone lived here, perhaps feeding on berries and sheep milk, drinking the water that trickled down the rock face of the gorge.

Just then she heard a footstep behind her. She turned quickly, expecting to encounter the hermit whose home this was, embarrassed and flustered by her own curiosity.

And so her eyes met the eyes of God.

*

The cave is still there, at the top of the gorge, gazing down through a cleft in the cliffs to the ever-changing ocean. Its smooth internal stones are blackened, now, with damp and moss, its floor littered with the debris of ages. Ivy, may and blackthorn clamber over the surrounding rocks, swept landward by the sea winds. In its opening grows a single elder tree, an ancient specimen, tortured and furrowed, its soft bark peeling, yet still it sends forth shoots of fresh growth, green leaves basking in the sun, creamy inflorescences in spring, clumps of juicy black berries in autumn. Amongst its upper boughs weave the twigs and branches of a hazel tree. From a distance, they seem to be dancing together, the elder and the hazel, embracing each other, flowing in slow-moving waves of love.

DICTIONARY

My first encounter with the *Concise Oxford Dictionary* nearly put me off words for life. I had to shift a hundred and twenty of the damn things. Weighty buggers! Real strenuous work, I can tell you. (Page 1378. "**Strenuous** *adj.* **1.** requiring or using great effort. **2.** energetic or unrelaxing." Too true.) I nearly gave myself a hernia, as my old man's always saying whenever he has to lift anything heavier than a pint of Guinness. (Page 635. "**Hernia** *n.* (*pl.* **hernias** or **herniae**) the displacement or protrusion of part of an organ through the wall of the cavity containing it, esp. of the abdomen." Sounds nasty.)

It all happened one miserable Tuesday morning, a few days before the end of term. We were enduring a maths lesson when the Headmaster stuck his head around the door,

"Coupla volunteers?" he asked, hopefully.

Obviously, volunteering to help the Headmaster in front of the whole class was the last thing any self-respecting pupil would dream of doing, but we were in the middle of one of those tedious end-of-term quiz-type-things that teachers think we might possibly enjoy as a treat from normal tedious lessons, so Mike and I stuck our hands up. What the hell! We were past caring.

One of our school traditions was the presentation to each leaving pupil, during the final assembly, of a hardback copy of the *Concise*

Oxford Dictionary. Apparently the considerable dosh required for this uncharacteristic act of generosity had been supplied, years before, by some rich local philanthropist. (Good word, that, don't you think? Page 1025. "**Philanthropy** *n.* **1.** a love of humankind. **2.** practical benevolence, esp. charity on a large scale.")

"May this hallowed tome inspire and facilitate your further assaults on the lofty heights of academia," the Headmaster would proclaim in his farewell speech - or some such pompous twaddle. No one ever paid any attention to anything he said.

I knew, from mates who had left in previous years, exactly what happened to all those dictionaries. First thing, all the leavers dashed around getting all the other leavers to autograph or write obscene messages on the inside covers. Then they got lugged home and stuck on a shelf or used as a paperweight or a doorstop or something. Maybe a few creeps actually read them. No doubt one or two obsessive types started at **a**, then **aardvark**, and, over the summer holidays, worked their way fastidiously through to **zymurgy**. (Page 1632. "*n.* the branch of applied chemistry dealing with the use of fermentation in brewing etc." Bet you didn't know that one, did you?) For the most part, though, the first thing all those dictionaries were used for was titillation. (Page 1463. "**Titillate** *v.tr.* **1.** excite pleasantly. **2.** tickle.") Sooner or later, everyone discovered that this authoritative book of words contained a veritable feast of rude words that most kids had never before seen in print. Boys, of course, started with the female genitals - quim, fanny, cunt, yoni, and so on. (Yes, they're all there. Take a look, if you haven't already done so.) Girls, presumably, delved into the assortment of phallic synonyms. Then both sexes investigated the abundance of terms for the act of sexual intercourse, before venturing into the excretory functions. Some – like me, I will confess - investigated such linguistic delicacies as **fellatio** (page 494) and **cunnilingus** (page 328). That, for most, was the extent of their summer holiday reading.

Anyway, the Headmaster led Mike and me to the assembly hall and pointed at a huge pile of cardboard boxes on the floor.

"Just empty that lot and stack the dictionaries neatly on the table on the stage, will you? Good lads. I'm off to put my feet up for half an hour." (Actually, he didn't say that last bit, but I bet he thought it.)

A hundred and twenty bloody dictionaries! You any idea how much a *Concise Oxford Dictionary* weighs? I'll tell you. (I took the trouble to stick mine on the kitchen scales.) Just over three and a half pounds. (Or one and three-quarter kilos, if that's what you prefer.) So 120 dictionaries at 1.75 kg each - isn't it amazing how maths comes into everything, just as all our maths teachers promised us - means that Mike and I shifted 210 kg from the assembly hall floor to the table on the stage. I weigh about 70 kg, so that's three times my own body weight. It just goes to show, it never pays to stick your hand up when the Headmaster asks for volunteers. That was one valuable lesson I learned that day.

Here's a bit more maths, in case that last bit got you in the mood. I noticed that the blurb on the back of the dictionary mentions that the book contains two million words of text. (Well, you notice things like that when you're lugging 120 of the damn things up a flight of steps onto the stage.) 1.75 kg of book packed with two million words. That means each word weighs 0.000875 grammes, a little less than a milligramme. How about that for a totally meaningless and utterly useless piece of information? The power of maths to change your life really is staggering.

Two million words, eh? (That's not two million different words, of course. No doubt some of them, like "a" and "the" and "and" and so on are used quite a few times.) The blurb doesn't say how many different words are defined, but it does tell those of us who are particularly interested that there are 140,000 separate meanings. (Lots of words, as we all know, have lots of meanings. Take shag, for instance - to take a random word that I just happened to look up. (Page 1271) Five completely different meanings. Mind boggling, don't you think? Here they are, because I'm sure you're dying to know: "**shag** *n*. **1.** a rough growth or mass of hair etc. **2.** a coarse kind of cut tobacco. **3.** a cormorant. **4.** *v. & n. Brit. coarse slang* have sexual intercourse with, *n*.

an act of sexual intercourse. **5.** (usu. in passive, often foll. by *out*) exhaust; tire out." Like Mike and I were after heaving all that lot onto the stage: totally shagged out. So, next time some teacher gives you a bollocking for using a word like "shag", you might like to politely point out that you were referring to a common sea bird or a type of tobacco.)

It took Mike and me about a quarter of an hour to shift those dictionaries onto the stage. (120 x 2 million = 240 million words. Not bad going, when you look at it like that - shifting 240 million words in a quarter of an hour.) After that, there were still twenty minutes of our maths lesson remaining before lunchtime, but it didn't seem worth going back to it. Mike slipped out of the stage door for a quick fag. I made myself comfortable on the Headmaster's chair on the stage (the only one with armrests and a cushioned seat), picked up the nearest copy of the *Concise Oxford Dictionary* and started aimlessly browsing. You wouldn't believe how interesting such a boring looking book can be, although there's not much in the way of plot, so far as I could make out, and it's a bit short on pictures. (They say a picture's worth a thousand words. Maybe the old COD would be better if it just contained two thousand pictures instead of two million words.) You can open it anywhere and, pretty soon, you're lost in some bizarre definition of a word you've never heard of. Some detain you for no more than a few seconds. (Here's the first I turned to: page 1099, "**prosopopoeia** *n.* the rhetorical introduction of a pretended speaker or the personification of an abstract thing." How's that for a completely incomprehensible definition of a word you can't pronounce and are almost certainly never going to use?) Some set your thoughts rambling all over the place. Like my second attempt at a random selection: page 332, "**cuspidor** *n. N. Amer.* a spittoon." A nice word, that. Cuspidor. Actually, it wasn't entirely new to me. I'd heard it many times before. My old man has this annoying tendency to spontaneously burst into song when washing up or strolling about the house or sitting on the bog or whatever. He likes to pretend he's an opera singer, Pavarotti or someone, and he'll launch into these well-known opera tunes but, not speaking Italian or whatever damn foreign language it's written in, he'll adapt things a bit with alternative words. His favourite is the toreador

134

song from *Carmen*. (You'd know it if you heard it: really catchy little tune. I sometimes even catch myself humming it.) He gets the first word right but, after that, his version grows a little different from the original:

"To - re - a - dor

Don't spit upon the floor.

Spit in the cuspidor,

That's what it's for."

(Well, that's my old man for you: totally bonkers.)

I asked him, once - back in the days when I genuinely cared about his state of sanity - what a cuspidor was. "A spittoon," he told me. "A container for spitting in. They used to have them in the old days on the floor of pubs and suchlike places."

And here, courtesy of the *Concise Oxford Dictionary*, was confirmation that he wasn't completely off his head. (The derivation, in case you're interested, is from Portuguese *cuspir*, 'to spit')

Off to page 1342 to look up **spittoon** - I couldn't believe that such a thing existed - and there it was, between **spittle** and **spitz**. "**Spittoon** *n.* a metal or earthenware pot with a funnel-shaped top, used for spitting into." Can you imagine anything more disgusting? How big is it? I wondered. Teacup size or bucket size? And how much spit does it take to fill it? I imagined this big stainless steel pot sitting on the middle of the floor in a crowded pub, the men turning around, every few minutes, and aiming a good, juicy gob into it, a satisfying "ping" as it struck the metal. How often was it emptied? I wondered. Every night or only when it was full? And whose job was it to empty it? Perhaps someone was especially employed to go round all the pubs at closing time and empty the contents of spittoons. What a job - spittoon emptier. "What d'you do for a living?" "I'm a spittoon emptier." Not exactly going to win you many friends.

To be honest, I hate spitting. I'll readily confess to a fair few bad habits, but spitting isn't one of them. And I hate people who spit in public. (Deliberate spitters, anyway. Some people can't help it. We used to have a history teacher who'd spit and slobber every time he spoke. The kids at the front of his class always used to wear raincoats throughout his lessons. I remember, he sat opposite me at lunch, one day. I purposefully didn't say anything to him, not wanting to get him talking. Then he leaned over and said, "Passsss the ssssalt, pleassse," and my lunch was splattered in a spray of his unedifying spittle. I couldn't eat any more of it.)

It's funny, don't you think, how we have such an aversion to substances emerging from other people's bodies? We don't necessarily mind our own, but we shrink back in disgust from other people's. And, when you come to think about it (which isn't often, it's true), there are quite a huge number of different types of extruded bodily fluids. Here's a more or less complete list that I compiled in my head while turning from **cuspidor** to **spittoon**: spit, snot, shit, piss, sweat, puss, earwax, puke, semen, blood, tears. (Have I missed any?) They're all rather revolting substances, aren't they? If we got any of them on our hands, we'd wash them pretty damn quick. (Except for tears, I suppose, which don't really have the same quality of revulsion. "Tears are the wine of angels," my old man always says, whenever Mum gets a bit weepy. I don't rightly know what it means, but I always think it sounds nice.)

The funny thing about all these excreted bodily substances is they all come out of different apertures. Spit and puke both come from the mouth, piss and semen from the penis, then it's shit from the anus, snot from the nostrils, earwax from the ears, tears from the eyes, sweat from sweat glands, puss from sebaceous glands, blood (in the case of females) from the vulva. (I hope you're impressed by my use of the correct anatomical terms. Biology lessons weren't completely wasted on me.) The only substances to enter the body go in through the mouth, while things come out through any one of nine different sorts of openings. Strange, isn't it? The body is like some giant plastic bag with all these gross substances slopping around inside it – plus billions of squirming bubbles of sticky cytoplasm. Imagine giving someone a cuddle. (Alice, for instance, who's probably the most cuddle-worthy girl in the Universe, if I may be allowed to express my personal opinion). You're only a matter of centimetres away from all this

136

revolting matter. You're squeezing a huge bag of noxious gunge. Every time we walk around, we've got pints of shit, piss, blood, spit, snot, semen, puss, puke and so on slopping around inside us. No, I've had enough of all this. I don't want to imagine Alice's body as a bag of disgusting substances. Turn to another page.

Page 579. "**Gnat** *n.* **1.** any small two-winged biting fly of the genus *Culex*. **2.** an insignificant annoyance. **3.** a tiny thing." Fair enough, but why spell the damn thing with an unpronounced 'g' at the beginning? What's the sense in that? It's just a tiny thing, that initial 'g', but it's an insignificant annoyance. The 'g' at the beginning of gnat is a gnat but it's a gnat. Funny language, English.

Try another. Page 964. "**Orthotone** *adj.* (of a word) having an independent stress pattern, not enclitic nor proclitic." Come again? I mean, who writes this stuff?

And then the bell rang, signifying the end of our strenuous maths lesson. I'd just spent twenty minutes browsing aimlessly through the *Concise Oxford Dictionary*. A single word could set off a huge train of thought, trundling its way through a strange mental landscape. Amazing thing, the human mind. Amazing things, words. And to think, there are two million of the buggers in this single book. I could quite easily spend the rest of my life reading nothing but the *Concise Oxford Dictionary*.

Time for some lunch. Think I'll seek out that beautiful bag of body fluids called Alice and, over lunch, regale her with tales of my latest career aspiration. Page 783: "**lexicographer** *n.* a compiler of dictionaries."

THE DEATHS OF
PRIVATE NEMO

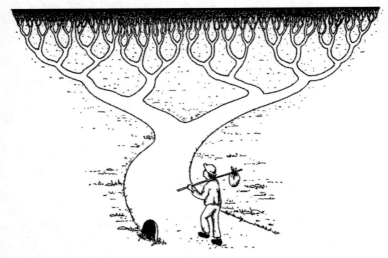

D ouglas Nemo, whose education omitted the study of classical
languages, was fifteen before learning that 'Nemo' was Latin
for 'Nobody'.

He took his revelation to his father.

"Nonsense, boy," replied Adam Nemo. He had three sons and,
always a little uncertain of the identity of each of them, he referred to
them all as 'boy'.

"So where does the name Nemo come from?" the boy persisted.

"Surely you've heard of Captain Nemo from the Jules Verne book.
Now, no one could accuse him of being a nobody."

In fact, neither Douglas nor his father had read the book, although
they'd seen the film. Douglas had been unimpressed by the far-
fetched underwater antics of his namesake, the captain of the Nautilus.
Far more inspiring and worthy of emulation was Charles Pooter, the
comic hero of the Grossmiths' "Diary of a nobody", the book that
Douglas had been secretly reading, enwrapped in his history text-book,

during a particularly boring lesson on the Dissolution of the Monasteries.

"A-ha, a nobody for Nemo," the history master had declared, whipping the concealed book from Douglas's grasp and brandishing it in front of the class. Then, remembering that Latin no longer figured in the modern curriculum and observing that his clever pun had not elicited the titters of appreciation he had anticipated, he abandoned the brutality of Henry VIII, leaving Abbot Whiting hanging but not yet drawn and quartered atop Glastonbury Tor, and launched into a brief Latin lesson based upon the derivation of Douglas's surname. Douglas, acutely embarrassed, was comforted only by his adolescent awareness that he was not a figure that mattered in the social structure of his peer group and that no one but himself and the history master were in the least bit interested in his name. In fact, no one else in the classroom seemed even remotely aware of the sudden shift in their teacher's monologue from Tudor England to ancient Rome. The history master sighed, Douglas's blushes faded and the execution of Abbot Whiting resumed.

But Douglas was moved, for the first time in his life, to ponder further on his name and its unfortunate Latin translation. His father, he had to admit, was, if not exactly a nobody, certainly not a somebody. His personality was as grey as the clothes he habitually wore, his opinions conventional, his hobbies confined to reading the paper, watching the television and growing fuchsias. His job involved sitting at a desk in a local government office – Douglas knew no more of it than that, nor did he ever wonder what affairs occupied him during those seven desk sitting hours each day. His father's life history, as far as he was aware, was sadly devoid of adventure or incident – apart, that is, from his meeting, as a young man, with Douglas's mother, Mary, nee Ampleforth. It was generally assumed that the two were attracted by the mysterious law of opposites. She was loquacious, exuberant, articulate, intelligent, the focus of a large circle of friends, in appearance striking if not strictly beautiful: a woman who made an impression on the world. And he was... Well, he was her opposite in every way: reserved, sullen, unsociable, narrow-minded and seemingly anonymous. One would be hard pushed to imagine a less likely match. The details of how, when, where and why they met and married, and how they stayed together through two decades, were matters tacitly ignored in the Nemo household. Most matters were tacitly ignored. Adam Nemo was not a great believer in conversation.

Douglas's maternal line, the Ampleforths, boasted a splendid collection of heroes, men of substance, women of culture and eccentrics galore. The Ampleforth family tree was ample indeed.

The Nemo ancestral archive was much sparser. Douglas's unremarkable father was the only son of Arthur Nemo, accounts clerk, himself the only son of Joseph Nemo who died in the Second World War.

Douglas had once quizzed his father concerning the wartime death of this distant forefather, hoping to hear a tale of bravery and distinguished service. But Joseph Nemo had never even set eyes on the enemy. He was killed by malaria protozoa, his only wound the bite of a mosquito that pierced his neck as he disembarked from a troop carrier in Bombay harbour. No one in the family could remember much about Private Joseph Nemo. He had no war comrades to tell cheery stories of his exploits: India had been his first posting. He left a recently married wife who barely knew him yet bore the growing embryo of Arthur Nemo in her womb. By the time the baby was born, she had virtually forgotten about his father and the very brief romance that had left her married, pregnant then widowed in rapid succession, but she retained the strange family name he had given her. The Nemo name spanned the Twentieth Century like a thin, barely noticeable gossamer thread.

*

The history lesson discovery of the meaning of his name initiated a radical change in the developing world-view of the teenage Douglas. He began to think of the past as the primary influence upon the nature of the present – an obvious enough idea, but a crucial one when it first explodes into a young and receptive mind. Things don't just happen: they have a vast history stretching back to the beginning of time itself. All things are linked by unimaginably complex chains of cause and effect. Perhaps, thought Douglas, the past was worthy of greater consideration than he had yet given it.

He took his musings to his mother, who, unlike his father, was capable of extending conversations beyond two or three staccato exchanges.

"Reincarnation," was her response. "It's time we looked into your past lives."

Douglas was unaware of the plurality of his lives. Indeed, he was only just beginning to realise that all this stuff that was going on was what was commonly known as a life – and, furthermore, that it was his life, the life of Douglas Nemo. Living once was miracle enough. Had he lived before?

His father would have dismissed the question immediately. Adam Nemo was a no-nonsense C-of-E Christian of the comfortable armchair variety, intolerant of anything that was not traditional, English, conservative and moderate. He attended church once each Christmas and at the christening of each of his sons. That, he considered, was the adequate exercise of his spiritual duties. The void preceded him and Heaven awaited him. Between the two, this life had been given to him to survive as best he could. Such were his religious views.

Douglas's mother, however, following the way of the Ampleforths, cast her spiritual net widely, happy to embrace any idea that seemed sufficiently contrary to those of her husband. She dabbled in Buddhism, Hinduism, Islam, Paganism and Native American shamanism. She wallowed in a string of New Age sects, philosophies, gurus, teachers and mind/body/spirit bandwagon entrepreneurs. Her pick-n-mix coat of many colours fitted her perfectly. She was the darling of the local alternative religion community.

She introduced Douglas to Sasha, a close friend – some said lover – who made a living as a past-life regressionist. Sasha outlined the general principles of the reincarnation business in a manner suitable for a youthful newcomer to grasp. To Douglas, the idea sounded perfectly reasonable. Suddenly popping into existence out of nothingness was a tricky concept to "get his head around", to use his mother's terminology. But many lives separated by many deaths, like waking days separated by nights of sleep: that was a notion with which he could happily live.

"So dream," said Sasha. "Allow your unconscious mind to trawl through some ancient memories. See what bubbles up. Bring me a grain of sand to work on and I will create a pearl."

Douglas had dreams of violent death – again and again – nightmares from which he would awake with a scream and sit bolt upright in his bed, sweat pouring down his face.

"Good," said his mother. "Sasha will be pleased."

Douglas lay back on a cushioned couch, the air thick with incense, the only light from a dozen candles, a constant background sound of trickling water. Sasha had no trouble placing his subject's pliant young consciousness into a state of hypnotic regression. His first life emerged in a matter of minutes.

He is a Norman foot soldier at the Battle of Hastings. He feels the cold wind and salt spray of the Channel crossing, in the fleet of William of Normandy. Then comes the march from the stony coast to the grassy slopes of Senlac Hill to meet the army of Harold, the two forces facing head to head, adrenalin rising, awaiting the first command.

"Fire!" – or whatever was the French equivalent. Douglas was regressing in English.

The sky darkens with arrows. Shields are raised as the two armies charge at each other. He holds his sword aloft, poised to strike, a warrior's yell screwing up his face. This is it – his first real fight, his first frantic foray into the valley of death. Death or glory! For William, for Normandy, for the pride of Private Nemo!

An arrow falls out of the sky and sears into his eye: a moment's burning pain and then darkness, too quick even for a final thought. He drops into the mud of Senlac Hill – a nobody, his pointless death totally eclipsed by a much more famous arrow-in-the-eye expiration, as every school child knows. The Battle of Hastings rages on. His body is trampled under a thousand feet, looted by the English peasants at day's end, picked apart by ravens as the new day dawns, nameless, unrecorded in the annals of history, forlorn and forgotten.

"Oh dear," said his mother, when Douglas had returned to normal consciousness, recalling every detail of the end of his former existence.

"A strange life," said Sasha, an elfin man with bushy black eyebrows and a white goatee beard.

"A strange death," said Douglas. "I was hoping for something a little grander, a little less painful."

"Death is usually a painful affair," said Sasha who had been privy to the tales of many deaths upon his hypnotist's couch.

"As is birth," said Douglas's mother, recalling not her own but the three subsequent births in which she had been the prime mover.

"But perhaps the stuff in between could be a bit more pleasant," mused Douglas, whether thinking of his past or his present life.

*

The second session with Sasha - a week later in his very cosy bachelor flat around which, Douglas noticed, his mother knew her way unusually intimately – took the young subject back to another battle.

"I am a serf in the entourage of a great knight," he recounted from the depth of his hypnosis. "My clothes are of coarse wool, my feet bare and I carry a stout pole and a long knife hanging from my belt. I am with a few dozen others, although I sense that I hardly know them. I have the feeling that the knight is lord of the manor in which I live. He has taken one young man from each of the villages on his land. I'm supposed to feel it an honour to have been chosen, but, in fact, I am resentful. I am scared, even. I am homesick for my peaceful village, my family and friends. We tramp through damp, lifeless woods, following our master who rides a black horse."

"King Arthur, perhaps?" Douglas's mother suggested, hopefully.

"I know no name. But now we converge with many other knights and their companies, encamping in a large clearing in the forest, close to the high stone walls of a castle. A siege is to begin. The word goes

143

round. Tomorrow we are to storm the castle, to avenge a wrong done long ago.

"Three siege towers have been built, thirty feet high, enough to reach the castle battlements, hastily erected on huge wooden wheels, massive structures made from the oaks of the forest. The next day, I am assigned to a team of pushers beside one of the towers. We heave the thing out of the cover of the trees, the dark walls of the castle just a stone's throw away. And suddenly stones are being thrown, from both sides, and arrows singing through the air, and shouts and screams and the smell of tar and blood and smoke. Still pushing beside the huge tower, I can only hear – not see – the thick of the battle. But then the wheel at my side collapses into a hidden ditch and the whole structure topples in my direction. I try to jump aside, but my foot is caught on something. I look up to see the blue sky disappearing behind the immense wall of the falling tower. A wave of fear. A wave of pain – is it pain? I don't know. It's all so quick. In a moment I am crushed into the muddy ground, my life extinguished."

He fell silent. His eyes, opening slowly and staring up at the ceiling, were glazed with tears.

"Oh dear," said his mother. "Such misfortunes in your past lives! Whatever did you do to deserve such things!"

"Come, come, Mary," Sasha rebuked her. "You know full well that the workings of provenance are infinitely complex. We cannot be blamed for the lives in which we find ourselves incarnated."

Nor the names we inherit, thought Douglas Nemo.

*

None of them ever doubted – Sasha, Douglas or his mother – that these past-life regressions should continue.

"We have a receptive and sensitive subject here," Sasha confided in Mary, "with real tales to tell. I am enthralled. Usually my clients recall themselves as heroes of battles, famous historical figures or, at least, in the close company of famous figures. They have names, lives and family histories. In Douglas, we have only deaths."

This was something that concerned Mary only mildly. She had hoped that her son's reminiscences might be less bloody and morbid, more indicative of a great soul, but this apprehension was swamped by her pride in Douglas's achievements upon the hypnotist's couch. Sasha's enthusiasm was her reward. He made detailed notes on each session, discussed them at length with Mary and hinted at a possible paper - a joint venture, even - in the reincarnation journal, Come Again? Douglas's case was important and worthy of wider exploration and exposure. What mother would not be pleased?

Adam Nemo, of course, knew nothing of all this. He would not have forbidden it: he was not a censorial man, least of all in connection with Mary's strange, "alternative" pursuits. But he would have mocked and scorned and probably advised his son, in a tone guaranteed to repel, to "Grow up, boy!" Had he met or heard talk of Sasha, he would instantly have branded him a charlatan, extracting money from weak-minded people by playing on their hopes and fears – such, at least, would have been the unmistakeable message of his body language: his mouth would have muttered a curt, "Pleased to meet you." But Mary made sure that they never met.

Douglas himself, whose images flowed so effortlessly in the relaxation of Sasha's couch, longed for more. These scenarios that he recounted were not dreams, but neither were they daydreams. They possessed a quality that he had never before encountered in his inner world, akin to fantasy yet beyond the control of his will. Of course he would have chosen to be at William's side as he celebrated victory on Senlac Hill. Of course he would have loved to have been one of the first to breach the castle ramparts, rather than be crushed to death by the falling siege tower before the battle had even begun. But his fantasies had followed plots not of his own creation. He was carried, it seemed, by the irresistible torrent of his own imagination. He was actually re-living history – albeit no more than a few unsavoury and traumatic snippets of it. And, under the influence of Sasha and his mother, he quickly became convinced that what he was experiencing were real memories rather than fictional fantasies. He was not one: the

145

unique, God-created soul that his father's Christianity supposed him to be. He was legion.

Or, at least, he was part of a legion, as the next session revealed. This time he regressed to First Century Britain: a field of marshy grass on the fens of East Anglia, as it would later be called. The Roman legion was fighting to establish supremacy over the Iceni, the bloodthirsty heathens of this God-forsaken island. They were led by a woman – Boudicca or some such name, according to the centurion. What hope did a woman have against the might of Rome?

The former "I" of Douglas stood in line with his century, shields raised, swords yearning for blood, sandaled feet rhythmically stamping to keep warm in the sodden grass. He'd never seen Rome, never basked on the shores of the Mediterranean. The legion was all he knew, memories of a shepherding family high in the mountains fading like the images of a dream. Now he was a soldier, Private Nemo of the Roman legion, marching across the Empire at the command of generals he had never seen, ready to fight for the glory of Rome, although, so far, all he had done was march.

The line of figures across the marsh was charging, the air heavy with the ugly screams of men of whom he knew nothing. Leading them were chariots, their horses splashing through the wetlands, their riders with wild hair and blackened faces, swords and spears aloft, challenging – for reasons unknown – the might of the legion.

The Romans started to advance, chanting in unison, the standard at their fore. Douglas, in the front line, thought for a moment only of his home in the green mountain pastures, his mother, her face a blur, at the door of their stone hut, the sheep bleating, the sky vast and pure. Suddenly a chariot was hurtling directly towards him. He leapt aside and swung his sword in an arc above his head, hoping to strike the chest of the charioteer and dislodge him – or her – from the vehicle. He didn't look down; never saw the rapidly revolving steel blades protruding from the wheel hubs. The chariot, in a shower of blood, cut a wide swath through the legion. Douglas fell, wondering what had unbalanced him. His head hit the ground and he found himself staring at a leg, severed at the knee, lying in the soaking grass like a small

146

branch from a tree. He didn't register that it was his leg. There was no time for pain. The body of another soldier, a friend perhaps, a stout fellow, fell lifeless upon him, his shield pushing Douglas's face into the pool of water that had formed in the rut cut by the chariot's wheel. Blood spurted from the open artery at the end of his thigh. The swoon of unconsciousness darkened over him. It is possible that he drowned.

"Oh dear," said his mother. "Such ignominious, bloody deaths. My poor boy, what lives you have led. We must hope for better this time around, eh?"

"Come, come, Mary." Sasha wrapped a comforting arm around her shoulders and, while Douglas's eyes were still closed, deposited a quick kiss on her neck.

Mary clasped his hand on her shoulder and squeezed her gratitude and affection. In former lives, they had discovered, he had been an Egyptian high priest and she the daughter of a pharaoh. They had loved in ancient times, lived long on the banks of the Nile amid the splendours of a glorious civilisation, and, when death finally came, it was wonderful and the stuff of legend. Entombed in the dead pharaoh's pyramid, they had made love one last time upon the altar stone then drunk from the phial of poison the priest had secreted in his robe. They died in each other's arms in the scented candle-light while the pharaoh's most loyal servant gently strummed his lyre. Blood and mud had not featured in their past-life regressions.

*

After his Roman ordeal, Douglas had had enough. He couldn't face another death. It wasn't the pain or the dread that bothered him – these feelings, like his lives, were extinguished in a moment – but the overwhelming sense of waste that tormented him as he returned to his normal consciousness. Why lead such a feckless, transient, nameless life just to die so miserably and pointlessly, unburied, unmourned and without, it seemed, ever having achieved anything worthwhile? Even to have clashed swords with the enemy, perhaps to have killed a few, to have stood and fought side by side with his comrades – that would have been something. But who would have remembered him in his former lives? And why? He had done nothing. He was a nobody.

His father, the taciturn Adam Nemo, had always considered ambition to be a quality required only in moderation, to be pursued and enjoyed a little in one's youth but never to be flaunted or overdone. Mary Ampleforth had once been ambitious – until she met Adam Nemo. He tended to think that ambition had not been one of her finer features. His own modest aspirations reflected, without any magnification, those of his generation: a decent, easy and secure job, a wife, a few offspring, a comfortable home, a small car, a European holiday every year or two – these were the extent of his dreams and, to give credit to the man, he had achieved them all by middle-age and desired nothing more than their perpetuation.

Douglas's sights rose only a little above the level of his father's. He wanted a woman, certainly – his hormones were bubbling furiously – and he wanted a home of his own with no one nagging him to get up or shut up or tidy up or buck his ideas up. (He had yet to learn that his desire for a woman was incompatible with this ambition.) As for a job: he was more concerned with the size of the salary rather than in what it consisted. He'd have sat at a desk all day, as his father did, if the pay was good enough. But what he wanted above all was a modicum of fame, a small crumb from the table of celebrity, if only for a day, or even for fifteen minutes. He wanted to be somebody, to transcend his pitiful name.

Fame, he realised at an uncommonly early age, requires either very good fortune or very good looks or outstanding talent. His past life experiences suggested that good fortune was not a current that flowed strongly through his various incarnations, although perhaps, according to the law of compensation with which his mother had attempted to console him, the tide was due to turn. In his present life, good looks or talent had not yet penetrated the spottiness of his adolescent face, nor the mediocrity of his school grades. Neither fame nor a good career appeared to be lying just over his horizon.

At the age of seventeen, he joined the army. Fighting had figured in his past lives, he thought, so why not in this one? He would never be a sporting hero or an academic hero or a cultural hero, but maybe he could still make it as a war hero. Anyway, the pay was better than anything he could have hoped for sitting behind a desk.

His father gave his approval. "Sound career choice, boy. Good opportunities. And a chance to see the world – or a few war-torn parts of it, at any rate."

His mother was more hesitant. While the back pages of the Ampleforth family album boasted several military types, the influence of Sasha had nurtured the seeds of pacifism in her. But, shining more brightly, she valued above all things the freedom of the individual to make his own choices in life. Do what thou wilt shall be the whole of the law: this was the essence of her New Age creed.

"Try not to kill anyone, Douglas," she said as he left the family home for his training camp. "And try not to get killed yourself."

"Will do," said Douglas, practising his Attention! pose and army salute.

His first sergeant-major proved to be familiar with the Jules Verne classic.

"Private Nemo, eh? Well, let's hope, for all our sakes, that you never make it to captain."

"No, Sir!" shouted Douglas, who had learned all his responses from American army movies.

"So, you never thought of becoming a sub-mariner, then?"

"No, Sir!"

"And please don't shout, Private Nemo. We're not in an American army movie."

"No, Sir!" shouted Douglas.

His first posting was to Afghanistan. The province to which his platoon had been assigned was described as "sub-critical". Stark mountain scenery: dust and sand: a shortage of trees. On his second day in Afghanistan, the commander asked for volunteers to accompany a minor BBC journalist to a village in the foothills from where the Taliban had recently been routed.

"Yes, Sir!" shouted Douglas.

He sat in the back of the land rover, rifle in his arms, imaging himself as 'shotgun' on a Western stagecoach, on the lookout for bandits. The driver had assured him that he'd made the journey many times without any hint of trouble. Approaching a deeply fissured buff in the hills, they heard the boom of an artillery shell.

"Still a few pockets of resistance," said the driver. "Don't worry. They'd be exceptionally lucky to hit us out here in the open."

But the shot was exceptionally lucky. The instant the driver finished speaking, even before Douglas had a chance to contemplate the notion of luck, the land rover exploded into a thousand pieces of jagged metal, the body parts of its occupants scattered far and wide across the desert sand. The sun beat down. Silence reigned for many minutes, broken by a solitary scavenger crow noisily flapping its wings as it circled overhead.

*

Douglas's mother had left her husband by that time, changed her name back to Ampleforth, and, after a lengthy retreat in Egypt, she was living with Sasha in his cosy bachelor flat. Adam Nemo called her with the grim news of their son's latest death. They shared a long silence on the phone.

Two hours later, sitting in his favourite armchair, Douglas's father watched the six o' clock news. "BBC reporter killed in Afghanistan," ran the headline. He watched as the highlights of the reporter's broadcasting career were reviewed and assorted well-known colleagues praised his courage and skills and reflected, with severe faces, on how he had been a thoroughly pleasant and dedicated chap with a renowned sense of humour. After ten minutes, the report concluded with the solemnly spoken words, "Also killed in the artillery attack were the driver of the land-rover, Corporal Jack Hopkinson, and guard, Private Douglas Nemo."

Adam Nemo, alone in his armchair before the television, swallowed back a sob. "That's my boy," he proudly whispered to nobody.

WALL STREET

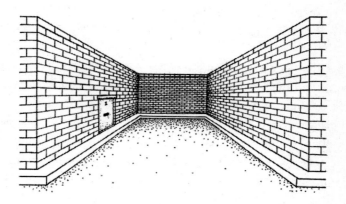

They called it Wall Street because that's what it was: a street with no other features than walls, a cul-de-sac some fifty yards long with a brick wall to the left, a brick wall to the right and, at the far end, where one might have expected something more interesting, another brick wall. All the walls were uniform – twenty feet high or thereabouts, regular terracotta bricks – except for one, the left hand wall, which, thirty yards along, bore a single door: just an ordinary, nondescript wooden door, white paint peeling a little, a brass "Number One" screwed to its centre above a letter-box slit of regulation size.

Every morning, the postman delivered a single letter to the occupant of Number One Wall Street: always a plain white envelope, A4 size, addressed in a neat hand to, "The Occupant, Number One Wall Street". The postman never wondered – he was not an especially curious man. His job was to deliver letters, not to speculate on their senders, their recipients or their contents. Although, over the years, he did begin to think it rather strange that no one but him ever seemed to venture along the abruptly terminating length of Wall Street, nor even give it any more than a quick glance as they hurried past its unwalled entrance. The city had no time for Wall Street. What use was a street that led nowhere?

The postman's name was Phil, a quiet man who carried a cacophony of troubled thoughts in his mind, like a grossly overweight parcel in his sack, sapping his strength. His life story was strewn with too many tragedies to be told of in this short tale. He was a man waiting for something to happen.

The idea slowly grew in Phil that some strange mystery lurked behind the door of Number One Wall Street and that the letters he delivered each day bore secrets that could sway the fate of nations. He kept his fantasies to himself. Like a priest, a postman is morally bound to be silent about the correspondences that pass through his hand or the snatches of conversations he hears through open letterboxes. (But never did he hear a sound emerge from the letter-box of Number One Wall Street, and peering through, as he surreptitiously did once or twice, he could detect nothing but blackness beyond.)

One day there was no letter. Through habit, Phil had walked to the door of Number One Wall Street before he realised that he had nothing to deliver. He stood there for a while, feeling a compound of bewilderment and disappointment. Reluctantly he turned, swivelling on the heels of his postman's shoes, and was about to retrace his steps along Wall Street when, most unexpectedly, the door flew open and there stood a Mohawk Indian warrior in full battle dress, a loincloth of buffalo hide, a head-dress of eagle feathers, a string of beads, teeth and claws around his neck, a stone tomahawk in one hand, a long bow in the other, a quiver of arrows slung across his back, his dark face painted with streaks of scarlet and blue.

Phil the postman took a step back and, naturally enough, froze in astonishment.

"No letter today, then?" questioned the Mohawk in a firm but gentle voice.

"Sorry, no," replied Phil.

The warrior nodded slowly. "Run out of words, I expect." There was a look of loss in his eyes, turning swiftly to acceptance. Then his weather-beaten face cracked into a warm smile.

The postman, too, had run out of words but found a responding smile. The smile sizzled between the two faces for a few seconds, an exchange of tacit understanding, a holy communion which Phil experienced as a sudden clarity, sweeping his normally agitated mind clean of its accumulated debris.

As for the Mohawk, his smile softly faded and the features of his face settled into a look of timeless equanimity.

"Farewell," he said in a deep and distant voice.

Then he closed the door, retreating into the darkness within, and was never seen again.

THE QUIET FRIENDSHIP
OF TREES

Some of my best friends are trees. Many of them live in the grounds of the local park. I visit them often, to see them change with the passing seasons, to share with them the joys of sun or shade, of wind or rain. We spend many quiet, happy hours together. Sometimes I tell them of my troubles - usually I confide my deepest feelings only to the solitary oak or tulip tree in the middle of the parkland - and they listen in silence, paying close attention like good friends should. They understand, I'm sure of it. I can sense their empathetic response; maybe in a fluttering of their leaves or a whisper spreading through their twigs. I'd happily listen to their troubles, too, but of course trees don't have troubles. They accept everything uncomplainingly, fully aware of the perfection of all that happens. Perhaps that's what I love so much about trees: their absolute tolerance and openness. They are divine beings, dwelling in the sanctity of the present.

My wife thought I was strange, perhaps insane. My love of trees, she believed, was a sure symptom of my insanity. How can that be? A symptom of my infidelity, maybe, but not insanity. Trees are the most sane beings on our planet. How can a relationship with a tree be anything other than a healthy blessing? But Miranda and I never talked about it. Trees were the unmentioned "other woman" in our marriage.

As it turned out, she was the unfaithful one. She ran off with the bloke next door. I always thought he was a fairly decent chap, a friend almost - not quite in the same league as the park trees, but we used to chat amicably enough over the garden fence. Then, one day, he left his wife and ran off with mine.

We consoled each other, his abandoned wife and I. Quite innocent, at first, you understand: just a few meals out, watching telly together, companionable heart-to-heart talks over late night glasses of port in her front room. Then I'd hop back over the fence to my empty bed, she to hers. Turned out we were both rather glad to be out of our marriages. They'd run their course. Whatever passion had once ignited them was long since spent. We even agreed that our two lost spouses were a good match for each other. There's generosity for you. No grudges, no recriminations, no longings to turn back the clock. Neither of us, we confessed, had shed a single tear when our partners left. It was as though two married couples had been walking along two roads, and, when the roads crossed, we'd simply swapped spouses and walked on.

She was a tree surgeon, my neighbour's ex-wife. Have you ever before come across a female tree surgeon? No reason why not, of course, it's just that it's not a career option that most women would consider. I once considered it for myself. I imagined diagnosing arboreal ailments and effecting gentle therapies: a few medicinal herbs planted in the surrounding soil, perhaps, or a restorative balm rubbed into the bark. But tree surgery, I discovered, mainly involved the amputation of limbs - entirely without anaesthetic, I might add - and mainly for the cosmetic sensibilities of the tree owner rather than for the health of the tree itself. I decided it wasn't for me. Besides, I'm a bit on the heavy side, none too agile and I've no head for heights. I prefer to confer with trees strictly at ground level.

But Yvonne, my neighbourly tree surgeon, was as nimble as a squirrel, and as fearless. Health and safety demanded the use of ropes

155

and harnesses and suchlike, but she didn't really need any of that paraphernalia. The first time I saw her scale a hundred foot ash, gliding effortlessly up it like a monkey, I thought: that's the woman for me. And - I'll be frank with you here - that very night I put my arm around her as we sat together on her sofa, and she turned her face to mine, and we kissed - just gentle, like, at first, but then with ever-increasing relish and ferocity - and...

Miranda, my ex-wife, knew next to nothing about trees. She could just about distinguish a holly from an ivy, or a monkey puzzle from a magnolia, but that was pretty well the limit of her arboreal knowledge. No, we were not at all well matched. My idea of a Sunday afternoon trip out was a walk in the woods. Hers was a visit to the local "factory outlet shopping centre".

But Yvonne was totally different: an intimate familiarity with all our trees - native, parkland and ornamental. Latin names and all. To be honest, she knew a darn sight more about trees than I ever did.

And, while we're being honest, I must shamefully admit that this rather annoyed me. Crazy, isn't it, but regrettably true. It's a sad fact that men tend to dislike being out-classed by a woman when it comes to something in which they think they've got some expertise. Take a more common example than the tree thing. Supposing you're a bloke who's mad keen on cricket. You meet a woman who's also a fan. Great, you think. Something in common. But then, gradually, you realise that she knows much more than you. She can name entire England squads going back decades - not just name but quote batting averages and bowling statistics. In short, her encyclopaedic knowledge makes you look something of an amateur, a dabbler. Now, come on, be honest. Wouldn't that piss you off just a little? Especially if she was foolish enough to contradict you in public. And especially if she was right and you were wrong. Like this, for instance:

"Beautiful cherry tree," I said. We were at a garden barbecue party with some friends of mine - real people, not trees.

"Actually, it's an almond," Yvonne corrected me. "Prunus dulcis. Even without its flowers, you can tell from the leaf shape and the colouration of the bark."

I mean, come on! That's a bit much to take, isn't it? At least Miranda only tutted and rolled her eyes when I started going on about trees.

After that, of course, Yvonne was the centre of attention.

"You seem very well informed," commented one of my friends.

"I'm a tree surgeon," said Yvonne, and that was it. Time for her star turn. Expressions of surprise, innumerable questions, exchanged anecdotes - everyone, it seems, has a story about an experience they've had with a tree surgeon - and, inevitably, requests for her opinion on "a rather sickly willow in my back garden" or "the best way to deal with Cupressus."

Why is it that people are defined by their occupations? "I'm a tree surgeon," she says and everyone wants to talk to her. Yvonne's ex-husband, Bill, who ran off with my wife, is a car salesman. Soon as he mentions the fact, people start asking him about the price of their own car or whether he can get any good deals on this or that fancy model. Even Miranda, who's a nurse, invariably elicits a plethora of hospital stories as soon as she mentions what she does. As for me, I'm a wages clerk at the local quarry. No one ever says, "Oh, how fascinating. Tell me about it."

It's all vanity, I suppose. Arrogance. That's what really annoyed me about Yvonne's superior knowledge. I secretly enjoyed the fact that Miranda was an ignoramus when it came to trees. I might have a boring, uninspiring sort of job, but at least I could commune on a first name basis with our woody cousins in our parks and hedgerows. I think I was even glad that she preferred the "factory outlet shopping centre" to the woods. We agreed to differ and we each did our own thing. It suited us both fine.

With Yvonne, however, as we became increasingly close and spent more and more time together, I noticed a rising irritation in myself. Sunday afternoons, for instance, we'd always take a walk in the woods. Hand in hand. Very romantic. But I began to miss my lost solitude. I actually preferred to be alone when out walking. And all my favourite tree friends in the park, it turned out, were also her friends. But she knew them more intimately, their histories and idiosyncrasies. She'd worked on many of them. And, ridiculously, it seemed to me that they looked more favourably upon her company than mine. I was jealous.

Just as her husband, Bill, had stolen my wife from me, so Yvonne was stealing my friends from me. Our little affair was sailing into turbulent waters.

So, apparently, was Miranda and Bill's.

"What I don't know about cars isn't worth knowing," was his favourite phrase, and he'd follow it, given half a chance, with a verbal deluge of car related facts - all the usual stuff about turbo-charge and torque, alloy wheels and "0 to 60 in so many seconds" and what have you. Miranda wasn't in the least bit interested in cars. In fact, she was marginally more interested in trees.

Bill was a trivia freak when it came to anything mechanical: cars, trains, computers, mobile phones, DVDs, MP3s, digital this, satellite that. He was a gizmo fanatic.

"He could bore for England," Miranda told me, when it was all over. "He could talk the hind legs off a donkey."

So could Yvonne, come to that. Silence, for her, was an empty space crying out to be filled, whether through talk or music. At home, the radio was always on. Walking in the woods, she kept up a constant conversation - more usually a monologue. I'm a quiet walker. I'd sooner listen to the sounds of the trees. Yvonne preferred the sound of her own voice. Even when climbing, high in the canopy, wielding her chainsaw, she wore earphones attached to some electronic contraption in her pocket, pumping out music to drown the whine of her awful tool of butchery. Pink Floyd's "Careful with that axe, Eugene" was her favourite, she claimed. She hoovered up silence as though it was litter polluting her environment. I tended to be a litterbug, strewing silence wherever I went.

Miranda came back to me. Quite suddenly, there she was, ringing the doorbell, asking if she could come in. She was contrite. She begged forgiveness and I forgave her. To be honest, I was glad to have her back. Bill returned to Yvonne. I've no idea what passed between them, but for days afterwards we could hear them through the wall, both jabbering on at full speed and full volume, neither of them paying any attention to what the other was saying.

Occasionally I'd see Bill in the back garden. He'd nod. I'd nod back. Fine. At least I was spared his gadget obsessed waffle. Yvonne studiously avoided me. That was fine, too. I was not sorry that our brief spell of intimacy was over. We were short-lived glitches in each other's lives.

Shortly after we got back together, I took Miranda to see my old friends in the park: the oak tree, the majestic copper beech, the tree of heaven, the mulberries, the tulip tree. We greeted them all.

"They don't say much," Miranda remarked.

"Right," I replied. "That's what I like about them."

She smiled - a rare smile. We're well attuned to each other, now, Miranda and I. Seems like our little dalliances with the neighbours have made us stronger, more tolerant, more open. Like the trees. Sunday afternoons, we often picnic together, in the park, inviting one of our quiet leafy friends to join us.

VISIONS OF JOHANNA

"...Lights flicker from the opposite loft.
In this room the heat pipes just cough.
The country music station plays soft
But there's nothing, really nothing to turn
    off.
Just Louise and her lover so entwined,
And these visions of Johanna that conquer
    my mind."

"You're spouting crap again, Bob."

"Yeah, it's what I do best."

"Ha."

I heard her monosyllabic laugh coming from the bed in the corner, then the sound of rustling sheets as she unravelled herself from the limbs of her lover and walked through the darkness to my perch on a breakfast bar chair beneath the attic room's only dormer window. The half-moon threw a wide, oblique beam of white light across her path and, as she stepped through it, I saw that she was naked, her skin glistening. I hated it when she did that. She knew her body drove me crazy. She bent down and plonked a quick peck of a kiss on my forehead before retrieving her clothes from the floor.

Her latest lover released a gentle snore – an unappealing, balding lump of a man: I didn't even know his name. He'd live to regret his late night encounter with me and the temptress Louise. We were a couple best avoided on the streets of this city.

Johanna, my beloved, has a rare, platonic beauty. Louise was different: she oozed sexuality and a subtle mist of pheromones. She was a nimble mover, a sweet talker – and a great cook, I must say. I was a good hustler and an as-yet unrecognised poet. We rubbed along well enough together.

I stared out through the window as Louise dressed. They had candles burning in the attic across the alleyway. Occasionally I saw the flickering shadows of moving figures. Looked like a cool scene was going down. Actually, it wasn't country music that I heard coming from that loft in the middle of the night. It was Beethoven. The fifth string quartet in A major. I lied about the country music. I'm a congenital liar. I can't help it. It's how I make my living. And I tend to keep my familiarity with the music of Beethoven a closely guarded secret which is why, using a pinch of poetic licence, I transformed it into a country music station playing softly. The heating pipes were definitely coughing, though, and it was cold in that flat. And Johanna, as always, was dancing through my mind.

You're probably wondering what we're into, Louise and I. Sex? Drugs? Rock-n-roll? All three, really, and more besides. There are a lot of sins out there, and a lot of sinners who'll happily part with a lot of money to satisfy whatever desires drive them. Sometimes I like to think we're performing a public service.

"He's out for the count," said Louise, doing up her blouse and nodding her head across the room in the direction of the bed.

"You sure?" I reached for my jacket, slung over the breakfast bar.

"He's gone. Now let's get out of here."

A delicious cocktail of vodka, orange juice and a hefty dose of powdered barbiturate had done the trick, as it always does. It had taken longer than most, with this fellow's rather weighty constitution, which was why Louise had had to play a little further down the lover road than usual. We always referred to them as her lovers. It was a kind of sick joke, really. She claimed she loved everyone – men, at any rate. Except that she didn't love me. She thought I was a bastard – not an unreasonable opinion, I have to admit. It's not exactly a path with a heart, making money out of other people's weaknesses – but it certainly pays well.

Louise and I, we feed the needs of sinners. Lust is Louise's speciality. I'm into avarice. I can always spot them: thick wallets, craving to make them even thicker. I'm a slick talker and Louise is skilled in the arts of seduction, distracting them from the crap I spout. It's about making big money from a comparatively small investment – they can never resist the thought of that. It never occurs to them that

161

if it was as easy as I make out, then why wasn't I stinking rich? A feigned altruism: that's my trump card. I pretend I'm a good natured chap who wants to share my great gift. And this is the thing: they're so greedy, so fixated by that shining pot of gold, that they fall for it. And for Louise's very persuasive charms, of course. We're a hot team.

We spot our target in some pub or club and move in with our well practised routine. If all goes well – as tonight – we get ourselves invited back to his place, usually some poncey bachelor pad, where we further hypnotise him with Louise's delectable teasing and my fast-buck banter. Then I introduce, from my fancy briefcase, the cocktail makings and slip the barbs into his while Louise does her titillating. We down them in one – "It's the only way, man!" – and wait for the effects to kick in. This is when my siren-like partner manipulates her victim to the bed and they disrobe and get down to the preliminaries while I slink off to some dark corner and leave them to it. She likes this bit, so I let her get on with it, even though it strikes me as not strictly necessary. As I said, lust's her speciality.

Once he's under, it's thanks for the hospitality, thanks for your wallet and anything else around the pad that's worth nicking, goodbye and sleep well. Simple as that: our methods are not particularly sophisticated. Basically, we're a couple of thieves, rip-off merchants. I can't understand why anyone works for a living.

Yeah, we're as bad as them – course we are. But Louise enjoys the thrill of it and I enjoy the money and we know they'll never call the cops. No one likes to admit that they've been fleeced by a whore and a con man – at least, nor the types we choose. That's pride for you. That's another sin on our side.

"I'll just check he's okay, Bob," she says, as we're about to leave. She's careful like that. She doesn't want any harm to come to him. Well, they played at being lovers for a while: not strictly in the carnal sense – she always withheld for long enough for the drug to kick in - but she's a bit of a softie, really, my Louise. She bends over him and gives his sleeping lips a lingering kiss.

Beneath her reckless persona and her vixen looks, she's got a kind heart. At least, that's what I like to think, but I suppose I don't really know her. We're just business partners. And she doesn't really know me. She thinks, I suspect, that I'm a selfish, immoral, work-shy hustler with grand ideas of being a poet or rock star or something. She thinks I'm a dreamer. Or maybe she thinks I'm only in it for the money.

She's wrong. I do it all for Johanna. While Louise frolics with her latest victim, I skulk in the corner, way off from the action, and I gaze out of the dormer window and dance among the stars or sing love songs to the silver moon or skip across the scuttling clouds or compose strange lines of poetry to the dead of night. And I wrap my mind around visions of Johanna, and I feel her cleansing kiss, placed lightly on my forehead, I feel her forgiveness for all my many sins, I feel her loving kindness embracing me, her unconditional, non-judgemental acceptance of exactly who I am with all my faults and fantasies. She lifts the sins from my soul, my Johanna. She is my redeemer, my inspiration. She saves me from myself.

Ah, Johanna. Maybe one day you'll step out of my dreams and into the real world. Maybe one day I'll finally meet you – or someone like you - and I'll give all this up and start to lead a good, wholesome life. Maybe one day.

So we leave Louise's lover to his long, sinless sleep. Outside, the streets are empty, the moon and stars lost behind a low bank of cloud, leaking drizzle.

"...And Louise holds a handful of rain, tempting you to defy it."

"You're spouting crap again, Bob."

ARTHUR'S TALE

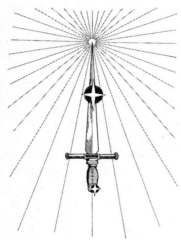

"**E**very home should have one," proclaimed Arthur as he dished out the final course of the dinner party - nothing fancy, just spotted dick and custard. My Arthur loved traditional English cooking.

"Have what?" asked one of the guests who hadn't been concentrating on Arthur's inebriated ramblings.

"A ghost story, of course. Every old house needs its own ghost story."

And if it hasn't already got one, then invent your own, I thought, which was basically what Arthur had done, with a little help from a local legend. But I kept my thoughts to myself. It was, after all, just a bit of harmless fun.

"The extraordinary thing about this house," he continued, warming to his favourite topic, "is that it lies inch perfectly on the straight line that connects Cadbury Castle - the ancient site of Camelot - with Glastonbury Tor."

"Really?" our guests exclaimed with varying degrees of feigned or sincere amazement. It was a curiosity, perhaps, but hardly a revelation. But more was to come.

"King Arthur, as I'm sure you all know, was intimately associated with both these places. He lived at Camelot and he was buried at Glastonbury, the mythical Isle of Avalon."

The dinner guests nodded their agreement as they tucked into their puddings.

"Now, here's the legend," continued the great king's namesake, "which, I might add, is recorded in many books concerning the doings of Arthurian times. Every year, at midnight on the night of the summer solstice, the ghosts of King Arthur and his most trusted knights, dressed in shining armour, gallop on ghostly horses along the line from Camelot to Glastonbury. Right through this house. In through the French windows, which point directly towards Cadbury Castle," (here he gestured theatrically at the windows) "along the hall and out through the front door, on to Glastonbury Tor. Every year. Twenty-first of June. Exactly midnight."

Our guests stared at him, their meals temporarily forgotten. Well, you can't help being intrigued by a tale like that, can you? Especially when you're munching your way through spotted dick and custard, sitting at the very table across which the glorious Knights of the Round Table come charging in full battle regalia.

"So have you ever witnessed this spectacle?" asked one of the guests.

"Most assuredly. Almost every year, as Jenny will confirm."

Please don't include me in your fantasy, I thought. But I smiled and said nothing.

"What, you've actually seen them?"

"Not seen, as such," replied Arthur, "but certainly felt: a mysterious presence, a total empathy with the spirit of King Arthur. It lasts only a moment but it's unquestionably real. Some years, it's just a smell - sweating horses and leather and polished metal - suddenly engulfing the room and lingering for hours after. Honestly, this is a remarkable place to be on the night of the summer solstice. Not for the faint-hearted, I might say."

I smiled and, with a quick, raised-eyebrow glance at Arthur, indicated that he'd probably gone far enough. We all returned to our puddings as I steered the conversation back to more normal subjects.

Well, what harm was there in letting him exercise his imagination? He had few enough pleasures as he slipped into rather crotchety old age. Since retiring, cooking had become the only activity to which he applied himself with any gusto - an activity that I was only too happy to relinquish after forty years. Hosting dinner parties - for random selections of neighbours and acquaintances - was his great joy. Good, plain, English cuisine, he called it. Plain, it certainly was. And now those dinner parties were enlivened by the gradual elaboration of his home-grown ghost story. I humoured him and supplied confirmatory nods as he told the tale to new guests. I have to admit that his conversation at social gatherings had always been a bit on the dull side. At least this latest tale of his added a certain sparkle to meals dominated by blandly boiled vegetables and stodgy puddings.

Eventually, Arthur's ghost story somehow reached the attention of a certain Dr. Watts, a psychology lecturer at Bristol University who was researching paranormal experiences. He paid us a visit and listened, his tape recorder running, while Arthur once again added yet more embellishments to his well-practised routine.

"So what d'you think?" asked Arthur when his tale was told, his grey eyes glowing with pride.

"What I think is irrelevant," replied the doctor, no doubt accustomed to dealing with over-zealous ghost spotters. "I'm a scientist. Without objective evidence, your story is nothing more than that - a story. I've already checked on a map and you're right about the positioning of your house, between Cadbury Castle and Glastonbury. And certainly the legend of King Arthur's solstice charge is well known. But without some collaborative physical evidence, your account is, well, how can I put it..."

"Are you accusing me of lying, of making it all up?"

Of course, many people had listened sceptically but never before had he been directly challenged. Well, you've got to be a bit tolerant of your host's foibles and eccentricities when you're sat at his dinner table, haven't you?

"No, definitely not," the doctor reassured him. "I'm here to investigate your claim. And, with the agreement of yourself and your wife, I propose that we conduct a serious investigation."

Arthur felt appeased and he sat back to listen. As for me, I began to feel a little nervous that his fantasy would be exposed as a sham under the glare of scientific scrutiny.

"What I'd like to do," continued the doctor "is set up a few instruments to monitor conditions in this room on the night of the solstice. See if we can detect anything unusual."

"What sort of thing?"

"Energy changes, temperature fluctuations, background radiation, that sort of thing. You see, even ghosts must possess some kind of energy. If they really do exist beyond the human mind, it's reasonable to suppose that they leave some measurable trace. That's what my work's all about and I've developed an arsenal of pretty sensitive instruments. If there's any unusual energy involved in a haunting, then I've got the gear to pick it up."

"Splendid," said Arthur. "Although I can't guarantee you'll detect anything. Some years we feel a lot, some years almost nothing."

"Of course. That's the trouble with ghosts. A fickle bunch. And I've found that they're not too keen on scientific instruments. But our understanding of such phenomena as you report will never advance until we can establish a definite scientific basis."

"Quite so," said Arthur who had worked as a civil servant for forty years and, though he knew little of science, was thoroughly committed to the importance of rationality.

"So, it's a month until the solstice," said Dr. Watts. "Would you be agreeable to me coming down with my equipment and spending the night in this room?"

"Happy to assist the cause of scientific research," replied Arthur and I could see that he was busy composing the next instalment of his dinner party monologue. "Anything we can do to help?"

"Well, yes there is, as a matter of fact. You see, I've come to believe that receptive minds are essential conditions for paranormal manifestations. Apparitions don't happen by themselves. They need human observers. And the more primed and open those observers can be, the better."

"Well, we're receptive enough. What more can we do?"

"Steep yourselves in Arthurian ideas. Get into the right mood, the right frame of mind. Read a few books. Watch a few films. Transport your imaginations back to the Dark Ages. Get the feel of the times."

So that was how we spent the sunny weeks of early June. We sat in the garden and read Mallory and Tennyson, 'The Once and Future King' and 'The Mists of Avalon'. We studied textbooks on the historical Arthur and on the development of the Arthurian legends. We watched videos of 'Monty Python and the Holy Grail' - which didn't seem quite appropriate - and 'Excalibur' - which astounded us with its brutal realism and otherworldly mystery. We visited Tintagel and Caerleon and the site of King Arthur's grave in Glastonbury Abbey – "Hic jacet Arthurus Rex." My Arthur even bought a suit of armour and an old sword he discovered in an antique shop and set about shining them up until they gleamed like the king's battledress and faithful weapon in 'Excalibur'. Like many before us, Arthur became enchanted and obsessed and even I, I must confess, fell under the spell of those ancient days.

On the day of the solstice, Arthur felt unwell. His chest was tight and he had difficulty breathing. Since retiring, his asthma had grown worse. I knew that he could do without the anticipated excitement of the night ahead, but I knew that nothing short of death would induce him to miss it.

Dr. Watts appeared with a vanload of electronic equipment and transformed the dining room into a mini laboratory. Arthur looked on, quietly bemused.

By nine thirty, as the sun was setting, everything was set up - cameras, microphones, sensors, a computer and two VDUs showing a continuous display of every conceivable physical condition within the room.

We ate a light meal but none of us had much appetite.

"Pre-match nerves," said the doctor.

In my case, I think it was more anxiety that the expected anticlimax of the coming night would take its toll on Arthur's fragile state of health. Perhaps Arthur felt the same. Or perhaps not. I thought I knew my husband well, after all these years, but lately he'd seemed to be in a world of his own. As if he really believed in the reality of his own fantasy.

By ten o' clock he was becoming wheezy.

"Better lie down for a while," he conceded.

I tried to follow him upstairs but he insisted that I should stay with the doctor.

"Mustn't let ourselves down," he said, enigmatically.

At eleven, Dr. Watts opened the French windows and the front door, allowing a clear passage for anything that might pass through. We took up our positions in the dining room, the doctor in front of his computer screens.

The sky clouded over, concealing the moon and stars. The house was pitch dark apart from the eerie green glow of the VDUs. Then a wind started blowing from the south. I wedged the doors open to stop them banging shut.

By eleven thirty, the storm that had been threatening for days finally broke. The sky lit up with sheets of lightning. The menacing roar of thunder crept ever nearer. The doctor and I stood at the French windows and gazed out, whatever apprehensions we might have had concerning our strange vigil magnified by the growing ferocity of the storm. Then the rain started falling, the first large drops exploding on the stones of the patio. Within minutes it was torrential.

By midnight, the noise was deafening, the thunder virtually continuous, the rain hammering down on the patio, the gutters and drain pipes overflowing. Forks of lightning ripped through the black sky, one after another.

Suddenly, in a moment's brilliant light, we saw it. Standing alone at the far end of the garden, on the line that joined Camelot with Avalon, a shining, armour-clad figure stretched the magic sword Excalibur high above his head - a gesture of triumph, of mystery, perhaps even of farewell. The shimmering vision remained for a second before blackness reclaimed the night and a mighty boom shook the house.

"Oh, my God, it's Arthur!" I screamed. "Whatever's he playing at? He'll catch his death out there in this rain."

I rushed out into the garden, soaked to the skin in seconds. Dr. Watts was with me, his powerful torch sweeping the lawn where the apparition had stood. There was nothing there.

"He must be hiding in the bushes," I yelled. "This time his game's gone too far."

We raced around the garden for a few minutes but the blackness of the night and the unremitting shroud of rain made our search impossible. Eventually the doctor dragged me back inside, dripping wet and shaking like a leaf, then he rushed across the room to consult his screens.

"All's well," he informed me. "Nothing's registered on the monitors."

"Damn the monitors," I screamed. "Where's my Arthur?"

Then, as though with a single mind, we both made for the door and scrambled up the stairs.

Arthur was lying on his back on the bed, a slight smile upon his white face. His eyes stared vacantly up at the ceiling. The sword and the suit of armour, polished to perfection, stood upright in the corner of the bedroom.

The local doctor pronounced a sudden, massive heart attack. Time of death was set at shortly before midnight.

I served spotted dick and custard at the wake following the funeral. Arthur would have liked that. No one mentioned his favourite ghost story. I think it best, dear Arthur, not to dwell on the gulf between fantasy and reality, nor that strange hinterland between life and death.

HAPPY FAMILIES

Two families lived in the flat upstairs. They weren't unreasonably noisy, but of course there were lots of comings and goings, the children yelling and crying, the men stomping over the wooden floors, the constant jabber of conversation, the whir of the washing machine, music and television. I'm a quiet type. All they would have heard from my flat would have been the drone of Radio 4 voices or the occasional chamber music concert. I lived alone, with three decent sized rooms and a kitchen to rattle around in. Upstairs, in the same space, lived eight people - four adults and as many children - all crammed into three rooms.

The wives were identical twins: Belinda and Melinda. Their mother, so I believe, was called Linda and she had always longed for a daughter to whom she could give her name. When a pair of daughters came along, she was forced into some hasty improvisation - hence Bee and Mel, as they came to be called. Most people who didn't know them too well, like me for instance, had trouble distinguishing them. Even in their twenties, they were identical, not just in looks and personality but, most annoyingly, in the way they wore their hair and the styles of their clothing. I addressed either or both of them as Linda, to be on the safe side, and either or both of them would giggle - in identical ways - and never complain about my lack of discrimination.

"Morning Lindas," I'd say, as we passed in the communal hallway, and they'd giggle together and respond in unison, "Morning Louise",

171

emphasising the final 's' sound, and then they'd giggle some more. Lovely ladies, though. You couldn't dislike them.

Their husbands, most confusingly, were both called Pete, but, unlike their spouses, they were totally different in appearance. One was short and tubby and, I must say, distinctly unattractive in the face, but a pleasant enough character. The other was tall and slim with a moustache that didn't suit him and a habit of constantly clearing his throat as he walked through the hallway.

As to which Pete - tall or tubby - belonged to which Linda - Bee or Mel: that was a mystery I left unresolved. Nor did I ever get to grips with the precise parentage of the four children - two of each sex, all between the ages of three and seven: noisy but charming, and always very polite to me, the little lady who lived downstairs.

They invited me up for Christmas dinner, knowing that I was alone. I hesitated at first - I like being on my own - but I couldn't really tell them that I didn't want to subject myself to the jovial dinner-table banter of eight extrovert souls, so I said yes and even took up a bottle of wine and some chocolates for the children.

All went well throughout the turkey course. I was even beginning to enjoy myself a little, and the young ones had soon got used to having a rather strange stranger at their crowded table. But then one of the Lindas asked me about my own family and, fuelled by a few glasses of wine, I was fool enough to launch into my unsavoury history.

So I told the collected company all about how my father had abused me, how I still bore the scars of his belt on my back, and how my mother had finally left him, taking me, their only daughter, only six years old, to some seedy bedsit in some seedy town where he'd never find us. And then I described the night, one miserable year later, when my mother died of a heroin overdose, lying in the bed beside me.

"I stayed with her for two days," I told my silent, staring audience of eight. "Then, ravenously hungry, I wandered out into the street and was caught stealing fruit from a greengrocer's stall. After that I was taken into care. My father never showed up and I ended up drifting through a succession of foster families, none of whom could cope with my moods and tantrums or, as I became a teenager, my self-harming tendencies."

I picked up my wine glass and shrugged my shoulders, as though shrugging off the trials of my past, and I attempted a little smile - I've never been much of a smiler.

It seemed that my tale had rather put the dampeners on the proceedings. The children just gazed silently at me: four pairs of wide open brown eyes. One of the Lindas wiped a tear from her cheek. The other, sitting beside me, rested a sympathetic hand on my knee and refilled my glass. For a few moments there was a rare silence around that Christmas dinner table.

Then tubby Pete slapped his thighs very forcefully with both hands and said, with splendid joviality, "Well, families, eh! 'Who'd 'ave 'em!"

And at that, the tension snapped and we all burst into hearty, inexplicable laughter: Bee and Mel, the two Petes, the four boys and girls, even me. We laughed till tears flowed down our cheeks. And tubby Pete kept slapping his thighs. And tall Pete vigorously twirled the ends of his moustache. And one of the children blew on one of those coiled up paper-whistle things: oh, what a noise we made!

Then each and every one of those eight members of two families, one by one, completely spontaneously, came to my place at the table, flung their arms around me and gave me a big hug.

And I felt so happy that, despite my earlier intention to leave as soon as was civil after we'd eaten pudding, I ended up staying all afternoon and well into the evening.

Now we've organised a far more even distribution of bodies amongst the rooms of this house, upstairs and down. I keep my own bedroom and my radio, but now I live in the midst of two happy families.

THE BAKER OF GLASTONBURY

Kaph, a mild-mannered fellow with a happy heart, was the sort of man upon whom the angels delighted in bestowing subtle gifts.

His boyhood peers were all named after saints – James, Christopher, Patrick and the like - but Kaph's father, a relisher of word-games and acronyms, decided to name his second son after the qualities of all saints: K for kindness, A for awareness, P for patience and H for humility.

Kaph himself was unimpressed. Untutored in reading or spelling, he thought his name sounded like a girl's. But he never had the chance to question or rebuke his father for his choice. Naming his newborn son had been the wordsmith's last act before leaving to become a soldier. Kaph's mother never knew in what country her husband had died, fighting what enemy, and for what cause. She was too busy, scraping a tentative living for herself and her three young children in a lowly corner of London town.

There was no place in Kaph's early life for education, play or contemplation. He worked the streets and stayed alive. Yet still he felt a destiny within, a fragile inkling, tickling at his heart, blowing on the kindling of his spirit. This was no great destiny – the sort that shapes the fate of nations. Kaph knew that he was an ordinary man, his talents no more nor less than any man's, but he felt sure that he had some mission to fulfil, some meaning for his being in the world.

The feeling grew, a constant tune in the background of his mind, until one day, while strolling aimlessly along the bustling thoroughfare of London Bridge, a gift was granted to him....

*

His attention alights upon a single white feather tracing a figure-of-eight in the air before him as it gently drops to the ground at his feet. He bends to pick it up, marvelling at its delicate form, and, looking up, sees the shimmering outline of an angel standing before him. The vision lasts no more than a fleeting moment - time enough for Kaph to feel the spark of destiny ignite within him, time enough for the delivery of a message, implanted in his mind with a clarity that is beyond all doubt, even though no words are spoken. He has been granted an angelic gift, and the gifts of angels, of course, are not material things but events in the inner depths of consciousness. The gift is simply two apparently mundane bits of information: a time and a place. The place is the market square of the town of Glastonbury in the Shire of Somerset. The time is noon, the day of the Summer Solstice, fifteen years hence.

So convinced is Kaph that he has been graced with a vision of his destiny, that day upon London Bridge, that he resolves to abandon all that has once been his life - albeit that "all" amounts to very little - to pursue whatever might be. His mother, who by this time has married an apothecary's assistant from Walthamstow and has started to reproduce again, does not try to stop him. London tries its best to detain him but does not succeed. Kaph sets out, by foot, on a long pilgrimage through the byways of England, bound for Somerset. And many are his adventures upon the way, but now is not the place to tell of them.

He arrives in Glastonbury a penniless and emaciated wretch, his clothes threadbare, his hair matted: barefoot, forlorn and desolate. He sits beneath the market cross, weary and dejected, yet not once does he bemoan the fate that has drawn him here.

A baker takes pity on him and offers him a stale roll, left on his barrow at the end of the day. Kaph takes it gratefully, paying for his

175

meal with friendly conversation, the only currency he possesses, and the baker, himself weary from a hard day's work, lingers a while and hears Kaph's tale. And this goodly man is so touched by the vagrant's words that he invites him to sleep the night in the warmth of his flour shed.

The next day, the baker bids him work for his breakfast, and this Kaph does willingly, keen to honour the baker's kindness. He works all day, well used to hard labour, and again, that night, sleeps in the shed upon dusty sacks of flour.

Now Kaph is not a big man, but the baker's attention is attracted to his strong, stout hands.

"He has a baker's hands," he tells his wife. "Hands to kneed and pummel dough, to tear it into loaf-sized lumps."

Their daughter listens. She is named after St Catherine, her name shortened to Cath. And it pleases her that the young man called Kaph should glance at her from time to time as they both pursue their chores, for she is not a pretty girl, but she has a pretty mind and she longs to find a man with whom she can feel something in common – even if just a like sounding name. Kaph's great gift – not given by the angels but, he likes to think, from his long gone and unremembered father – is to see beyond a plain body into a pretty mind. He becomes captured by Cath, the baker's daughter.

Enchanted, too, does he become by the subdued pace, the quiet streets and the greenery of the market town. And by the mouth-watering smell of baking bread that pervades the bakery, the fine dust of flour that covers every surface, the yeast fermenting in the cellar, the comings and goings of delivery boys and housewives.

"I like it here," he tells the baker, who makes no suggestion that, after a week or more in the flour shed, Kaph should be moving on his way. The baker likes to have another pair of stout hands to help him through his labours.

Here I will leap a few handfuls of years - for this story is but a short one - and state only that Kaph becomes the baker's apprentice and works with him each day, preparing dough, baking bread, pies and cakes and selling them in the market place.

And, as will be anticipated, Kaph and Cath, the baker's daughter, fall in love, in due course marry and are blessed with two children and a happy life together. When finally the baker hangs up his apron, Kaph, like a dutiful son, takes over the running of the bakery and proves himself to be as fine a man as his benefactor.

The day comes when fifteen years have passed since that fateful morning on London Bridge, the day of the Summer Solstice. Kaph arises, as usual, at dawn, kindles the fire in the oven and tears the dough he has prepared the previous evening into loaves and rolls and sets them a-baking, thinking only that, on this sunny, festive day, the country folk will be flooding into the town and the demand for bread will be greater than ever. At eight of the clock, he loads his barrow with mounds of crisp, brown loaves and heaves it along the cobbled streets to his customary spot in the market square. There his trade is brisk and jovial and, so engrossed is he in his marketing and chattering, that he gives not a thought to the bells of St John's as they chime the hour of noon. As afternoon wears on and the crowds drift away, his barrow is empty of all but crumbs. With a merry heart he packs up his stall and begins pushing his barrow on the journey home.

The bells ring out at four o' clock and suddenly Kaph recalls that the time of his destiny has come and gone. He stops in his tracks, looks at his empty barrow, scratches his balding head and thinks of his wife Cath, awaiting him at home with a hot meal, his two children playing in the yard, the flour shed where he spent his first night in Glastonbury, the dough that needs mixing for the morrow.

Just then the gift of a white feather floats down from the sky, traces a figure-of-eight in the air and gently lands on his empty barrow. And Kaph feels, in his soul, the smile of an angel.

177

PAPER, SCISSORS AND STONE

"**M**orning, Miss Nosegay. Today's the day, then."

"Morning Mr. Biddle. Indeed it is."

She watched from her desk as Mr. Biddle removed his overcoat and hung it on the coat-stand along with his umbrella, turned to the mirror, straightened his tie which didn't need straightening, smoothed his moustache with the thumb and forefinger of his right hand and prodded at the bridge of his spectacles with the middle finger of his left hand. She had watched the same routine at the beginning of every working day for twenty-three years, a daily reminder of the honest and dependable character of her employer. Had Mr Biddle glanced at Miss Nosegay - although this was not part of the routine - he might have noticed something more than admiration in her eyes, concealed behind her thick lenses, a twitch of longing on her lips beneath the downy grey moustache which it never occurred to her to remove.

"You have the document ready, Miss Nosegay?" he said as he sat at his desk and made minute adjustments to the array of pens around his blotter.

"I've just removed it from the safe, Mr. Biddle."

She stood up and carefully flattened the back of her grey skirt before crossing the office and laying a buff folder in the centre of his blotter. He waited for her to return to her desk before opening it.

"For the attention of Mr. Giles Biddle," he read aloud the title of the sealed envelope he withdrew from the folder. "To be opened only on 8th August in the year 2002 or in the event of Mr. Jake Grimley's death, whichever date is sooner."

He glanced at his desk calendar which, as always, Miss Nosegay had set to the correct date before he arrived. "Today's the day, then," he repeated.

"Indeed it is, Mr. Biddle."

He removed his paperknife from the desk drawer, opened the envelope with a decisive slit and withdrew a single sheet of folded A4 paper. As he unfolded the sheet, he looked up at Miss Nosegay. "You, too," he said, "have waited five years to read the contents of this letter, perhaps not with the same personal interest as myself but with, I venture to suggest, a certain measure of curiosity." (Miss Nosegay lowered her eyes in embarrassment. Curiosity, she maintained, was not an appropriate quality for a solicitor's secretary.) "Therefore I propose, as a mark of respect towards our long-standing working relationship, to read aloud the words of my old friend Jake Grimley, for your edification as well as my own." (Miss Nosegay looked up, overwhelmed by the generosity of her employer's gesture.) "Assuming, that is," he added in a mumble, "his writing style avoids the usual vulgarities of his speech."

He cleared his throat and adopted the voice he always used when reading out legal documents, which was, in fact, although he didn't realise it, indistinguishable from his normal speaking voice.

"Dated the 8th August 1997. Headed notepaper of Luxcombe Hall.

"Dear Biddle. So you're still alive, then? (Unless you're not and some other lackey at Biddle and Swayne is reading this, in which case it won't mean much to him.) But I assume that the wholesome ways you've always pursued have carried you safely into your sixties. As for myself, I'm not so sure. Perhaps I'll snuff it before the twenty-first century gets under way, in which case what follows is rendered rather irrelevant. My will, by the way, is deposited with one of your rivals and will, in any case, come as a disappointment to you. I've left Luxcombe Hall to some obscure charity. But I hope it won't come to that. I have more interesting plans.

"So, assuming that we're both still in the land of the living, this is what I propose. After fifty years, it is time we met again. We have some unfinished business to discuss involving - I'm sure I don't need to remind you - some paper, scissors and stone. Why today? you may ask. Because it was on this very date, fifty years ago, that the paths of our boyhood destinies finally diverged. A suitable date, don't you think, for us to rectify the mistakes of the past and for me to teach you a long overdue lesson, you old bastard. (My apologies, Miss Nosegay. I only report what is written.) And where shall we meet? Neutral territory, I think. The old oak tree - you know the one. Two o' clock this afternoon. I'll be there, God willing. What about you, Biddle? I've hated you for fifty years, as I'm sure you know. Hate is not a feeling that mellows with age. On the contrary, it grows ever more warped and ingrained. It becomes a private pleasure to relish. Which is why I'm going to enjoy it for a further five years. And then, on this very day in the year 2002, I think it's time to finally lay it to rest. I trust you'll be there, Biddle. You always were an honourable chap. Except once.

"Yours, Jake Grimley."

Mr. Biddle refolded the letter and replaced it in its envelope. Then he leant back in his chair, rested his elbows on its arms and arched his fingers together.

"A mystery, Mr. Biddle," his secretary commented.

"No mystery, Miss Nosegay. Or, at least, the only mystery is why he's left it so long."

"But why the rendezvous at an oak tree? Why can't he come here, or you go up to Luxcombe Hall?"

"The oak tree's in the paddock at Luxcombe Hall. It's where we always met as boys. Perhaps it was the last place where we were ever happy together. Cancel all my appointments, this afternoon, will you please, Miss Nosegay."

"You're going, then?"

"Of course I'm going. When have I ever let down a client?"

"He's not exactly a client, Mr. Biddle. And he's not exactly - how can I put it? - the most savoury of characters." There was more than a hint of concern in her voice, overriding her natural reluctance to speak ill of anyone.

180

"The man's a scoundrel, Miss Nosegay, you're right. A drunkard, a gambler, a womaniser and an all round bad penny."

"And a murderer, perhaps," added Miss Nosegay, tentatively.

"Never proven," responded Mr. Biddle at once. "His wife was prescribed morphine after an operation. Women's troubles, I believe. How she came to receive a massive overdose, we'll never know. Gossip, Miss Nosegay, does not lie within the province of our profession."

Miss Nosegay accepted the mild rebuke and sought a rapid change of subject. "How did you come to know Mr. Grimley, Mr. Biddle?" Her employer, she knew, was always eager to impart the fruits of his vast experience, whether professional or personal, and she was ever the attentive receptacle of his reminiscences.

"We grew up together, Miss Nosegay. Same age. Both youngest sons of large, poor families. Both our fathers were killed in the war. Back in the early 50's we'd have been about eleven or twelve. That was when the parting of our ways came about. We were caught, one day, trying to trap rabbits in the grounds of Luxcombe Hall. The gamekeeper boxed our ears and dragged us up to the house to face Her Ladyship. I think Lady Felicity took pity on us, a couple of malnourished local urchins. She said she had a job going, mucking out in the stables, after school and at weekends. Trouble was, she could only offer it to one of us. Yours truly got the job, Miss Nosegay, and I don't think Jake has ever forgiven me for it. Of course, once I started work in the stables, I didn't see much of him, except at school. He fell in with a bad crowd. Petty theft, brawling, always trying to make a bob or two from some shady scam or other. Naturally we drifted apart.

"As for me, the stable lad's job was the making of me. I was a diligent worker, always willing to do whatever was asked of me. Lord and Lady Felsham took a liking for me - they had no children of their own, you understand. A philanthropic pair, I must say. Always doing their bit for the needy of the parish. I became their favourite. Eventually, recognising that I was a bright boy, they paid my way through private school where, if you'll excuse the self-aggrandisement, I was an excellent student.

181

"The rest you know, Miss Nosegay. Law at Durham. A junior clerk at Swayne, Swayne and Bedaglio, junior partner in Swayne, Bedaglio and Biddle and, finally, Biddle and Swayne. As you know, Lady Felicity passed away in the early Seventies and Lord Felsham was forced to sell the Hall in 1997. I was appalled when Jake Grimley purchased the place. His wife's money, no doubt. Some wealthy miller's daughter he'd come across in Bolton and ingratiated himself into the family fortune. As you said, Miss Nosegay, not the most savoury of characters. And to think that he's been living in Luxcombe Hall for the past five years! A strange world, Miss Nosegay."

"Tea, Mr. Biddle?"

"And a digestive biscuit, I think. Mustn't let ourselves grow maudlin, eh?"

"One thing that puzzles me," remarked Miss Nosegay as she carried the morning beverage and a saucer bearing a single digestive biscuit to Mr. Biddle's desk, "is the reference to unfinished business in Mr. Grimley's letter. Something to do with paper, scissors and stone."

"His little joke, perhaps," replied Mr. Biddle, allowing himself the rare luxury of a smile. "Fifty years ago on this very day, you see, we had a momentous decision to make. We had to decide which of us was to take the job of stable lad. We were standing in the drawing room of Luxcombe Hall. Her Ladyship, after reprimanding us for poaching rabbits, softened her tone and made her offer. There was a single job available in the stables. She knew nothing about either of us and it was to her great credit that she thought us worthy of such a position. To her we were just a couple of local scallywags. 'Who wants it?' she asked. 'Me,' we both shouted in unison. She looked from one grubby face to the other, unable to reach a decision. 'You decide amongst yourselves,' she said. She always was a ditherer. 'I've got a call to make. I'll be back in five minutes.' With that, she left us standing in the centre of the drawing room.

"How were we to resolve such a crucial dilemma? Rational argument would have been pointless. We both wanted the job with an equal fervour and, besides, rational argument is hardly the way eleven-year-old boys go about solving problems. A scrap would have been the natural course of action but, amidst the finery of the drawing room, a bout of rough-and-tumble seemed out of the question. It was Jake, I believe, who suggested handing the matter over to chance and I confess that I could see no better alternative. Neither of us had even a penny in our pockets to toss so we agreed upon a game of paper, scissors and stone. Best of three, of course, as always.

"I'm sure you know the game, Miss Nosegay. Or perhaps it was not a pastime in which young girls indulged. I'm sure it's got some more technical name but we always knew it simply as paper, scissors and stone. Right hands behind backs. At the count of three, both players withdraw their hand in the shape of either scissors, paper (a flat palm) or stone (a clenched fist). Scissors cut paper, paper wraps stone and stone blunts scissors. Simple as that.

"First round, Jake produced scissors to cut my paper. Second round, I came out with paper again and he had stone. So it was all down to the decider, our future lives, or so we thought - and so it turned out to be - hanging in the balance.

"We'd played this many times before, of course. We knew each other thoroughly, well aware of the preferred strategies of our opponent. But never had we played it for such stakes. A job, even part-time work mucking out stables, was quite a prize in those days. The tension mounted as we faced each other across the drawing room carpet, one hand behind our backs, each frantically trying to probe the hidden intent of the other. I'd used paper twice. Would he think I'd try my luck a third time? He'd offered scissors and stone. Would he go for paper this time? Or would he expect me to think this and therefore go for stone to beat my anticipated scissors? In which case, should I risk paper a third time? Endless mental deliberations. This was desperate stuff.

"At last we were ready. Together, very slowly, we counted to three and whipped out our hidden hands. I had stone. Jake had scissors. The job was mine."

"And what was his reaction?" asked Miss Nosegay.

"He stared in disbelief, but what could he do? I'd won, fair and square. Further argument was pointless. Lady Felicity came back into the room and I announced that we'd reached a decision. She never questioned it, relieved, no doubt, to have been spared that decision herself. She handed Jake a consolation apple from the bowl on the table and led me out to the stables to show me my duties. I noticed, incidentally, that Jake sneaked another apple into his pocket as we followed Lady Felicity from the room - a sign, of course, of further dishonesty to come.

"And that, would you believe it, was the last time I ever spoke to Jake Grimley. I was tied up with work in the stables every evening. At school, he'd stare daggers at me but never said a word. In a matter of days, we drifted apart completely. He fell in with the local gang of ne'er-do-wells and I... Well, you know the rest."

"So what's this unfinished business he mentioned?" asked Miss Nosegay.

Mr. Biddle shrugged and opened his palms. "Who knows what's in his mind? A guilty conscience, perhaps, about Luxcombe Hall. He knew, when His Lordship put it up for sale, that I was trying to raise the finances to buy it myself. But he put in a higher bid. Sometimes I think it was just to spite me, to get his own back after all these years. Maybe now he's settled down and wants to atone for the sins of his past, to rekindle, even, an old friendship. I think, Miss Nosegay, that today may indeed turn out to be a memorable one."

But his secretary was less optimistic. Leopards and spots sprang into her mind. "Are you sure it's wise meeting him alone, Mr. Biddle?" she asked, trying to disguise the concern in her voice.

Mr Biddle nibbled on his digestive biscuit. "Miss Nosegay, Jake may be, as you so delicately put it, an unsavoury character, but he is, I believe, a man of honour. Besides, what harm can ensue from a meeting out in the open, in the paddock of Luxcombe Hall?"

But Miss Nosegay was not so sure. Perhaps a call to her policeman cousin Sergeant McGilligan was in order.

*

184

Jake Grimley hadn't changed a bit, thought Mr. Biddle - except for his long trousers, of course, his hair - grey and very little of it - several inches extra in the waist region and a face as tough and wrinkled as a turtle's.

"You've not changed a bit, Jake" he greeted his boyhood friend.

"You're blind as well as stupid, Biddle," Jake Grimley responded, spitting out the solicitor's surname with venomous relish.

They stood facing each other beneath a huge oak tree in a neglected corner of the paddock, Mr. Biddle, his bald head shining in the afternoon sun, dressed in his overcoat, an umbrella hooked in the crook of his arm. Jake Grimley had opted, instead, to carry a shotgun - unbroken, Mr. Biddle noticed, and pointing at the ground rather too close to his feet.

Mr. Biddle forced his mouth into the closest shape it would make to a smile.

Jake Grimley glared back at him. "You came, then."

"Of course."

Jake looked him up and down. "You've done well for yourself, I hear."

Was that a hint of conviviality in his voice, Mr. Biddle wondered? He found himself glancing too frequently at the shotgun at Jake's side. He hated firearms of all sorts. "Mustn't grumble," he replied. "And yourself, Jake?"

"Don't try to pretend that you don't know everything about my life, Biddle. I bet you've got a bulging file on me in your cosy little office. All my convictions. All the charges that didn't quite stick. No doubt, like everyone else, you even suspect me of killing my wife."

"No, Jake, I don't."

Mr. Biddle tried to make it sound as sincere as possible but all he received in return was a snort of derision. "I married for money and that, apart from a wife who had the good fortune to die after only a year of my company, was what I got. Enough to buy Luxcombe Hall, much to your chagrin, and more besides. Never married yourself, Biddle?"

"Er, no. Married to the job, you might say."

"Poor Miss Nosegay, eh?" Jake's face cracked into a grin for the first time, causing Mr. Biddle a moment's perplexed reflection. "So, Mr. Renowned Solicitor, noted in these parts for your honesty and integrity, aren't you going to ask me why I invited you here?"

"No doubt you'll tell me in your own good time," replied Mr. Biddle, concealing, he hoped, a spasm of anxiety he felt every time he glanced at the shotgun.

"Fifty years ago to this very day," Jake began, "both our lives changed in the drawing room of that house, not a hundred yards from where we stand. An opportunity that you grabbed at heartily. Credit where credit's due, Biddle. You milked it well, I'll grant you that. Made a successful life for yourself. As for me, that day marked an opportunity lost - and a friend lost. I felt I was a loser and I started acting like a loser. Gave up on my schoolwork. Gave up on my family. Drifted into company and pursuits of which, let me tell you, I'm not proud. The more I heard of your successes, the more I despised myself. Not you. Not then. That didn't come till much later. And by then, the course of my life had been set, the colours of my personality established. I'm not a nice man, I know. And for that, I always have and always will blame you."

"Come on, Jake," beseeched Mr. Biddle. "It was a game of chance. I won and you lost. Simple as that. Do you expect me to apologise for winning?"

"I expect you," Jake's voice was steadily rising, "to apologise for cheating."

Mr. Biddle stared at the man and Jake stared back.

"I expect you, at the very least," his voice was calmer now, but firm, "to admit that you cheated."

Mr. Biddle opened the palms of his hands. "How can you cheat at paper, scissors and stone?"

"My thoughts exactly. Which was why, for years, I was prepared to grudgingly accept that you'd won fair and square. Lady Luck was on your side, that day. But then, back in 1997, as you know, I bought

Luxcombe Hall from that feckless fool Lord Felsham. It wasn't my intention to buy it, at first. Just thought I'd view the place, for old times' sake, you know. Particularly that fateful drawing room. I stood on the same spot of carpet where I'd stood forty-five years before and relived, in my memory, every detail of our game. Then, for some reason, I turned around. Directly behind me, above the fireplace, was a huge mirror. Ha! I even got old Felsham to stand where I had stood and clench his fist behind his back. I stood in your spot and there, in the mirror, was a perfect view of Felsham's clenched fist. All done with mirrors, as they say. You cheating bastard, Biddle!"

"But..." Mr. Biddle felt a flush spreading over his face and he fingered his shirt collar nervously. "I didn't even see a mirror behind you," he objected. "I was too busy trying to second guess your next move. You've got it all wrong, Jake."

Jake Grimley grinned. "'Fraid not, Biddle. It won't wash. The whole thing was just so obvious. God, you must have felt pleased with yourself, me with my back to a bloody great mirror. Which brings us to the point of our little meeting."

"Yes, the point." Mr. Biddle tried to steady his nerves. "I take it you have some proposal to make."

Jake's steely eyes had not left Mr. Biddle's for a moment. Now he glanced down at the shotgun at his side and twisted it a little in his hand, which did nothing to ease Mr. Biddle's fears. "I propose," he said slowly, "that we turn the clock back fifty years. I propose that we re-enact that decisive game."

"Fair enough. But why? What good will it do? It won't change the past fifty years."

"Oh, it'll do one of us a power of good. It's all a question of stakes, you see. Last time, the stakes were pretty high, you agree? This time, we'll make them higher still."

Mr. Biddle swallowed uncomfortably. He was not a gambling man.

"You win," continued Jake, "and I'll give you Luxcombe Hall. I've got the deeds here in my pocket. The place will be yours. I've no need of the damn ruin, anyway."

187

"Very generous of you, Jake. And if you win?"

"Then I take your miserable life." He raised the shotgun a few inches to emphasise the point.

"Oh, come on, Jake!" Mr. Biddle tried to force a giggle. "The joke's gone on long enough."

"No joke, Biddle. There's nothing I'd like more than to blow your head off, right here and now. It's been my dream ever since I discovered that you'd cheated on me. But I'm a sporting man. Unlike you that day in the drawing room, I'm prepared to give you a fighting chance."

"But..." He struggled to find some rational line of argument. "You'd never get away with it. My secretary knows that I'm here. This time, the charge of murder would undoubtedly stick."

"You suppose I hadn't thought of that? You think I care? Besides, I'll be out of the country in a matter of hours. I'm a rich man, Biddle. I'll take a long, comfortable retirement, somewhere in South America, I think."

"But why kill me? What will that gain?"

Jake shook his head and smiled. "You know, I really believe you can't see it. You don't understand the power of hatred. Perhaps you've never hated anyone in your life. Never loved, either, I suspect. Well, hatred can be a yearning as strong as anything. And the satisfaction of that yearning can be a man's highest goal. To kill you, Biddle, would be the crowning achievement of my life. No, I really believe that you can't understand the pleasure it would give me to pull this trigger and end your life."

"So why not do it now?" stammered Mr. Biddle, regretting his words even as they emerged. "Why all this silly pretence, this game playing?"

"Because I'm a gambling man. How d'you think I've made all my money? The thrill of the game, Biddle - something else you can't understand. Only this time we'll play it fair. No mirror behind my back. Just you and me and an outcome that neither of us can predict. Luxcombe Hall or your life. Excitement, Biddle! Have you never in your life felt it?"

"You're mad, Jake." It was the only coherent thought left in Mr. Biddle's tidy mind.

"Think what you like, Biddle. A few minutes from now, you'll either be a rich man or a dead man. Either way, I'll be gone from here and you'll never see me again. I'm happy with that. Aren't you?"

"How do I know I can trust you?"

"You trusted me last time and I trusted you. Did I argue when you came out with stone and me scissors? I accepted the outcome of the game then, even though you cheated, and I'll accept it again this time. As I said, I'm a sporting man."

"But..."

"No more buts, Biddle. I don't see that you've got a lot of choice in the matter. So let's get on with it. Best of three."

He put his left hand behind his back, his right hand still gripping the shotgun. Mr. Biddle slowly put his left hand behind his back, his umbrella still hooked over his right arm. This is utter madness, he thought. He made a flat palm with his left hand.

"One, two, three," they counted together and whipped out their left hands. Jake offered a clenched fist. The corners of his mouth twisted upwards, his eyes never leaving his opponent's.

"Paper beats stone. First blood to you, Biddle."

"This is utter madness," Mr. Biddle voiced his thought.

"Round two," announced Jake, placing his hand behind his back again.

Mr. Biddle made the scissors sign. He wasn't thinking. His mind was numb.

"One, two, three."

They both produced scissors.

"Round two continued," said Jake. "Come on, Biddle. You're one up. Your chance for a famous victory."

As Mr. Biddle replaced his hand behind his back, his mind suddenly whirred into action. Scissors again? he thought. Or would Jake expect that and go for stone? Or would Jake anticipate that thought and opt

189

himself for another scissors? Or would he try to confound him by choosing paper? How could he expect a logical response from a madman? How could he expect, come to that, any kind of logic or strategy to enter such a senseless game? He made a fist.

"One, two, three."

Jake triumphantly produced a flat palm and released an ecstatic whoop. He was grinning, now, his eyes shining with what Mr. Biddle took for demonic glee.

"All down to the decider," said Jake. "Just like fifty years ago. You ready for it, Biddle?"

Mr. Biddle nodded. How could he ever be ready for this? He was a lawyer, not a gambler. He did things by the book. He had never done anything without having a pretty good idea of the probable outcome. His heart was pumping wildly, his legs were shaking and his stomach felt so knotted up that he feared he might be sick. His left hand, furthermore, refused to form itself into any shape whatever, hanging limply behind his back.

"One, two, three," Jake counted slowly.

Mr. Biddle found himself revealing a flat palm: paper. It seemed to him that the world had suddenly shifted into slow motion as he gazed down at Jake's hand, his first two fingers opened into a wide 'V': scissors.

He heard him speak. "Bad luck, Biddle," followed by a short cackle, and he watched the barrel of the shotgun rising slowly from the ground, higher and higher until a gaping black hole, like an eye of death, was staring straight into his face.

Then he glimpsed Jake's finger moving on the trigger, very slowly pulling it back. And the last thing he knew, before his legs collapsed beneath him, was the sound of a very loud... click.

*

"That'll do, Grimley," came a gruff voice. "Put it down slowly on the ground."

While Sergeant McGilligan picked up the shotgun from the grass, Miss Nosegay rushed past him to the supine figure of her employer.

190

She fell to her knees beside him, grabbed his two cheeks between the palms of her hands and might well have kissed his puckered lips had he not, at that moment, opened his eyes.

"Miss Nosegay," he muttered, pushing himself up on his elbows, at which point Miss Nosegay threw her arms around his neck and hugged him.

"Oh, Mr. Biddle!"

"Empty," said Sergeant McGilligan, breaking open the shotgun and peering inside. "Both barrels empty. What's your game, Grimley?"

"Paper, scissors and stone," replied Jake, a wide smile creasing his face. "Have you never played it?"

*

The sergeant conceded, as they made their way, at Jake's invitation, across the paddock to the drawing room of Luxcombe Hall, that no crime had been committed. Threatening behaviour, Sergeant McGilligan suggested, but Mr. Biddle persuaded him that the whole thing had been a high-spirited prank in which they had both colluded. They all drank a glass of port.

"To the renewal of an old friendship," Jake proclaimed, raising his glass. "And perhaps to a lesson learned and a debt repaid."

"I'll drink to that," said Mr. Biddle.

"But Mr. Biddle..." objected Miss Nosegay, sitting very close beside him on the sofa. "What about the shotgun? He could have... You might have... Besides, you know you never drink in the afternoons."

"Today, Miss Nosegay, is an exceptional day."

He looked up at the mirror above the fireplace.

Jake followed his gaze. "You did cheat, didn't you? Come on, you can admit it now. This time, it was me who cheated. The shotgun was empty and, had you won the game, I had no intention of giving you the deeds of this house. I admit it. I cheated. How about you?"

"My entire life and reputation, Jake, are based on honesty and fair play. Do you seriously suppose that I could have founded all that on a lie?"

Mr. Biddle hauled himself up from the sofa and, as he did so, Jake Grimley saw him throw another quick glance at the mirror and noticed a flicker in his left eye that was very nearly a wink.

"Well, Miss Nosegay," Mr. Biddle announced, "it's time we were getting back to the office. We've got work to do. And perhaps later, Miss Nosegay, in recognition of your unswerving devotion to duty, this day, I would like to ask you to accompany me to a restaurant for dinner."

Miss Nosegay's response was delayed by only a second - a delay occasioned by shock rather than hesitation. "I'd be delighted, Mr Biddle."

OSMIUM

The music was still ringing in his ears, a constant background roar like the sound of the sea crashing on to a shingly beach, back in his home town. Even when he awoke, shocked into painful consciousness by the early morning traffic, he could feel the relentless beat of the drums, the pulsating twang of fuzzy guitars. He'd been dancing right in front of the main speakers, leaping up and down, his hair flying in all directions, completely out of his head, hour after hour. Somehow - he had no idea how – he'd found his way to a secluded shop doorway, unrolled his sleeping bag and crashed out. Now his head was pounding and his mouth felt so dry that he could barely move his tongue.

He found a cafe and ordered tea. He'd been there before: one of the regular stops on his daily round of wandering. They were well used to his type. No one commented on the state of his dress or his hair. No one seemed offended by the smell he was doubtless exuding. He hadn't washed or changed his clothes for days - weeks, probably.

He sipped his tea and began to feel a bit more human. At least now his tongue would operate - not that he had any words in his head to speak, nor anyone to hear them. He reached into the pocket of his denim jacket and pulled out the remains of his money, a ritual he enacted dozens of times each day. Two tenners and a handful of coins - all that was left from the savings account he'd emptied on the day he left home. Should last him a few more days, he thought: perhaps longer if he did a bit of begging. It'd come to that, soon enough. A few more days, and then... He felt no desire, no need to look beyond the next few hours, let alone days or weeks or years. Another cup of tea and a doughnut - that was where his vision of the future ended.

A girl sat down in the chair opposite him, a cup in her hand. She was one of his type. They exchanged a glance, nothing more. He put his money away quickly, pulled out his tobacco and prepared a roll-up.

"Can you spare one?" the girl asked. Her tone was not pleading. It was simply a straightforward question.

"Help yourself." He pushed the packet across the table and watched while she extracted a skin and a large twist of tobacco. "Hey, take it easy," he said.

She looked up at him for a moment then returned a little tobacco to the packet. Her hair was long and matted, like his, but her face was spotless and white. She was probably a year or two younger than him. Sixteen, maybe. Maybe not. What did it matter? She managed a brief twitch of a smile as she lit her roll-up.

"Cheers," she said, exhaling a cloud of smoke.

He sipped his tea. At least it was warm in the cafe. He thought he might just sit there for a while. Nothing else to do.

"What's your name?" she asked.

No one else had seemed particularly interested in his name. He hadn't used it for weeks. He knew that people like him never used their real names. They made up something. He could be anyone he liked. Here, he had no name, no past, no future.

"Osmium," he said.

She nodded. She could accept it. Why shouldn't she? But now, he felt like talking.

"It's a heavy metal," he said.

"Ah. What, like lead, you mean?"

"Much heavier than lead. Twice as heavy. Density twenty-two grams per cubic centimetre. Lead's only eleven."

"Really?" He could tell she wasn't interested.

"Heaviest metal there is," he continued. "Dense and impenetrable. See this cup. If it was full of osmium, you wouldn't even be able to pick it up."

"Yeah?" Was there a flicker of interest?

"Named after the Greek word for stench. How about that?"

This time he succeeded in evoking a smile.

194

"Atomic number seventy-six. Melting point three thousand Celsius. Pretty high, eh?"

"Fascinating. You know a lot about it."

"Course. It's my name. Anyway," he added, "I used to be into chemistry when I was at school."

His words dwindled into silence. Talking about school wasn't on. That was all part of what was. Another lifetime. Nobody on the streets talked about school.

"So you're into heavy metal music, are you?" she asked.

"Dead right. Heavier the better."

"Gives me a bloody headache," she said, turning away from him.

"Nothing wrong with a headache," he said. "At least you know you're alive."

"Big deal. I'd rather not know."

She gazed through the cafe window. He did the same. Nothing more to say. Conversations of more than half a dozen exchanges were beyond him. He'd never mastered the art.

Outside, the streets were getting crowded. Businessmen on their way to work. Rich bastards. What did they know about real life, he thought. What did they know about cold and loneliness and uncertainty and the feeling of inadequacy that he wore around his neck like a mighty boulder?

He looked at the girl's face. God, she was beautiful! Her brown eyes seemed to be focused on nothing, he thought, and now they shone with a sheen of tears. She was withdrawing into her own private despair. He wondered how long she'd been like this, living on the streets. A wave of formless pity came over him, like the pity he only usually felt for himself. Yes, he could love this girl, he thought. And maybe she could love him too. Surely such things were possible. Her hand was resting on the table. He reached over and, not really knowing what he was doing, rested his own on top of it.

"Back off!" she snapped, snatching her hand away.

She glanced at him for an instant, then returned her vacant gaze to the window.

"Sorry," he murmured, staring down at his cup.

"Me too," she said, after a few seconds, and turned to look at him again. No one had ever looked at him like that before. Absolutely no one. It was as if he really mattered.

"What's your name?" he asked.

This time her smile was real. God, it was the most real thing he'd ever seen!

"Call me Lithium, if you like," she said. "The lightest metal. Soft but reactive. Touch me and I'll burn your fingers. I did chemistry at school, too, you know."

*

They spent the day together. Not that they did much, but he reckoned it was the best day he'd ever known. He bought them both a big, greasy breakfast. She ate half of hers then dashed off to the loo to throw up. They strolled down to the river. She approached a few tourists and got a couple of quid. The sun came out and they sat in the park, smoking his tobacco and a tiny lump of hash she had hidden in her knickers. They took a ride on the Underground, twice around the Circle Line. He told her about the heavy metal pubs where he tended to spend the evenings, making a single lager last for hours, occasionally dropping a tab of acid or E or anything else he could get his hands on and dancing himself into oblivion. She took him to the camp beneath the viaduct where she usually spent the nights, wrapped in cardboard.

He told her that he'd walked out of his home when he was seventeen and that he'd been on the road for a couple of years. It was a bit of an exaggeration but she didn't question it. She told him that her mother had moved in with a bloke she hated. He'd burst into the bathroom, one day, when she'd been taking a shower and he'd tried to fondle her until she'd screamed so loudly that he'd hit her in the face. She'd left home that night and never been back. He believed her. Their pasts bonded them, two disillusioned teenagers, adrift in a hostile world. He told her that one day he'd make it as a heavy metal guitarist, that he was brilliant on the guitar, and, if he failed at that, he'd become a research chemist. She said she thought he'd be good at that. She said one day she'd be a writer and tell the world what it was really like to be a homeless kid on the streets of London. They'd call themselves Osmium and Lithium, the rock star and the writer, and, one day, they'd be the stuff of legends.

He never touched her again. They'd be friends, she said, nothing more. She didn't want anything physical. And all he wanted was to be with her, night and day. As they lay together, that night, in her grubby cardboard box beneath the viaduct, he listened to her breathing and sniffed her body. He gazed at her sleeping face and felt so happy that he longed to hug her, to press her against his body and never let her go. But he never touched her again.

The next day, they made a supreme effort to tidy themselves up and went to the Tate Gallery. It was warm in there. They could stay all day. He was entranced by the Pre-Raphaelites. She fell in love with Turner. That evening, they changed their plans and decided they'd become great painters instead.

When it rained, she stayed in her cardboard box.

"You know how lithium reacts with water," she said.

"Hydrogen gas and the alkali lithium hydroxide," he replied.

"So you go out today and get us some money. I'm staying in the dry."

"Osmium is immune to water," he said. "Nothing can touch me."

He went to The Embankment and managed to beg enough money for a few cans of lager, a bar of chocolate and a pizza. When he returned to the viaduct, her box was empty.

"She went off with some bloke," an old woman told him.

He stared at her in disbelief.

"Well, what did you expect?" The old woman gave him a toothless grin. "She's a pretty girl and you're hardly God's gift, are you?"

He stayed there, beneath the viaduct, for two weeks but she didn't re-appear. His money was gone and he couldn't face begging again. He hadn't eaten for days. He returned to his favourite heavy metal pub and danced in front of the speakers, imagining her there with him, leaping up and down, smiling her beatific smile. He danced on, a frenzy of chaotic motion, until he'd shaken himself free of all feelings. Then he collapsed on the floor.

An ambulance came and took him to the nearest casualty department. When he came round, he gave an address in Brighton. A few hours later, his parents arrived. They smothered him in tears and affection. His mouth was so dry that he could barely say a word as they drove him home.

He never forgot that brown-eyed girl called Lithium. A year later, he went up to Oxford to study inorganic chemistry.

DOORBELL BLUES

The doorbell roused her from drowsy absorption in the daily affairs of a group of unnaturally good-looking Australian teenagers. She leaped to her feet as it rang a second time, straightened her blouse and ran the fingers of both hands hopelessly through the mess of her uncombed hair.

Slippers? No time for slippers.

She charged out of her flat in her bare feet, and hurtled down the three flights of stairs as it rang again.

Yes! she thought. A visitor!

She ran through the possibilities to herself as she raced along the cold flagstones of the empty ground floor hall. Mary, inviting her out for a drink? Or Valerie? She said she'd pop round sometime with the CD she'd borrowed. Or Mike, perhaps? Had he really meant it, in the pub the other night, when he'd said he'd like to see her flat? Or...

The Parcel Force man held out a small book-shaped package and a clipboard for her to sign.

"Name of Mitchell?" He didn't return the welcoming smile that Jenny had fixed to her face before opening the door, didn't even look at her.

"Er, no," said Jenny, letting her smile flop.

"Sign 'ere, anyway."

She did as she was told, the delivery man walked off and Jenny closed the door, threw the parcel onto the pile of unopened mail on the communal hall stand and trudged back up the stairs.

Back in her armchair in front of the tele, she contemplated what to do with what was left of the day ahead. No point in the pub. No money and, anyway, the few locals she knew only went there at weekends. She didn't fancy sitting at the bar with her lager trying to think of clever things to say to the barman. Back to the computer? A few more hours' work on the translation before getting some food? She didn't much fancy that, either. Anyway, Countdown would be on soon. Bit of intellectual stimulation. At least she could have an imaginary conversation with Carol Vorderman. Better than talking to herself. Just about.

Then the doorbell rang again and she was flying down the three flights of stairs, hastily composing her face into a look that said, "Great to see you. Come on up." Mary, this time, surely? Or Valerie? Mike, even?

The double-glazing salesman was a few sentences into his patter before realising that Jenny didn't look the buying type.

"You the owner of this property?" he asked.

"I rent the attic flat. Come up, if you like. I'll make you a cuppa."

Unaccustomed to such courtesy, the salesman withdrew, giving Jenny a suspicious glance.

After Countdown she put her shoes on and took a walk in the park. It was a decent day and there was a fair crowd about - lovers arm in arm, couples with kids, groups of office workers strolling home. The only single people were dog-walkers. And Jenny, trying to give the impression that she was on her way to meet someone. She circled the park once and headed back to her flat, cheering herself up with the thought of the frozen, individual spaghetti Bolognese that sat alone in her icebox, and the crumpled cushions of her armchair whose unused partner she had pushed into the corner of the room so as not to have to stare upon its emptiness.

Was this what she had anticipated when she moved to the city? Don't let your social life distract you from your work - that had been her mother's typically motherly advice. Parties, night-clubs, lively conversations in pubs, boyfriends, visitors constantly interrupting her - those had been her mother's fears. And Jenny's hopes.

Her job was translating English textbooks into Portuguese and a bit of vice versa. It had seemed like a good line of work, if a rather solitary one, for a languages graduate with no particular desire to move to Portugal or Brazil, and working from home had always suited her. It was her father who had kept muttering about still living with your parents at the age of twenty-three. Besides, a small Somerset village was hardly the place for an ambitious, beautiful, fun-loving, single girl (well, single, at least), hardly the hub of civilisation. The city was the place to be, where the real movers and shakers hung out.

So who had she met in three months? Mary, a part-time hairdresser with a probable drug habit. Valerie, a supermarket check-out girl obsessed with Robbie Williams. And Mike from the local pub, a spotty computer nerd who took an unhealthy interest in her breasts. Plus the odd delivery man and double-glazing rep. What was she doing wrong?

Half way through her spaghetti Bolognese, the doorbell rang again. Must be Mary this time, she thought as she charged down the stairs, her mouth still full. Or even Valerie would be company of a sort.

The front door swung open to reveal a tall, bespectacled young man with short curly blonde hair and a toothy grin.

"Oh." He seemed taken aback. Or was it a reaction to the fixed, open-mouthed gawp she always wore, expectantly, on her fruitless dashes to the front door, her teeth stained with Bolognese sauce? "Jenny, isn't it?"

She nodded and wiped her mouth closed with the back of her hand.

"I'm James?" What was the question mark for? she wondered. "Second floor flat? I forgot my key?"

"Oh. Right." Recognition dawned. They had met once or twice on the stairs.

"Sorry to disturb you," he said. "Eating dinner, were you?"

"It's okay," said Jenny.

He squeezed past her. She shut the door and followed his trail of aftershave down the hallway. Nice chap, the thought began to form itself in her mind. Very nice, at least compared to double-glazing salesmen and parcel deliverers.

"Silly of me to forget my key," he said, glancing over his shoulder and giving her a smile that seemed to sweep away, in an instant, all memories of the loneliness of the day, of the previous three months - all the loneliness, in fact, of the previous twenty-three years. "It's been one of those days. One hassle after another. Glad to be home."

"Right. I bet." Was that really the best she could do by way of small talk? Her solitary lifestyle had deprived her of the power of normal conversation. But there was nothing normal about following such an alluringly masculine scent - not to mention such a firm bottom - up those stairs which normally she descended with such hope and ascended with such dejection.

"You live on your own?" she asked as they climbed the first flight of stairs.

"Yeah." Was that a happy Yeah or a lonely one? "You, too?"

"Yeah," said Jenny and, though she tried to disguise it, there was no doubting that it was a lonely Yeah. "Just me and the old PC. I work from home."

"Ah," he said. "Lucky you."

"You fancy a quick coffee?" she ventured as they climbed the second flight of stairs. In the pause that followed, an express train of thought rattled through her head. Far too forward of me. Course he doesn't want a coffee. Or, rather, he doesn't want to come into my flat. Why should he? He's just had a hard day at work. And why should he be interested in someone like me? Oh, well. Back to the armchair. Nice chap, though. Very nice.

They stopped at his door on the second landing.

"Rather have a bottle of wine," he said, pulling one from a carrier bag in his hand and giving her a look that could melt a polar ice-cap. She returned his look, into and then rapidly away from his eyes, and suddenly the remains of her day exploded into a fleeting shower of delightful possibilities.

He followed her up the final flight of stairs. Now it was his turn to look at her bottom and this thought caused Jenny's legs to shake and her stomach to flutter uncontrollably.

She led him into her flat, quickly turned off the tele, dumped the remains of her spaghetti in the kitchen, frantically scoured the cupboards for her spare glass and, finally, pulled the second armchair into the middle of the room, alongside her own.

"Nice flat," he said, looking around as she struggled clumsily to open the bottle. "You must get lonely stuck in here all day on your own."

"Lonely? No. Not me. Never."

MR PERKINS
GETS IT WRONG

"I love a story with a happy ending," said Mr Perkins. "Don't you, Mrs Firth?"

Irene was so taken aback at being addressed at

such length by Mr Perkins that she almost forgot to scan his card before taking the book he presented. Normally, their exchanges comprised precisely three words each: "Morning Mrs Firth." "Morning Mr Perkins." Or, on exceptional days: "Nice weather today." "Lovely, isn't it."

She glanced up at him for a moment, then returned her attention to the matter of issuing his book. A response was called for. A simple agreement, thought Irene, would lessen the significance of the occasion and, besides, she didn't share Mr Perkins' opinion.

"Personally, I find sad endings far more true to life," she ventured. "Happy endings leave me dissatisfied. Give me Thomas Hardy, any day, rather than Jane Austen."

She handed Mr Perkins his book - Doris Lessing's Love Again: an odd choice, she thought - and glanced at him again. The charming smile and slightly mischievous twinkle in his eyes always disconcerted her.

"And I took you for a secret romantic, Mrs Firth," he said.

Irene flushed, although she tried desperately not to, and turned to her next customer.

From that point, their relationship - as Irene liked to imagine it - progressed through a series of very brief weekly discussions over the library counter.

"I'll try something more modern, this week," said Mr Perkins, handing over Ian McEwan's Enduring Love. "D'you know this one?"

"Excellent beginning," replied Irene. "Unfortunately the conclusion doesn't live up to the initial promise."

The next week, it was Captain Corelli's Mandolin.

"Saw the film," said Mr Perkins. "Wonderful love story."

"The ending in the book is rather different," said Irene. "I hope you won't be disappointed."

This time, their eyes met for more than the customary instant. Mr Perkins was smiling, as usual, and Irene found her own mouth involuntarily opening in response. She had one of those faces that is utterly transformed by a smile, like the sun suddenly bursting through a grey mass of turbulent clouds; a haggard face, one might have called it, etched with the usual trials and traumas of fifty-five years of living. Yet when she smiled, her years slipped away like a dusty drape from a fine piece of antique furniture. She should smile more often, thought Mr Perkins, but he didn't dare say it.

The library had been the mainstay of Irene's life for fifteen years, ever since her husband had left her to raise an illegitimate family with some bimbo from his office who had probably never read a book in her life. The shame of it had struck her more forcefully than the sense of loss. Nothing could remain private in a small town. She had hated all the tacit sympathy and the whispered gossip behind her back.

At least the library was frequented mainly by people who kept their thoughts to themselves and who rated literature well above soap opera. The regulars, like Mr Perkins, were mainly her age or older and she felt an affinity even for those women who headed straight for the romantic fiction shelves or men who borrowed nothing but thrillers and westerns.

The trouble with Irene's face was that even when she was content she looked miserable, even when placid she looked angry and even when being friendly she appeared hostile. It was a face that suited her profession, she fancied - authoritative and stern. A single glare across the room was enough to silence the giggles of school kids on the computers, sending banal e-mails to each other. And rarely did a reader object when she tapped masterfully away at her own computer at the counter and informed them that they owed a hefty fine. She was accorded respect by the regular library users, yet few - save Mr. Perkins -offered her conviviality. And even fewer ever considered the woman behind the austere librarian's facade.

"Where's your bedroom?" a little boy once asked her as she scanned his books.

"I don't live at the library," she had replied.

"Don't you?" He had gazed at her incredulously and even his mother had seemed surprised that she might have a life beyond the library walls.

A life populated mainly by books. Each evening she read in her armchair, escaping into other people's imaginary worlds. Each night, in her bed, she sank into a sea of fantasies, of heroic adventures and undiluted passions.

And now she found Mr Perkins creeping into her fantasies. She thought of him increasingly often, of his twinkling eyes and chubby, childlike smile, wondering whether he was enjoying the latest books he had borrowed. She imagined him sitting in the empty armchair opposite hers, both quiet but companionable, immersed in their books, occasionally looking up and acknowledging each other's presence.

Tuesday mornings were his time - had been for fifteen years. Straight over to the crime section, five minutes browsing then one, maybe two books if they were thin, up to the counter, a quick "Morning Mrs Firth" then off. She knew virtually nothing about him. Many years before, she had overheard a local gossip telling her friend that he was a widower, that his wife had died young from cancer, that he lived alone. She discovered a little more by surreptitiously peeking into his record on her computer: his address - a nice old house in a leafy cul-de-sac - and age - just a few years older than her.

What puzzled her, now, was why his reading tastes had suddenly changed. Was it simply that he had exhausted the crime shelves? Or had some newly arisen need inspired his venture into general and romantic fiction? And was this change connected with his new-found sociability, the spring in his step as he marched across the library carpet, the looks he gave her which, she had to admit, evoked an unfamiliar flutter inside her?

After Captain Corelli, it was Birdsong.

"Not too racy for me, I hope," he commented as he handed it to Irene.

"A wonderful story," she said. "You'll enjoy it." But then she recalled the explicit sex scenes and found herself blushing.

"And a happy ending, I hope?"

"Not exactly."

When he returned the book, the following Tuesday, she couldn't meet his eyes, and when he came up to the counter clutching The Handmaid's Tale, she flustered with the scanning wand and ended up date stamping her thumb.

"What agile hands you have, Mrs Firth," he said. "I appreciate fine hands on a woman."

She gave him a brief, coy smile and turned away at once. He left the library quietly whistling to himself.

In his reserved, gentlemanly way he's trying to woo me, she thought. She felt flattered and, though she refused to indulge the feeling, even a little excited. The subtle evolution of their relationship was like a gentle weekly serial. She found herself looking forward to the next instalment.

At home, she hovered, one day, before her mirror, attempting to see herself as others saw her. Yes, in ways she matched the stereotype of the country librarian, just as Mr Perkins clearly fitted the typical image of the widowed, well-off, retired civil servant. But she hated stereotypes: they painted such drab, superficial pictures of real people. Surely the conventional persona of Mr Perkins concealed a grand and fascinating soul, just as her admittedly stern and unexciting face belied the total woman she felt herself to be, this seething cauldron of unspent passions. Beneath the surface, she dreamt dreams of heroism and wonderment. Alone in her room, the person staring at her from the mirror was not a librarian but a universe of possibilities.

The next week, she noticed Mr Perkins consulting the popular psychology section in the corner and she gave him a quizzical look when he presented his choice: Getting what you want out of life.

He appeared bashful, trying to disguise a self-conscious smirk. "Just trying to improve my chances," he murmured. "You're never too old to make a new start, eh Mrs Firth?"

"Indeed not, Mr Perkins." And she rewarded his confidence with a beaming smile.

"Oh, please call me Ralph, Mrs Firth."

"Then you must call me Irene," she said, an invitation she had not given to another library user in fifteen years and one which, she felt, signified much more than the natural development of a casual friendship.

"I should be honoured to do so," he proclaimed and gave a little heel-clicking bow of the sort that Mr Darcy might have given to Miss Bennett.

They exchanged a parting look which, in reality, lasted no more than a few milliseconds but, for Irene, bordered on eternity.

The more she thought of Mr Perkins - Ralph - over the following week, the more his image transformed itself, in her mind: a dozen years dropped from his age, his clothes became more elegant, his conversation more eloquent, his personality no longer that of a taciturn and rather reclusive pensioner but now a dashing, sophisticated and very eligible gentleman. She took the thought of him to bed with her and, oh yes, it felt good to lie beside him.

The following Tuesday was a day she would not allow herself to anticipate. She had begun to rebuke herself whenever she found her thoughts lingering on him, and yet the temptation of indulging those thoughts was sometimes too much to resist, like the image of a half finished bar of chocolate in the kitchen cupboard which, once it had entered her mind, would give her no peace until it was satisfied.

As it happened, the following Tuesday was a day she would henceforth desperately try to forget.

In waltzed Mr Perkins with a lady on his arm. Irene stared for a moment then busied herself with a pile of leaflets on the counter. She could hear her own heartbeat and felt sure that its ferocity must have been audible throughout the quiet library.

"Ah, Good morning, Irene," said Mr Perkins, with more than usual chirpiness and a distinctly self-satisfied smile. "My book returned. Getting what you want out of life. A most enlightening read. You should try it yourself."

"Perhaps I will," she muttered, barely able to raise her eyes to look at him.

"And may I introduce Ursula," he continued, "who, I am delighted to say, has recently consented to be my wife."

Irene accepted this news in a moment. Be calm, she told herself. Be professional. She looked up and took in Mr Perkins' companion in a single glance. Fat woman, she thought. Dyed hair. Too much make-up. Trying to look forty when she's clearly nearer sixty. Totally unsuitable.

Irene forced a smile that barely ruffled the lines of her face. "Well..." she began then realised that she had not the slightest idea of what to say.

"Saturday, twentieth of July," Mr Perkins announced. "Just a small registry office do but I hope you'll do us the honour of coming."

Irene found her voice at last and heard herself saying, "Busiest day of the week, Saturday. I couldn't possibly, I'm afraid."

"Shame," said Mr Perkins. "I know how much you like a happy ending."

You've got it all wrong, Mr Perkins, thought Irene. You know nothing about me, do you? I hate happy endings. So unrealistic. A sad ending is so much more true to life.

SYNCHRONICITY AT GLASTONBURY

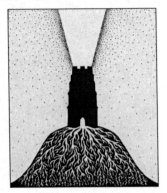

The man knew my name - not my real name but that secret name by which Sophia had called me in a dream, many years before.

"Kaph," he spoke, gruffly but firmly.

I opened my eyes at once, too drowsy to be more than mildly surprised. He was standing above me, shielding me from the sun and the blue sky so that he appeared as a black silhouette, his face a dark blur. I sexed him more from his voice than his appearance. His age completely eluded me. He moved and the stabbing shock of the brilliant sun forced my eyes shut. By the time I reopened them and sat up to look around, he was gone, dissolved into the milling crowd.

Had I imagined him? That was my first thought but I dismissed it immediately. Despite my predilection for numinous dreams, I have always been acutely aware of the modality of my perceptions. Dreams may be very real experiences for me but I have never confused them with the reality of the waking world. My second thought, for I am prone to a natural and, I think, healthy scepticism, was that I had misinterpreted that single word he spoke: Kaph, my dream name. Perhaps he had said something else, perhaps merely coughed or grunted. I dismissed this thought, too, with a certainty that was more intuitive than rational. But who knew that name? Only Arthur and Chris, and I had seen neither of them for years.

By this time I was wide awake, rapidly returning from the pleasant solitude of a mid-afternoon doze to the hectic pandemonium of a crowd of a hundred thousand. The Glastonbury Festival in full swing. From my viewpoint, lazing on a grassy hillside in the so-called 'Sacred Space' at the southern tip of the site, the whole event assaulted my fragile senses: a mass of coloured tents sprawled over the surrounding hills and fields, vast numbers of people meandering along the paths, the distant bass thud of music on the stages, the closer cacophony of strumming guitars, bongo drums and shaking tambourines, of voices laughing and shouting, the pervasive smells of chips and burgers, wood smoke and skunk weed.

The first day, I had tried to get into the spirit of it all, merged with the crowds, sampled the musical and theatrical fare on offer, wandered amongst the stalls, as varied and exotic as a Moroccan market place, bopped in the litter-choked arenas to rock bands I had never heard of and even attempted to leap up and down to the heartless electronic rhythms of the dance music that seemed to have forgotten the concept of melody. I drank my share of cider and smoked the odd spliff whenever one was passed my way by a convivial stranger. I suppose I was trying to recapture something of my past, those long-gone days when a scene like this, enjoyed in a stoned haze in the company of like-minded friends, would have been the high point of a lazy summer.

By the second day, after a restless night in my tent, surrounded by drunken insomniacs, I felt more inclined to observe rather than participate and to accept, with no more than a fleeting sadness, that, at some point over the past decades, I had slipped into a different generation. So I headed for the Green Field area and this Sacred Space - a couple of ironic misnomers - where bemused kids and hardened, brain-addled old hippies 'chilled out' on the grass while innocent looking drug dealers wandered amongst them, plying their wares. "Pills", "Skunk", "Hash cakes", "Mushrooms". And, finally, that unexpected word, rousing me from my careless lethargy, "Kaph."

He had gone, whoever he was, but the word still echoed in my head, the name conferred upon me in a dream - the most vivid dream I have ever experienced - by Sophia, Goddess of Wisdom, the archetype of mysterious femininity, who had graced my dreamscape with a sublime presence that had touched my soul. Like a knight errant, I had just returned from some heroic adventure, the details of which have long since faded. Sophia awaited my homecoming, greeting me like a lover and a mother combined, knowing me - and I her - with a compassionate thoroughness that I have since searched for and failed to find in a dozen more worldly women. "You are Kaph," she proclaimed and the warmth of her voice and the familiarity with which I received that name filled me with tears that propelled me back to wakefulness.

For years I carried my name as my most intimate secret, neither questioning it nor wondering at its meaning. Eventually I shared it, one evening of close colloquy, with Arthur and Chris, the two speechfriends of my youth who, for a while, had walked beside me along life's narrow path before drifting off into their own peculiar byways.

Arthur asked me to spell it, which I did for the first time, for some reason opting for a 'K' rather than a 'C', a 'PH' rather than a double 'F'.

Arthur, a connoisseur of meaningful acronyms, smiled and granted me an insight into a mystery that should have been, but wasn't, obvious to me. "The four characteristics of a virtuous life," he said. "The goals of our quest."

I saw it at once, for we had talked many times of personal development, of nurturing those qualities that give access to the Kingdom of Heaven, the gates of Enlightenment. Kindness. Awareness. Patience. Humility. These were the aims of the way we travelled, the ideals to which we aspired and, more often than not, failed to achieve. To be kind, to be aware of each moment, to patiently accept the vagaries of changing circumstances and to be humble in all one's dealings with others. A simple formula, we believed, for a true and lasting happiness. And now my very name encapsulated these qualities. I would never forget them, nor ever have.

I looked down at the grass where the man had stood. How could he have known, I wondered, the meaning of that short syllable? I am a believer in synchronicity, in the strange potency of meaningful coincidences. I believe that the patterns of our lives are integral parts of a far greater pattern, that God, the weaver of destinies, holds countless billions of threads in his hand yet he moves his needle with a single motion. We creatures, so concerned with the minutiae of our individual lives, focus on the particular and fail to see the larger picture of the cosmic tapestry.

There, lying on the grass beside me, was a small wooden ornament, a disc or, rather, half a disc for it had been broken in two, no more than an inch across. I picked it up and examined it and might have discarded it at once, dismissing it as one of the thousands of hippy trinkets on sale at countless stalls throughout the site at Glastonbury, were it not for the design it bore, crudely etched and stained in the smooth wood. It was a seven-pathed labyrinth - or, rather, half a labyrinth - echoing that mysterious symbol that stretched back into the depths of prehistory, the Cretan labyrinth, recurring throughout the world, in the temples of long-dead American civilisations, in the graphic language of the Asians, in the cathedrals of Christendom. I had traced my finger around the same labyrinthine path carved in stone in the enchanted Rocky Valley near Tintagel and followed the same design around the slopes of Glastonbury Tor. This, for me, was the symbol of the journey that all men must make, into the heart of themselves then back out into the world.

Yet was this anything more than another random coincidence? Had the man who called out "Kaph" - if that, indeed, was what he had called - dropped this broken disc at my feet? And if so, what did these events signify? How was I to interpret them? I have always been a seeker of strangeness but, more in the mould of Scully than Mulder, I have always looked for the rational explanation rather than the miraculous. Here, the rational explanation amounted to invoking that woolly and ultimately irrational concept known as blind chance. But the alternative, that these strange signs held some secret meaning for me, was equally unacceptable.

I pocketed the disc and made my way back into the heart of the festival. It would have been a futile effort to try to find the man who had initiated this bizarre train of thought, whose image in my memory was completely without definition, but my senses were alert, on the look out for... for whatever. I imagined that, as it was for the mythical Questors of the Holy Grail, one sign would lead to another, but how was I to distinguish a sign within this maelstrom of sensory input?

I strolled among the tents and stalls of the Green Fields where every conceivable manner of healing and prophecy and spiritual experience was proffered, for a price, and the words 'Alternative' and 'New Age' were proclaimed like royal warranties. Nothing arrested my attention. I jostled with the crowds to an arena where jugglers and acrobats displayed their skills and children with painted faces skipped and giggled through the hordes of curious adults. I stood awhile in the entrance of a marquee while a group of energetic teenagers banged out their raucous music. Then I found myself in a small, tree-lined enclosure full of huge tepees. The ambience here was quieter, less frenetic. Men and women, many in Native American attire, sat around campfires, some cooking, some carving wood or stringing beads, some lying on the grass, recovering from the excesses of the previous night.

The tepees fascinated me. Some stood twenty feet high, cones of taut canvas, white or adorned with colourful designs, a dozen stout poles protruding from their peaks with pendants flapping in the breeze. I peered into the doors of those whose flaps were open, admiring the spacious interiors, the floors lined with rugs and animal hides.

"Come on in." A woman sitting on a small stool beckoned to me, noticing my curiosity.

Rather self-consciously, for I felt that I was intruding into her home, I ducked under the flap and sat beside her on a woven rug. She watched me closely as I gazed around, my eyes growing accustomed to the relative gloom under the canvas, my nose vexed by the scents of burning joss sticks and patchouli oil.

"I'm Kath," she said, her smile so warm that my shock at hearing that name evaporated in a moment and I smiled back at her.

"My name's Kaph. With a 'PH'." Why did I say that? I had not spoken that word to another since the days of Arthur and Chris.

She nodded, pleased, it seemed, but not unduly surprised by the similarity of our names. In her hippyish society, I presumed, such odd names were commonplace.

"You like my tepee?" she asked.

"Love it." But my attention was fixed on her face, not exactly pretty but certainly alluring, draped by two plaits of blonde hair that reached to her lap, her eyes ultramarine, intense and vibrant. She was about my age - mid forties - her complexion and the wrinkles around her eyes and lips attesting to a life spent outdoors.

"You live in it all year round?" I asked, suddenly aware that I was staring at her.

"All summer. We travel the circuit of festivals and fruit picking."

"Ah," I said, realising the divergence of our lifestyles and feeling a pang of envy for the imagined freedom of hers.

It was then that I noticed the pendant dangling from her neck, lying on the tanned skin of her chest. It was a wooden disc - or, rather, half a disc - pierced and hanging on a thong. The emblem it bore was a seven-pathed labyrinth.

She looked down and cupped her hand over it. Or perhaps she was modestly concealing her cleavage from the uninhibited curiosity of my stare.

I reached into my pocket, produced my newly found semicircle of wood and handed it to her. As she took it and turned it in the palm of her hand, I sensed that something weird was happening. The constant background noise of the festival appeared to subside into silence, the periphery of my vision faded into greyness and all my thoughts, like so many insubstantial bubbles, popped and disappeared. I watched the movement of her hand as she raised it to her breast and placed the

215

broken edge of my disc alongside hers. The two halves fitted perfectly. There could be no doubt that they were once an undivided whole. The labyrinth motif was complete.

Neither of us spoke. It was one of those special moments. When our eyes met, a shared understanding flowed between us. No, it was not an understanding but a mutual awareness that we were participating in something wondrous.

"Where did you get it?" she asked, her voice little more than a whisper.

"I found it," I replied, feeling embarrassed that I could furnish no more momentous explanation.

"You weren't given it?"

"Not exactly." I could have told her about the man who called my name but, for some reason I declined to analyse, I didn't.

"How long have you had it?"

"No more than an hour or two. And you?"

She lowered her eyes from mine, her hand still clutching the two halves of the wooden disc. "Five years," she said. "For five years I have been searching for the missing half."

I was keen, of course, to hear her story but she was reluctant to tell it. Perhaps, like my secret name, it was not a matter she felt inclined to discuss with a stranger. But I was a stranger no more. In giving her my half of the disc, I felt that a bond of intimacy had been established between us, like the first kiss of would-be lovers, and I think she felt it too.

"It was in India," she began, after a long pause. "I was staying at the ashram created by Sri Ramana at the foot of the holy mountain Arunachala. There were plenty of other Europeans there but, for the most part, we observed the code of silence. Then, one day, I went wandering in the scrubland on the lower slopes of the mountain. I lost my way and was soon overcome by the oppressive heat and the relentless ferocity of the sun. I collapsed and might well have died, alone in that dry, alien landscape but I awoke from my stupor to find a man pouring water from a bottle into my mouth. He had come to find me. I recognised him from the ashram - long black hair, a black beard, typical travelling type but something in his manner and bearing set him apart from the rest. The others, like myself, I suppose, were still searching. He had found it, whatever it was - peace, happiness, enlightenment, call it what you will. There was a remarkable self confidence in everything he did, a sense of equanimity that seemed to shine from him. I don't know. I can't explain.

"Anyway, he sat beside me and, once I had recovered, he started talking, launching into this incredible rap. We mustn't struggle against the circumstances in which we find ourselves, he told me. We are all parts of the Universe and we all have our parts to play in the unfolding of the universal drama called time. Everything, every person we meet, every object we encounter, every thought and feeling we experience is bound up in that drama and everything has its purpose and meaning. Every event happens only when the time is right. We can't know that great mystery but we can be certain that the part we play in it is as vital and necessary as any other part. This is why we must let the course of our lives be governed by intuition - which knows everything - rather than intellect - which knows only what it chooses to know.

"What could I say? He spoke a truth that was simple, obvious and unarguable.

"That was when he handed me the disc. One day, he said, you will encounter the missing half - the two halves are destined to be reunited when the time is right - and then you will be ready to enter the next act of the drama of your life. I asked him for some explanation but he could not, or, more likely, would not give me any. Don't anticipate, he said. Don't fantasise. Be patient and wait. Be as you are - the perennial teaching of Sri Ramana. And, with that, he led me back to the ashram. After that day, I never saw him again."

"What was his name?" I asked. I knew it was absurd but her brief description of the man and the way he spoke struck a distinct chord in my memory.

"At the ashram, they called him Arthur," she said. "We never used surnames."

Surely not my old friend Arthur! And yet my body, overriding the protests of my rational mind, was suitably convinced. My heart started racing, a current of tingling energy shot up and down my spine and the image of Arthur became so firmly fixed in my inner vision that I knew that no appeal to reason would ever dislodge it.

Arthur was always the otherworldly one of the three of us, not exactly our leader, for he was not the leading type, but the most self assured, the wisest, perhaps, the most committed to the path we travelled. We were all seekers of the miraculous, our ways entwined throughout the heady years of our twenties but, inevitably, pulled apart by the various changes that overtook us. Chris became entrapped in the world of drugs. I sought scientific knowledge as the means to understand the Universe. And Arthur split to India, the homeland of religious experience. We each thought our way was the right one. We talked and argued through many a long night but we each knew that our congress was fading, our paths diverging.

But surely not Arthur! I could not accept such an unlikely coincidence. Yet to deny synchronicity, as Arthur himself once said, is to reject a divine gift.

"What now?" she was saying, more to herself than to me. "For five years I've waited for this moment, tried to imagine what it might mean, how I would feel. And now..."

I tried desperately to think of something to say but nothing came. This entire situation had absolutely no precedent in my experience and even humour, which usually comes to the rescue in such circumstances, failed me. Her eyes grew vacant, as if she had forgotten my presence. What could I say? I was dumbfounded. It seemed that I had stepped into a world the mechanics and meaning of which I knew nothing, a world of utter strangeness. I felt that our destinies were somehow connected - although the very idea of destiny has such immense ramifications that I was powerless to analyse the feeling. I felt that this bizarre episode would bind us together, for a while, at least, but she seemed to be rapidly losing interest in me, absorbed in her private thoughts. The disc was what mattered to her, not me, and I realised then, as I had often realised before, that we are not privy to the forces and motives that drive others, nor can we seek to understand their secret, inner lives. We touch each other for moments only, then move on upon our idiosyncratic ways.

Suddenly she was on her feet, pushing aside the flap of the tepee and striding off, at quite a pace, towards the centre of the festival. What was she thinking? I had no idea. Or was she acting through an intuitive compulsion that even she did not understand?

And what could I do but follow her?

I quickly caught up with her and walked alongside. She glanced at me, nothing more, and in that glance I could detect not the slightest clue to suggest what she was doing or where she was going or, indeed, that she was aware of either herself. She is possessed, the thought crossed my mind. A magician's spell has come into play with the union of the two halves of the wooden disc, casting her into a hypnotic trance. The thought was not worthy of consideration, but no more reasonable explanation for her behaviour presented itself to me.

"Kath?" I pleaded with her.

She glanced at me again without halting her rapid march. Was it fear, this time, that I caught in her glance? Or was it the single-minded pursuit of some aim she had no intention of sharing? Or was she giving me notice of dismissal? Or was she beckoning me to follow her? I realised, then, that I could not interpret her look, that, quite simply, I did not know her. We had been together for only a matter of minutes. I took her, during the course of those strange minutes, for a friend but she was, of course, a complete stranger to me.

"Kath, wait," I beseeched her but she either failed to hear or ignored me.

By this time she had left the tepee area and was striding along one of the wide avenues of the festival site. Thousands of people seemed to be moving in both directions, like the pavement of a busy city in the rush hour. The vastness of the throng demanded an ambling pace but she moved with purpose, as though late for an appointment, constantly weaving amongst passing bodies. I fell a few steps behind her, keeping my eye on her blonde hair, her two pigtails flapping across her back as she walked.

Then I became aware of a young man approaching me, a pleasant looking, almost angelic, smiling face curtained with bouncing black hair. He wore a white T-shirt emblazoned with fluorescent orange lettering which I found myself reading as we walked towards each other:

"COMMIT ACTS OF RANDOM KINDNESS AND SENSELESS BEAUTY."

I side-stepped him in my haste to keep up with Kath. He stepped in the same direction. I twisted to the opposite direction. So did he. We came to a halt just in time to avoid a collision.

"Sorry" I said, automatically, and made to walk around him.

"It's cool, man," he said and held out his arm to stop me. In his hand he clutched a single red rose. I noticed that it was a perfect specimen, as though he had just plucked it from a bush. Its deep, almost translucent colour, tinged with streaks of orange, caught my attention for a moment.

"Take it," he said, smiling.

"No, no." I tried to get away. "I'm in a bit of a hurry."

"Please take it." His tone was firm but not compelling. He was offering me a gift. He wanted me to accept it with the same grace with which he gave it.

I looked up from the rose to the message on his T-shirt, to his eyes which shone with the delight of committing an act of random kindness and, in that moment, I recalled those words whose initials made up my name, words that I have long held to embody the ideals of our life on this Earth: Kindness, Awareness, Patience and Humility.

"Thank you," I said, taking the rose from his hand.

His smile widened. I might have taken him for a drug-crazed fool but the look in his face belied such a defamatory thought. This act of giving was, for him, a joy, a defining moment, perhaps. And what could I do, despite my haste to keep up with Kath, but share that moment with him? I smiled back at him and held up the rose to admire more closely. It was, indeed, the most exquisite rose I have ever seen. My gaze fell into the spiral folds of its luscious red petals, the lattice-work of veins on its sparkling green leaves. Its scent wafted up to greet my nostrils and transport me, in an instant, to the peace of a cottage garden.

"Be happy," the young man said before slapping my shoulder and moving off into the crowd.

I knew at once that I had lost my Kath. Ahead of me was a bobbing sea of heads, none of which I recognised. I tried to run but, after a few difficult steps, the avenue split into three, each awash with lazily drifting bodies. I shouted "Kath!" a few times but my voice was lost in the ambient din. A few people looked in my direction and walked on. Kath, after all, was not an uncommon name. Yet I knew nothing more about her. I considered retracing my steps back to her tepee and awaiting her return, but I knew, with a certainty that was devoid of all reason, that I would never see her again.

I stood in the centre of the path while people pushed past me and, finally, asked myself the question why. Why was I so anxious to stay with her? Why was I upset at losing her in the crowd? She meant nothing to me. We were complete strangers. I had found, by chance, a peculiar object lying in the grass. Then, by chance, I had met Kath. By chance, again (as if that little phrase explained everything and nothing), I had bumped into a grinning man who, in his eagerness to confer on me an act of random kindness, had caused me to lose contact with both Kath and the wooden disc. What had I lost? The hint of a mystery that I knew would never be solved, for, as Arthur used to say, mysteries are to be experienced, not to be solved. And what had I gained? I had gained, in my hand, a beautiful rose, a gift that had no use other than to be as it was. Very soon, in the summer heat, it would wither and die, but, right now... Right now it was the pinnacle of all creation, a vision of perfection.

I made my way slowly back to the grassy hillside, the 'Sacred Space' on the edge of the festival site. En route I bought a bottle of water in which I placed the rose and set it on the grass beside me. All the people I meet, I thought, have a purpose to play in my life and I in theirs. We are all connected, all bonded in a vast, unbroken circle. There is a pattern and a meaning behind the things that happen to us but it is an arrogance to suppose that our puny thoughts can ever perceive that pattern in its entirety or grasp that sublime meaning. Yet when our selfish thoughts drop away, when we look with pure awareness, when we act through kindness, when we wait with patience, when we feel with humility, then may we catch a glimpse. And perhaps a glimpse is all that we can take.

I lay back upon the grass and let my eyes rest on the blueness of the sky. At the centre of a labyrinth, I thought, the only way to go is out again. And this was my final thought as the scent of a single red rose accompanied me into a peaceful slumber.

THE COLOUR OF THE CALL

The call would come, not in words, nor even in sound. No, the call would be written across the sky in the colours of sunset. He would know it when he saw it – of that he had no doubt. He would recognise, at once, the one colour he sought. He could picture it perfectly in his inner eye: neither pink nor crimson nor violet, neither golden nor amber nor rusty brown, nor was it a mixture of these sunset hues. It possessed a quality of its own which no name could capture. He called it simply, "the colour of the call". Someday it would appear, a smear, perhaps, across the distant western clouds, an iridescence in the blueness, maybe just a faint hint upon the high wisps that turn slowly grey once the sun has slipped below the horizon, or a dazzling chromatic intensity within the orb itself. He would know it. All his life, since first he knew that he would be called, he knew that he would know it when he saw it. Sunset watchers had felt it within themselves for countless millennia, a purpose too fragile to hold, too insistent to ignore.

Each evening he climbed the hill and turned to face the sinking sun – southwest in winter, due west at the equinoxes, northwest in the coolness at the end of hot summer's days. Oftentimes the far-off hills would be hidden in mist or rain, the sky a dismal grey, the hour of dusk dragging slowly from day to night. But always he climbed the hill and watched and, though he saw not the colour of the call, the sun's farewell display rarely disappointed him and he marvelled, daily, that the world should be so beautiful, and he felt the Grace that is known by all sunset watchers.

Each day, before climbing the hill, he packed his bag with a blanket, fresh bread and water, his yarrow stalks and a few mementos of love. He never said goodbye to his family and friends, though he knew, as they did, that one-day he would not return from his evening watch. It was accepted that sunset watchers lived on the fringe of society. It was the way of things.

And one day, of course – to end this tale – he saw the colour of the call, incandescent in the low western sky. He knew it at once, as he had always known he would. No cry of jubilation, no feeling of ecstatic consummation. He smiled a little, shouldered his pack and set off down the wild side of the hill, away from his home, towards the leaving place of the sun, towards the unknown future.